# BACCANO! ∞

1934 Alice in Jails: Prison

## RYOHGO NARITA
### ILLUSTRATION BY KATSUMI ENAMI

"Firo, you said? It's hard to describe him offhand... He's a childhood friend; we grew up in the same rundown tenement. There's really nothing else to say."

"Well, he ain't too bright."

"If he has you saying that about him, Berga, there's no coming back from that. I think I would call him awkward rather than unintelligent."

"Yeah... How long's he been living with that Eris broad now, four years?"

"It's Ennis, Berga... It's obvious he's fallen for her, and yet he still hasn't even held her hand. He isn't Claire, but it does make you wonder whether they're actually members of the same species."

"Bet it takes them another fifty years to get together. Gah-ha-ha-ha!"

"Although... Well, his awkwardness may be dyed-in-the-wool, but he's more than just a shy dawdler."

"Yeah, if you ask me, he seems more like a hot-blooded type. A permanent kid."

"He's extremely clumsy with other people. Honest to a fault, you see. However...for that very reason, Firo can't betray others, and he's able to cry for someone else's sake. To grieve for them, to laugh with them. Yet, for his family, he can freeze his own heart and even lay down his

# Regarding Firo Prochainezo

The Three Gandor Brothers
Speak Their Minds

life... So he's well suited to being a gangster but not to being a villain. His personality is inconsistent."

"So he's a klutz at life, then."

"......"

"Oh yes. You say something, too, Keith."

"What, you were here, Keith? Gah-ha-ha-ha!"

"...He's awkward."

"Hey, Keith, c'mon, we were just saying tha—"

"He's so clumsy that he can't misrepresent himself. With him, what you see is what you get. Anything we could say about him is completely meaningless."

"Wha...? Keith, this is the longest speech you've made in ages, and you're negating everything we said?!"

"Are you maybe mad because we just talked around you the whole ti—? Whoa... Okay, okay, sorry, Keith. Just quit with the scary glare—"

(At this point, an icy atmosphere settles in to stay.)

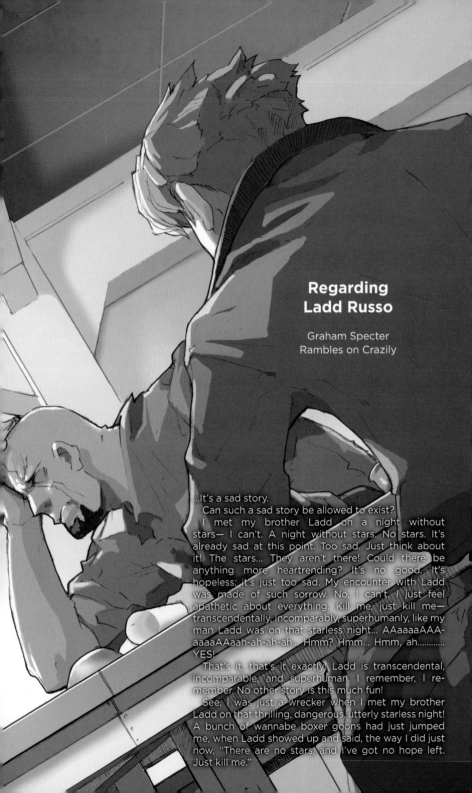

# Regarding
# Ladd Russo

Graham Specter
Rambles on Crazily

...It's a sad story.

Can such a sad story be allowed to exist? I met my brother Ladd on a night without stars— I can't. A night without stars. No stars. It's already sad at this point. Too sad. Just think about it! The stars... They aren't there! Could there be anything more heartrending? It's no good, It's hopeless; it's just too sad. My encounter with Ladd was made of such sorrow. No, I can't. I just feel apathetic about everything. Kill me, just kill me— transcendentally, incomparably, superhumanly, like my man Ladd was on that starless night... AAaaaaAAA-aaaaAAaah-ah-ah-ah... Hmm? Hmm... Hmm, ah...........

YES!

That's it, that's it exactly! Ladd is transcendental, incomparable, and superhuman. I remember, I re-member. No other story is this much fun!

See, I was just a wrecker when I met my brother Ladd on that thrilling, dangerous, utterly starless night! A bunch of wannabe boxer goons had just jumped me, when Ladd showed up and said, the way I did just now, "There are no stars, and I've got no hope left. Just kill me."

The moment the thugs looked at one another, my man Ladd meticulously, powerfully, and solidly wrecked the teeth of one of those bruisers with his fist. And what do you think he said?

"...It's like they always say: If you try to kill a guy, you can't blame him if you get killed instead."

And after that, he says...

"In other words, when I said 'Kill me,' you fellas got the right to kill me and be killed by me. Am I wrong?"

That's how Ladd thinks! He's insanely happy and terrific and dangerous and stupid and moronic and aaaaaaaawesome, see?

I'd cheered up real fast, and the other punks were all stunned, so I smashed their joints with my wrench. That's how my brother Ladd and I got to be pals.

I'm just a dumb guy with a little finesse, but Ladd's turned awkwardness into an art form! He's pouring all his talent into the areas of life where he's a total klutz!

That's what makes him awesome.

I mean, he was shattered and broken right from the start, but just look at the way he shines! Know what I mean?

## Regarding
## Huey Laforet

Elmer C. Albatross
Speaks Cheerfully

Hmm. Let's see. When I first met Huey, I think we were still about fifteen.

It seemed like he hated everything in the world, and he seemed to watch all of it from afar.

At first, he was hard on me, too, but as we talked, he gradually started to smile for me.

So Huey's a good guy. Everybody steered clear of him, and the only people he actually talked to were me and our alchemy teachers...but I can tell. He's a good guy. Even now, he's my best friend.

As a rule, all his smiles are fake, but sometimes he smiles for real.

At those times—and only those times—he says what he actually feels:

*"I want to destroy this entire world. You, me, and our teachers, too—until there's nothing left."*

The first time I heard Huey express himself honestly, that was what he said. It sounds like some painful stuff happened before I met him, but it is what it is, I think. It's not my place to tell you about it, so I can't give you any details...

But anyway, I replied, "I'd have a problem with that."

I told him if that dream of his came true, then I'd never get to see his sincere happiness once it finally did.

His happy ending is the one I want to see the most. Although, I mean, it's probably pretty selfish and rude to say I want to see somebody's ending, regardless of whether it's happy or sad.

But—I think it was after we'd first met Maiza and the rest and after we'd had a bit of an adventure...

*"I do still want to destroy this world."*

That was what he said, but...when he said it, his smile was fake! I was really glad.

He may not have fixed that habit of experimenting on people as objects rather than seeing them as human, though. That's just how he lives, I think.

He's an awkward guy.

Even so, I do want him to be happy. Or actually, that's exactly *why* I want him to be happy.

Because I know that clumsiness will let him find his awkward happiness along with everybody else.

# Regarding Victor Talbot

Nile Speaks Irritably from the Twenty-First Century

Let me just say this.

I have nothing to say about him. Nothing save for complaints, at any rate.

He was always strict regarding rules. Too strict. He gave contracts and regulations priority over his own emotions and spoke of them instead.

However, I venture to say this:

He was not so straitlaced that he could act only in accordance with the rules, nor was he an autocrat who relished binding others up in these rules.

I expect he had simply decided that, in order for everyone to enjoy the utmost equality in happiness, what was needed was the law.

You see, Victor was an intelligent fool. He was aware that there was no way for everyone in the world to live happily. So instead, he determined the best possible method of balancing the differences between individual mind-sets, values, and emotions was to restrict them with the law.

All that is fine. Those are normal thoughts.

However, in order to take all the grievances produced by those regulations onto himself, he voluntarily stepped into the role of a villain. Furthermore, the man is irretrievably warped. There was probably no way others could avoid seeing him as a tyrannical despot.

Let me just say this. A supremely clumsy man he may well be, but among the alchemists, he was a particularly human individual. On par with Zankurou.

The others—Elmer, Huey, Lebreau, Maiza, Szilard, and all the rest... As humans, they were somehow broken. Victor is naïve, but in a way, among them, he may be the most thoughtful toward others.

He is an appalling counterfeit of a villain.

Formerly, he attempted to keep the group of alchemists in check with rules, and at present, he is doing the same to the country of America.

He must have a deep liking for it: that nation and the people who dwell there.

He truly is...an awkward fellow.

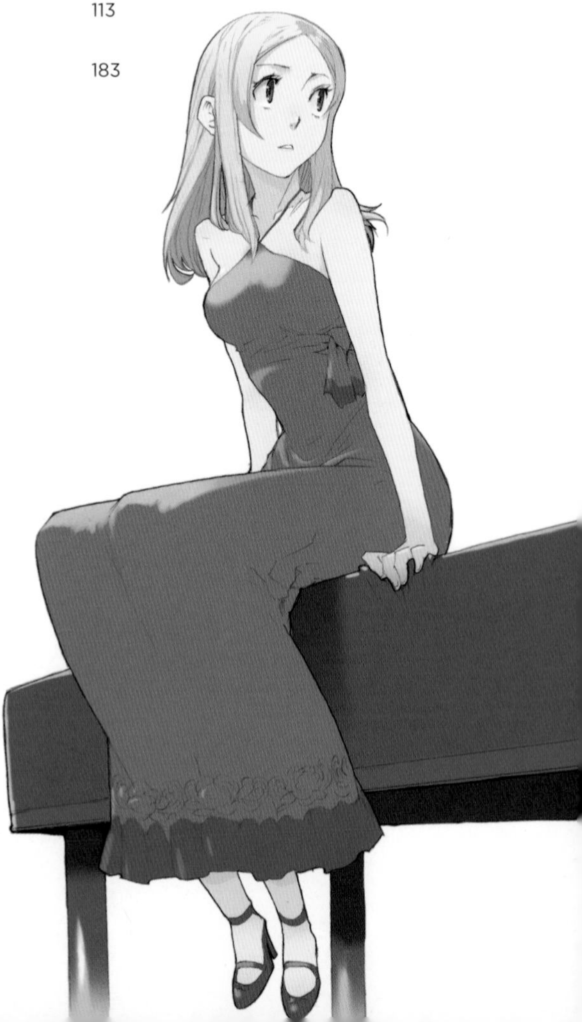

Design: Yoshiko Kamabe

# BACCANO!

## 1934 Alice in Jails: Prison

## VOLUME 8

## RYOHGO NARITA

### ILLUSTRATION BY KATSUMI ENAMI

YEN ON

NEW YORK

BACCANO!, Volume 8: 1934 ALICE IN JAILS: PRISON
RYOHGO NARITA

Translation by Taylor Engel
Cover art by Katsumi Enami

BACCANO! Vol.8
©RYOHGO NARITA 2006
First published in Japan in 2006 by KADOKAWA CORPORATION, Tokyo.
English translation rights arranged with KADOKAWA CORPORATION, Tokyo,
through Tuttle-Mori Agency, Inc., Tokyo.

English translation © 2018 by Yen Press, LLC

Yen On
1290 Avenue of the Americas
New York, NY 10104

Visit us at yenpress.com
facebook.com/yenpress
twitter.com/yenpress
yenpress.tumblr.com
instagram.com/yenpress

First Yen On Edition: August 2018

Yen On is an imprint of Yen Press, LLC.
The Yen On name and logo are trademarks of Yen Press, LLC.

Library of Congress Cataloging-in-Publication Data
Names: Narita, Ryōgo, 1980- author. | Engel, Taylor, translator.
Title: Baccano! / Ryohgo Narita ; translation by Taylor Engel.
Description: First Yen On edition. | New York : Yen On, 2016–
Identifiers: LCCN 2015045300 | ISBN 9780316270366 (v. 1 : hardback) |
ISBN 9780316270397 (v. 2 : hardback) | ISBN 9780316270410 (v. 3 : hardback) |
ISBN 9780316270434 (v. 4 : hardback) | ISBN 9780316558662 (v. 5 : hardback) |
ISBN 9780316442275 (v. 6 : hardback) | ISBN 9780316442312 (v. 7 : hardback) |
ISBN 9780316442329 (v. 8 : hardback)
Subjects: | CYAC: Science fiction. | Nineteen twenties—Fiction. | Organized crime—Fiction. |
Prohibition—Fiction. | BISAC: FICTION / Science Fiction / Adventure.
Classification: LCC PZ7.1.N37 Bac 2016 | DDC [Fic]—dc23
LC record available at http://lccn.loc.gov/2015045300

ISBNs: 978-0-316-44232-9 (hardcover)
978-0-316-44233-6 (ebook)

1  3  5  7  9  10  8  6  4  2

LSC-C

Printed in the United States of America

**Firo Prochainezo**
A young Martillo Family executive. Baby-faced and not happy about it.

**Ladd Russo**
The nephew of the Russo Family don. A bloodthirsty killer with several screws loose.

**Huey Laforet**
One of the immortals and Chané's father. He's currently in jail, but…

**Renee Parmedes Branvillier**
A manager at Nebula. A ——ing —— and ——, as well as a ——ish —— ——.

**Felix Walken**
A hitman with a legendary reputation in New York, except…

**Isaac Dian**
Same as always.

**Miria Harvent**
Same as always?

**Agent Edward Noah**
An enforcer with federal power who has it in for Firo. A paragon of an agent who takes his work seriously.

**Victor Talbot**
An immortal and Edward's superior. Foul-mouthed.

**Ennis**
A homunculus created by an immortal. Except for the fact that she is also immortal, she's no different from humans.

**Maiza Avaro**
A Martillo Family executive. An agreeable young man who's always smiling. Immortal.

**Czes**
An immortal boy. He's more of a schemer than his looks suggest, but he gets swept along by the people around him with surprising ease.

**Ronny Schiatto**
A Martillo Family executive. Has the eyes of a gangster. Demon.

**Misery**
An Alcatraz Federal Penitentiary bureaucrat. More accurately, he's connected to the Bureau of Investigation, not the jail.

**Jacuzzi**
The leader of a gang of young delinquents. An extreme crybaby. He'll be twenty soon, so he's thinking about his future.

**Nice**
Jacuzzi's girl. A bomb fiend who wears glasses over an eye patch. Lately, she's been really into Japanese fireworks.

**Chané Laforet**
Huey's daughter. A knife expert. Since she's given up her voice, she generally communicates by writing.

**"Vino"**
Real name: Claire Stanfield. A wanderer who sometimes works as a hitman. First and foremost, he's strong. That is all.

CHARACTERS

## Epilogue I     At the Information Brokerage

Where should I begin?

The locations featured at the beginning and ending of the tale I must relate today are incredibly vague, you see. Strictly speaking, *this matter* might easily have begun before my birth, and perhaps it has not yet ended.

There's no need to mingle emotion with information?

Just give you the facts, plain and simple? Ha! Don't be absurd!

Here's the thing, info broker. I ain't telling you this stuff because I want lettuce.

I desire completion… Yes. I wish to complete the information.

The dope I know ain't enough to complete this incident.

I think one must gather and spin many, many stories until, in the end, they form one shape.

Right, this information will combine many perspectives to create one set of facts.

Objectively reassembling it is a job for you information brokers— the gentlemen who've heard the tale—is it not?

Yes, as I've told you, I shall relate it accurately.

I'll give you hopelessly subjective information, all from me, by me, and for me!

"Don't get worked up," you said?

Haaaaah… Man, you don't get it. You just don't get it.

This excitement is a scrap of info, too, see?

Read between the lines, fella. It's written right there in the mood itself.

For example, say, ain't the way I'm so worked up startin' to paint a picture of the incident I'm about to go over?

Results always come with a side of emotion. Erasing that is a job for you newshounds. When we see it, we bystanders will accept that single result with a whole new set of feelings.

…Yes, that's right. In a manner of speaking, the past is a matter of the heart.

You folks eat *that kinda thing* to live, don'tcha?

You take that one result that people produced by mustering up blood and sweat and tears and wits and courage and shame and dreams and strength and emotions and pasts and hopes, and you leap on it, greedily devour it any way you please, change and degrade it, then expose it to the world.

…Hey, don't get your knickers in a twist. That was a compliment, a'ight?

No, it's no good. You won't do.

Call the vice president for me. Gustav St. Germain.

Him and the president. They're the only ones. Way back, I told them the same stuff. I was being sarcastic, but they both laughed and said, "Oh, you'll make me blush. Don't compliment me like that."

That, and Gustav pays well. The president's fine, too, but he's probably stuck in that mountain of documents like usual, yeah?

…Don't look so upset. I'm just pulling your leg.

I already know. Gustav's in Chicago right now, ain't he? Him and that half-pint photographer girl. They stayed in Chicago's Gansluck Hotel last night, and they had ham and eggs for breakfast this morning.

How do I know?

Well, because I just happened to be in that hotel.

I'm the waiter who poured the hotel's original blend, that aggressively bitter coffee, for your young lady photographer as she stuffed her face with ham and eggs.

The girl looked boggled, but she toughed it out and drained the cup.

…Now, don't give me that business about the times being inconsistent. Sure, it's not possible to get here from Chicago in a few hours.

Man, that's no good.

You really don't know anything about me?

What, me?

I'm… Let's see. I'm not sure how to put this.

A name? I've got several hundred of those.

Oh, no, no. I don't mean aliases. I have scores of actual names.

I have a body to go with each name, too.

I've got only one mind, though. Just one.

…Hmm, well, I wonder… Is it possible to count minds as one?

Minds are a curious thing. I can sense mine quite clearly, yet it's so vague I can't count it. Can you really say you have zero minds after you die or before you're born? In that case, what about when you're sleeping dreamlessly? Or when you're just spacing out?

Well, I suppose there's no point in thinking about it. That's simply how it is.

Nobody can prove that my mind and your mind are similar in the first place.

…Oh, right, yeah, that's right.

My name. Sorry 'bout that.

I know my speech style's all over the map. Don't let it get to ya.

My mind can't make itself up, see.

It's not sure whether it owes you respect or not.

It has as many ways of living as it has names and bodies.

However, there is a name that I go by. A name that all my bodies share.

This may be the start of a long relationship, so I shall make an exception and tell you.

It's Sham.

There's no need for you to remember it. I'm merely being diplomatic.

Well, that's all I want to say by way of background information. Thanks in advance for your assistance.

All right… Now then, let's start over.

Where should I begin?

During this incident, I was present in some situations and absent from others.

Let me make one thing clear.

This little episode is already over.

If you view it as part of one long-term, larger occurrence, it may not actually be over yet, but… technically, this "single" incident, which developed simultaneously in New York, Chicago, and just off the shore of San Francisco, does seem to be at an end.

I'll say it once more:

There were times when I was present and times when I was not.

What I would like to hear, in exchange for providing you with my report, is information about the locations from which I was absent.

That can wait, however. From the beginning of all this, then…

Well, though, I'm still not sure. Which beginning should I start with?

That's right: There were several events that can be termed "beginnings."

I'm truly not sure which I should relate first, but perhaps I'll start with a simple one.

With the story of a camorrista in an interrogation room…

A young executive from an organization that is not the mafia.

The name of this abject young man, who had been taken captive by the FBI, was—

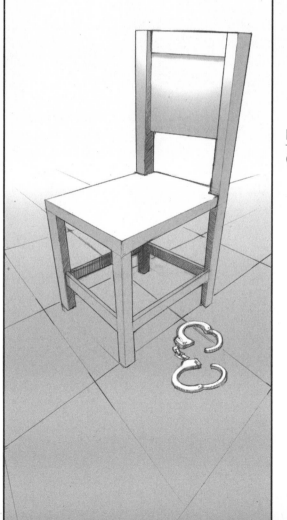

## PROLOGUE I
# CAMORRISTA

1934    A basement somewhere in Manhattan

"Firo Prochainezo."
"..."
A person had called his name.
His real name, the one his parents had given him.
Even though he'd heard it, the young fellow stayed silent. The man who sat facing him muttered with apparent satisfaction:
"You're a *sight* to behold. You look just like a Broadway star...in a comedy anyway."
"If you're jealous, I'd be glad to trade with you, Agent Edward."
With a complicated expression that held a mixture of anger and scorn, Firo Prochainezo raised his head, giving respect that was anything but.
His features made it hard to decide whether to call him a boy or a young man, and his wrists were firmly linked by dull silver handcuffs.
Firo's hands were currently useless, and the room he found himself in was cramped.
Even so, he couldn't tell what the room was supposed to be for or even what kind of facility it was a part of. The police had put him in a car and dropped him off outside Manhattan in front of a non-descript, ubiquitous brick building, and except for this room—the

first one he'd been taken to—he had no way of knowing what the place was.

The walls had no windows, only a lone mirror, and there was a sturdy door a good distance away from him. The walls were pale red brick and cold concrete, and the light of the electric bulb reflected off them to create an unsettling, lukewarm atmosphere.

Fine particles gleamed in that light. Imagining clouds of dust getting into his lungs, Firo began breathing more shallowly.

"This is a pretty crummy workplace for a guy who's moved up in the world," he continued after a time. "Although, I mean, it's perfect for a clod like you. Or, what, did your stubbornness bite you in the ass and get you demoted right off the bat?"

In response to getting lip from a kid who was clearly younger than he was, Agent Edward Noah, a fairly young member of the Bureau of Investigation himself, shrugged and continued to look down at the criminal in front of him.

"This interrogation room is a bit special. Sure, it's tacky, but you'll just have to deal with it."

"...You've changed, Edward."

"How so?"

"Way back when, even a little jab like that would have made you turn beet red."

The young fellow's acrimony didn't suit his boyish face, and Edward retorted with a barb of his own.

"You're the one who's changed."

"......"

"Way back when, you wouldn't have let the police take you in so easily, would you?"

The agent was a man Firo had been acquainted with for years, someone he was firmly unable to shake during all that time. So now, in response, Firo quietly looked away.

"...I didn't want to cause trouble for my family, that's all."

"I see, I see. That's just like you. To a sewer rat like yourself, I bet that piddling little syndicate is the only place that feels like home."

"The 'piddling' was uncalled for. Although, compared with the

Department of Justice's mighty Bureau of Investigation, most syndicates probably seem tiny."

His comment had been sarcastic, but it seemed to stir something in Edward, who responded to Firo frankly.

"As the Bureau of Investigation, we don't even have the authority to make arrests, but starting next year, both our name and our organization are going to change. The 'Federal Bureau of Investigation'… From what I hear, that's the name we're switching to. Grand yet simple. Well, I bet 'the FBI' is the moniker that ends up sticking."

"…You're gonna sound awfully pretentious. So you're slapping 'federal' on the front of it now?"

The Bureau of Investigation.

Originally, the organization had been no more than a small office within the Department of Justice. At present, though, it was something like a representative for all police organizations, with bases all across America.

J. Edgar Hoover, the current director, had stepped into that role in 1924, and since then, the organization had expanded rapidly. In just a few short years, it had gained enough might to make its name heard throughout the country. It was a large organization that had performed thorough investigations of the interstate gangs whose influence had increased during the Prohibition era, and it ruled over the United States as one of the Department of Justice's trump cards.

"This was a bad year for you people."

As Edward muttered, his expression was triumphant. He put his face right up close to the cuffed gangster.

"They passed the firearms act, and now you can't even kill one another in style. It must be real frustrating to put on your show of strength without your tools."

"I usually use my bare hands, so it's got nothing to do with me."

Put briefly, the National Firearms Act, which had gone into effect that year, was a proposal created to shave away the violent potential of the organized crime syndicates who were active behind closed doors throughout the country.

The law limited the possession of a wide variety of weapons and

accessories, from fully automatic weapons like Thompson subma-
chine guns all the way to shotguns whose barrels had been sawed off
to widen the spray.

"To think you'd ban silencers, too... Are you trying to make helpless civilian weapon makers hang themselves?"

"You think we want 'helpless civilians' manufacturing silencers,
tools for the sole purpose of assassination?" Edward continued to
display the composure of the law with but a light parry. "On top of
that, this is the first year since Prohibition ended. Wasn't that a huge
blow to your group? Speakeasies were your main source of income."

"I hate to tell you this, but whether they're undercover or out in
the open, business is booming at our places."

"That gambling den you run, too..."

"Look, you're the one who gets to gloat here. Would you quit constantly trying to pick fights?"

Just when irritation had started to show in the young man's face—

"Hi there... It's great to see you two getting along so well."

—the door opened abruptly, decanting three men into the little
room.

"Erm... I don't believe we've met before. I'm Bill Sullivan."

A man with sleepy-looking eyes greeted their captive with a
laid-back tone, then gestured to the two behind him.

"Uh... This well-built gentleman is Donald Brown. The one with
glasses is Allen Becker. We all work with Edward over there."

The agent who'd said his name was Bill spoke as if he was intro-
ducing friends. The two who stood behind him didn't move so much
as an eyebrow, and their expressions were stern.

"Hmm... I'm sorry we're so surly around here. It's a pretty stress-
ful job, you see."

With a slow gait that matched his voice, Bill sauntered over to
stand beside Edward, then read from the papers he was holding, as
if confirming their content with Firo.

"Uh, Firo Prochainezo... aged twenty-two. Single. Born in Hell's

Kitchen, New York. Italian father, American mother; both parents contracted tuberculosis and are no longer with us, correct? ...Ah, my condolences. After your mother died, you left Hell's Kitchen and drifted through New York... Then, although we don't know the particulars, like your father before you, you joined a mafia syndicate..."

"We're not mafia."

Even at the mention of his parents' deaths, Firo had remained expressionless. However, now, for the first time, he turned to face Bill. Shooting him an icy look, he said:

"We're Camorra."

$$\Longleftrightarrow$$

Firo Prochainezo was not an upright citizen.

He was what was commonly known as a gangster, a type of person deeply associated with the America of this particular era.

That said, he belonged to an organization affiliated with a system that was known as the Camorra in its home country of Italy. It wasn't connected to the mafia groups sweeping America at the time, represented by Cosa Nostra.

Unlike the mafia, which had begun in Sicily, this organization was mainly based out of Naples. Its organizational structure and what it traded in differed from the mafia as well, but in America, particularly among people on the right side of the law, the two groups were almost invariably lumped together.

Firo Prochainezo was an executive in one such organization, the Martillo Family, which controlled an extremely limited territory.

Even if he was an executive, he was still one of a dozen of that rank in their group—they made up nearly a quarter of the syndicate.

As the youngest of them, Firo had been put in charge of a small underground casino.

In a family emergency, he was prepared to immediately lay down his life, and at the same time, he was able to steel himself to take the life of an enemy.

This time as well, even as Edward brought him in for questioning, he hadn't made a single blunder that would have brought unnecessary suspicion down upon him. It was likely that if they tried to get some stopgap information on the underground casino or anything else out of him, he was prepared to keep everything securely under wraps and was fully confident that he could do so.

Beneath the mask of a baby-faced young man, there was a gangster who lived a violent life in the darkness of the city—and at the moment, he was glaring coldly at Bill.

That was Firo Prochainezo's hidden face.

⟺

"Ah... Camorra, right. 'Scuse me. I got that wrong on purpose."

Bill apologized, beaming, and Firo put on a tense smile as he identified the man in front of him as a definite enemy.

"...Be careful not to walk through our turf after dark, all right?"

"Thanks for the warning."

With a smile of ostensibly genuine gratitude, Bill went on as if nothing had happened.

"Erm... I think you've probably heard already, but we brought you in to ask about the *destruction of property* at Mist Wall last year. Nobody's issued an arrest warrant yet, so don't you act so high and mighty, either, Edward."

His delivery was so relaxed, you'd never have thought the guy was with the Bureau of Investigation. Firo scowled upon hearing the news, stole a glance at Donald and Allen, then looked back at the man in front of him.

*I don't like this guy one bit.*

That last comment, addressed to Edward, was something he wouldn't have said if he hadn't heard their earlier conversation. He'd probably been eavesdropping on what was going on inside this room.

"Bill, be serious."

Donald, the man with the square build, rebuked his partner for his attitude.

Possibly because they were used to this, Edward stood there looking indifferent, and the other man, the one with glasses, patted Firo on the head. He was wearing a disgusted smile.

"Just ignore that, all right? He loves getting sarcastic with little guys like you."

"Knock it off. I'm not a kid."

Firo jerked his head, shaking the hand off, and examined the offending, bespectacled figure.

As far as age went, he wasn't young, but he didn't really seem middle-aged, either. He was bursting with energy, and he seemed to be a man in his prime.

Pushing his glasses up smartly, the man sat down in the chair facing Firo before Edward could get there.

And then, he leaned back into it with a *creak*.

"…?"

The man's attitude was odd, and Firo gave him a quizzical look.

*Who did Bill say he was? Allen Becker?*

He was acting pretty self-important. Who was this guy?

*Is he pushing his luck because I'm a suspect?*

Firo was thinking this, unable to figure the other man out, when out of nowhere, he noticed that something seemed weird.

*What is it?*

He got the feeling he knew the man in front of him.

However, he was pretty sure they hadn't met before.

*That's right. In the twenty-some years I've been alive, I've never run into a guy like this.*

But he did remember him.

*Don't … tell me …*

Just as Firo realized what that meant, the bespectacled man spoke, smirking.

"Careless, Firo Prochainezo."

Smiling, he held up his right hand for Firo to see, opening and closing it.

"If I'd been hungry, right about now…*you would have been my lunch.*"

The man's words were the clincher, and Firo realized exactly who he was.

His memories had been right.

It was true that Firo had never met him before.

However—the man was definitely *in* his memories.

The memories of a man who Firo had once "eaten" with his right hand: the alchemist Szilard.

⟺

Firo Prochainezo wasn't an upright citizen.

Not only that; it was possible he wasn't even human.

Four years ago, Firo had been pulled into an incident involving alchemists, and he and his friends had been turned into odd beings known as immortals.

Any and all wounds regenerated immediately.

They didn't age to match the years they'd lived.

They were creatures compelled to live semi-eternally, whether they wanted to or not.

The only way they could die was by being "eaten" by the right hand of another immortal.

Even if they were packed into an oil drum and dropped to the bottom of the ocean, even if they were diced up and encased in molten iron, they'd be forced to keep living.

*That* was Firo Prochainezo's third face.

⟺

"The demon's rules for immortals are pretty fuzzy."

In front of Firo, who'd frozen up, the man who'd been introduced as Allen shook his head, his lips twisting.

"It's okay for somebody else to introduce me by a false name. Weirdly enough."

"Victor... Victor Talbot?"

Tracing a thread of information in memories that technically belonged to somebody else, he watched the man's past.

Victor Talbot.

As one of the alchemists, he'd summoned the demon and drunk the liquor of immortality, along with Szilard—the man Firo had eaten—and many other companions.

Apparently, he hadn't gotten along with Szilard or the alchemists that Szilard had eaten, because that was just about the only information the memories had on him.

However, judging by his arrogant attitude, it probably would be hard to find anybody who got along with him, period.

As he reached that conclusion, Firo belatedly paled at the thought that this man's right hand had been on his head a minute ago.

"Oho!" The kid had told him his real name without trouble, and Victor exhaled, sounding entertained. "Get a load of that. It's just like the intel said, then?"

Arrogance still intact, Victor glared cheerfully at Firo.

*"You're the one who ate that old bastard Szilard?"*

"……"

Firo responded with silence, but inwardly, he clicked his tongue in irritation.

*Dammit, I tipped my hand, and now he knows. Still... What did he mean, "like the intel said"?*

As if to head off the young man's doubt, Victor knocked on the desk with one hand and began playing his cards.

"Well, you know, there's what's-her-name, Ennis... The little chick who was the old geezer's clone."

"...!"

The moment that name came up, Firo stiffened.

At the same time, intense distress threatened to overwhelm him.

"...What about her?"

He knew nothing good would come of rising to the bait, but he had to ask anyway.

Ennis—the girl who'd once fought Firo as Szilard's underling.

Szilard had formerly had the power to easily take her life if he chose, but now, Firo held that privilege. However, he was very fond of Ennis, and to him—

"Ha! Don't get so jumpy. See, we knew that doll was stuck with the old guy—well, more like she couldn't live without him. And now that the geezer's gone, she's stuck with you. I'd figured Maiza ate him to avenge his little brother, but that part seemed fishy. So I tried asking a couple'a leading questions, and voilà."

"That was a dirty trick."

As Firo clicked his tongue, clear hatred made itself plain on Victor's face.

"Listen to you! That kinda stings, coming from troublemaking scum like you. Mafia or Camorra, you people are gangsters—enemies of the state."

His rimless glasses made him look like an intellectual, but the way he was talking said he was itching for a fight. He took a condescending attitude as he ranted at Firo.

"Listen up, punk. I'm gonna keep on playing hardball with you, so don't you come crying to me later and saying I didn't warn ya. Let me make one thing clear right now."

Smacking his right fist into his left palm, Victor the immortal let the young man in front of him feel the brunt of some terrifically personal sentiments.

"See, gangster bastards like you who strut around like you own the place, like you're the rulers of underworld society—I hate, hate, hate, hate, hate, hate, hate, hate, hate, hate, hate, hate, hate, hate, hate, hate, hate, hate, hate, hate, hate, hate, hate, hate, hate, hate, hate, hate, hate, hate, hate, hate, hate, hate, ha— *Koff* ... *kaff* ... *ghak* ... Ha... *Kaff* ... Ha, hate, hate, hate, hate, hate, hate, hate you from the bottom of my soul, you get me? Maybe some of you are good-natured, maybe some of you don't mess with people on the straight and narrow, maybe some of you think you're on fire for goddamned justice, but you're all the damn same to me. Why, you ask? Because fellas like you are what I hate, hate, hate, hate, hate, hate, hate, hate, hate, hate, hate, hate, hate, hate, hate, hate, hate, hate, hate, hate, hate, hate, hate, hate, hate, hate, hate, hate, hate, hate, hate, hate, hate, hate, hate, ha— *Koff …hack…ghak…!*"

Victor choked and coughed, on the brink of suffocating, and Firo eyed him with disgust.

"Don't keep going until you run out of air. And twice? Are you an idiot?"

"So what if I am?! At least I'm not you! This idiot's got the upper hand, and you can't do a damn thing about it."

"If you know I'm an immortal…don't you think I might jump you here and now and shove my right hand onto your dome?"

Victor's abuse was openly hostile now, but Firo had retaliated with a light verbal jab. He'd definitely been careless a minute ago, but under these circumstances, he'd decided that it would still be an effective threat.

His opponent was only about a yard away across the desk. If he kicked the desk up and went underneath, even with cuffs on, he still had a good shot at capturing his opponent's head.

Firo thought he'd see what the other man's character was like, based on how he responded to that remark.

Victor didn't change his attitude, and yet he didn't give him any openings or look away, either. He just gave a counterattack of his own.

"Don't make me laugh, you damn brat. You think you're testing me as an immortal or something?"

"What?"

"You sound like a perp being questioned for robbery. It's like you just told the detective, 'I'm gonna jump ya, shove my thumbs in your eyes until it gives you brain damage that leaves you crippled for life.' You think federal law bends over for threats like that?"

*Tch! I guess he's not just an overbearing moron.*

Firo made that call not because he couldn't argue with his sound logic, but because during that long reply, the agents had changed the mood entirely.

He must have sent them some sort of signal. Donald and Edward had circled around to either side of the desk, and at some point, Bill had lit a cigarette behind Firo's back. Victor had also slightly shifted his weight in the chair, swiveling his hips to the right.

If it came down to it, the four of them were probably ready to draw their guns and fire at once.

"Are you crazy? If you shoot from there, you'll take each other out."

He'd tried to sound as derisive as possible, but Victor answered instantly.

"They've already got orders to shoot me right along with you. Hurts like a bitch, but afterward, I'll just chop off your arms and legs, shut 'em in an iron safe so you can't regenerate, then let you scream at me to give 'em back while I pay you back double on your face."

"...Yeah, I guess you would."

"The ability to use suicide maneuvers freely is one of the *few* advantages we immortals have."

Victor's attitude was as domineering as ever, and Firo decided that continuing this war of words wouldn't get him anywhere.

So he resorted to violence instead.

With no hesitation, he grabbed the table with his cuffed hands, smoothly tensed his upper and lower body together like a spring, and flung the flat surface up.

The table hurled into the air.

It was a shabby-looking wooden table, but it certainly wasn't light.

Firo had thrown the table up in the blink of an eye, immediately killed his momentum, looked straight ahead at his target—and froze up.

In front of him, under the airborne table, Victor was nowhere to be seen.

*Where is he?!*

Before he managed to find him, the table stopped rotating in mid-spin, then dropped back to the floor in its original position.

He heard the sound of a hammer being cocked.

At the same time, a shiny black muzzle appeared in front of Firo.

"All right, sit down."

Firo slowly looked up—and there was Victor on top of the table, staring down at him right along with the barrel.

Victor gave Firo a smirk, which then became a grin as he spoke.

"I see. Yeah, it's just like they said: You're quick to fight, and you're pretty confident in your strength and agility, too."

"…Can everybody in the Bureau of Investigation do circus tricks?"

"Hunh… Stuff like this is indispensable when it comes to arresting vicious criminals and enemies of the state. Everyone who's gone through formal training can do it… easily! More splendidly, swiftly, beautifully than I ever could!" Victor cried triumphantly.

But all the surrounding agents broke in at once:

"Uh… No, sir, I can't."

"Quit raising the bar for new recruits on your own say-so, please."

"Assistant Director Talbot, I wish you'd hurry and get down. You're getting the table dirty."

"…Fine. Damn, you people are no fun."

Sounding a little embarrassed, Victor put his gun away, quietly jumped down to the floor, and resumed his seat.

"…Well, uh, see…the actual jump went the way I'd planned, but landing on the table was an accident."

"…Huh."

"……"

"……"

A meaningless, awkward silence passed between Firo and Victor.

After a few breaths, Firo sighed and picked up the conversation again.

"So let's move on. You made a big fat deal out of hauling me in for my involvement in the damage to the Mist Wall… What exactly are you trying to get me to do?"

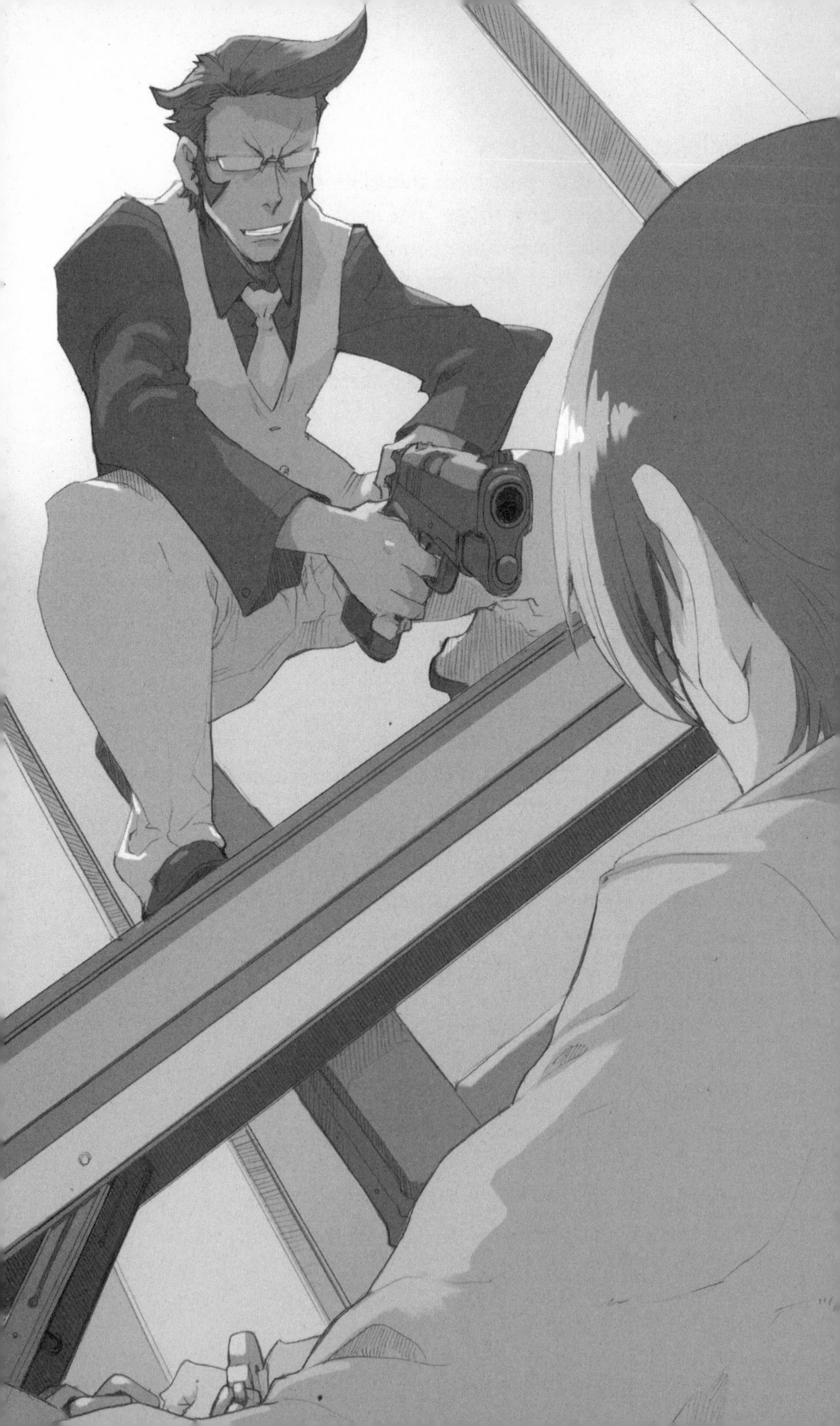

Firo, who had been pulled into a certain incident the previous year, was considered a witness to an explosion that had occurred in a high-rise building known as Mist Wall.

The event was several incidents at once, in which humans and immortals from multiple organizations had become entangled in complicated ways, driven by varying motives. In the course of the grand, closed affair, they had assembled in a building owned by Nebula, a vast organization, and had been confronted with a variety of facts.

Led by a man named Christopher, Ennis and Firo had been instantly transported from outside the incident to the inner circle.

Of course, they knew who had actually caused the explosion. However, for a little while, the police strangely hadn't said a thing to them.

According to Maiza, an upper-level executive in Firo's syndicate, it sounded as though some politician with ties to that building had put pressure on them, but…

A year had passed, and just when he'd let down his guard completely, they'd hauled him in.

*For the love of … I guess I probably should have taken precautions on my end, huh?*

Firo cursed his own boneheadedness, and Victor smiled brightly as if to mock him and replied with a seeming non sequitur.

"Well, I just thought I'd suggest you take a little trip."

"A trip?"

"Yeah, to flowery San Francisco, on the West Coast. A vacation surrounded by sea and sky… Sounds great, doesn't it? If you're lucky, you just might meet one of your world's big stars, and you'll get to spend time in perfect silence, since nobody there talks to one another."

Firo had a bad feeling about this.

To people like him, who lived in underworld society, *West Coast*, *San Francisco*, and *surrounded by sea and sky* were loaded phrases, especially when heard from a G-man. The last half of what he'd said had been so blatant that he didn't even feel like trying to think about what it meant.

There were a nauseating number of hints, and they focused Firo's thoughts on one place.

And then, wearing his breeziest smile, Victor made one last, hopeless remark, turning that hideous premonition into a reality.

"Ever hear of Alcatraz?"

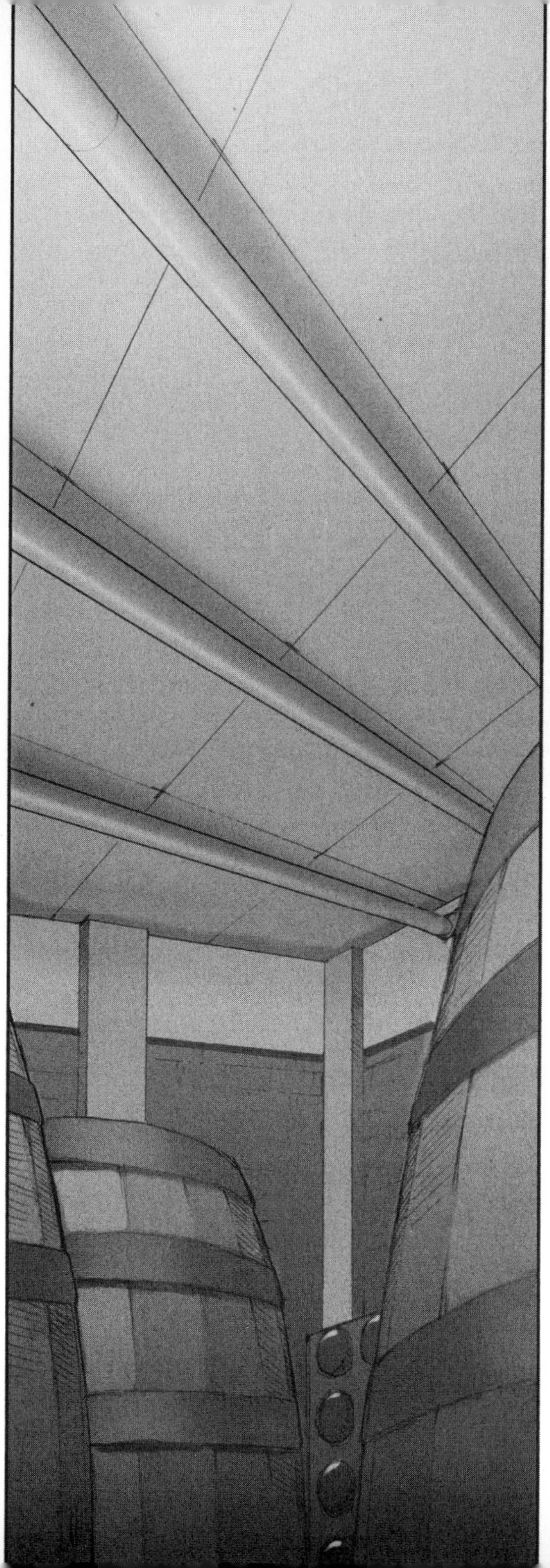

## PROLOGUE II

# BRUISER

In the basement of a certain tavern        Private room

You want to know about a con who got sent from my prison to Alcatraz?

Oh, I see. Yeah, you can't talk about that stuff openly, that's for sure.

...Still. I was a rank-and-file guard, and I only just quit. We called 'em by numbers; I don't remember much about any of those guys. Well, anybody who'd get shipped to Alcatraz would have made more of an impression on—

Huh? Number 302010?

......!

......

Ha...ha-ha...

Ah... Yeah, yeah.

Yeah, yeah, yeah, yeah, yeah!

Him! Yeah, him I remember perfectly. The number was an easy one, but more importantly, uh, I guess I just... I mean, there's no way I could forget that guy.

I know his real name, too. I got curious, see.

Ladd... Ladd Russo, I think it was.

They said he was a nephew of Placido Russo, the don of the Russo Family in Chicago.

It was murder or robbery or something like that... Apparently, they nabbed him on several counts, but I don't know any of the details. To prison guards, they're all just animals we're calling prisoners, and we're supposed to call them by their numbers, equally. Maybe the perp's real violent, or maybe he's just a thief, or maybe he's a gangland kingpin, but in the cooler, they're all nothing but numbers...officially anyway.

What is it actually like? I dunno. It probably depends on the jail and the prison officers, and I can't just go around talking about that stuff.

That's not what you want to hear, though, right?

Number 302010... That Ladd fella. Isn't he what you're asking about?

Yeah... You're thinking I'm a weirdly cheerful, shallow guy, aren't you?

When I was a guard, I tried to be a capable type. The serious, quiet guy who put wordless pressure on prisoners. But, see, the thing is, y'know, we're talking about *him* now, after all, and that really makes me want to completely distance myself from who I was back then. See? You get me, right?

Back when he first got to the prison, I kinda threw my weight around when I did his physical exam, too. To teach 'im, "You people are criminals now—ditch your pride; you're underdogs; you're here to apologize and keep on apologizing for the trouble you caused us and the general public with your lousy Mickey Mouse crimes, see."

Ah, no, the other guards don't take it that far. I mean, shattering the other guy's pride is an important job, but...

Me in particular, I was especially, uh, well... I pushed my luck a bit.

No matter how famous a criminal they'd been on the outside, in here, I outranked them. When you think about that, you know, of course you wanna act big. I mean, there were swarms of hoods right there, and I could sneer at them without worrying about a thing.

Well, see, that's why.

I said so a little bit ago: I'm acting all casual-like because I want to get as far as possible from *the me I was back then*.

You don't understand what I'm getting at?

... Well, uh, yeah. I'll get to that later. Later.

So, about Ladd.

The guy was weird in all sorts of ways.

When he was first admitted to prison, he looked incredibly chipper.

I figured he was some big shot with a lawyer and planning to get himself released right away, or maybe he'd started something with some other mafia on the outside and had come here to get away.

Well, it's a decent place to run and hide. If your enemies are powerful, though, they'll just get a hitman into prison. The guys in question may be able to tell, but there's no way for us to pick 'em out from the rest.

But you know, when I asked the other guards, they said he wasn't anything like that. Plus, all sorts of stuff about him smelled *fishy*. I hear he caused a bit of trouble on a train... and then the whole thing... was totally covered up, or so I hear.

Nah, I dunno. I don't know anything about that situation. It's like there was some sort of pressure from the country itself ... That kind of stuff didn't make it around to me, and he didn't talk about any of the details.

Yeah, he was a quiet guy.

He had the look of a lively fellow, but he didn't say much of anything that didn't need to be said. Sometimes we gave him permission to make phone calls to the outside, but he didn't talk about anything particularly hinky.

He did his prison work quietly and well, and I guess he was what you'd call a model prisoner.

He'd injured his arm real bad somehow, and it was always wrapped in bandages... Well, long story short, it was a prosthetic. We checked it over carefully, thinking he might have some tool in there that he could use to break out, but there was nothing. It was just a prosthetic, and the joints didn't even move that well. Only, it was attached directly to his arm or to the bone… Yeah, I'd never heard of a prosthetic like that, either, but from what the rumors said, his bones were stripped bare even though they were still attached, and they'd used 'em just like that. My pals who did his physical thought it was real spooky.

I thought bacteria and stuff might get in there and give the live parts gangrene, but he was surprisingly peppy.

He didn't cause any trouble. He just spent his days as a convict. He actually did hard labor voluntarily; he really was a model prisoner. We couldn't have him using a screw off his prosthetic arm to pick a lock, so we watched him like a bunch of hawks.

He didn't do anything that stood out, though. Time just passed by; nothing happened.

—Until that one day.

He suddenly changed—well, he showed his true colors—a few months back.

It was just about the time Alcatraz switched over from being a military prison to being a regular one.

I think you probably know already, but, well, here's the thing.

That place ain't normal.

You can't commit a crime and go straight to Alcatraz, for one. It just doesn't happen.

Inmates from ordinary jails get sent to the island afterward.

It's a West Coast paradise, famous for housing the worst trouble-makers from all the other prisons.

Well, at the prison I used to work at, the most dangerous guy by a long shot was this fella named Gustavo.

You know the Runorata Family, right? They're one of the bigger outfits in this area.

Gustavo used to be one of their executives. Apparently, he caused some kind of trouble that led to getting his elbows checked by the cops.

He had this seriously nasty scar at the base of his throat. Ordinar- ily, you'd figure a wound like that would've put him six feet under. Just like with Ladd, though, it didn't even look like it had made him any weaker.

The guy was a real mad bull. When a guard lobbed some stupid taunt at him, he ripped his handcuffs apart, just like that.

"...Whoops, these sorta fell to pieces on me. That ain't safe. Get me some new ones, wouldja?" he said without a care in the world.

The guard couldn't do a thing, and the big lug just leered at him.

Of course, he caused problems in stir, lots of 'em, and we had our hands full with him.

None of the other prisoners could beat him in a fight, plus they were scared of him, so they didn't even try to rat him out to the guards on the sly. He acted like he was king of that place.

But then, this one day...

The guy went on a rampage in the mess hall. The fight started over some stupid thing, like how the guy in front of him had laughed at him or something.

We took our billy clubs and surrounded them, and as you'd figure, they calmed right down. Well, there were officers waiting outside the gun ports behind him with rifles at the ready. They pretty much had to.

I let 'em have it.

I started feeling kinda sadistic, and, well, it felt good, and I told 'em, all condescending-like:

"Do you fellas want to get dumped into Alcatraz? They don't even have books or newspapers on that rock, so if anybody feels like going loony you just keep right on getting your exercise this way."

That's what I said.

Well, Gustavo probably knew the rumors about that place. Several of the other guys clammed up, too, like they'd gotten cold feet.

Yeah, frankly, I was feeling real good right about then.

It was tops. So fantastic I might have gotten the wrong idea and thought the world was mine.

That's when it happened.

"Alcatraz...?"

One guy walked up to me.

Right. It was Ladd.

"What would a fella have to do to get sent to this Alcatraz place?"

To be honest, I was a little surprised. This was a model prisoner, a guy who didn't usually talk at all, and I hadn't thought he'd speak to a guard armed with a sap in a situation like that.

They don't encourage conversation between prisoners and guards. Some jails actually ban it. I answered, though. Ladd didn't look like he knew what sort of place Alcatraz was, and I thought it'd be a good chance to hit the other guys who weren't in the know with a good, solid threat.

So I told him. I took the stuff about how horrific Alcatraz was, all the rumors that had gotten worse over time, and I padded it even more.

He'd gotten real quiet, and when I saw that, I started feeling great...

"Well, we're planning on recommending the worst troublemaker in this prison for that place. A chicken like you should just keep your head down and stick to being a model prisoner," I told him.

And then...

And then, see... Uh... Well...

He smiled.

Grinned at me just like that. Like he was really and truly happy.

*What's with this guy?* When I saw that smile, I got hit with this sudden uneasy feeling.

He wasn't even looking at me anymore. He turned around without a word, went straight back to his own seat, and started eating again, like the trouble with Gustavo and the other guys hadn't even happened.

Right then, I felt it in my gut... This real nasty hunch. It was just, how should I put it...? Just a bad feeling. There's really no other way to describe it. It was like that feeling you get when you're up on a high bridge, and you look down at the valley floor and you think,

*Hey, I wonder what it would be like if this bridge suddenly vanished and I fell from up here?* And then you imagine it, and your whole body sort of shrinks up. It was just like that moment.

But I wasn't up on a high bridge or on top of a building. It was just the inside of a prison. Plus, he was a prisoner. I was a guard. There shouldn't have been anything in there to scare me, but...

In that moment... when I saw him smile, I really did feel fear.

That night, that terror jumped me in physical form.

I heard there was more trouble in the dining hall, and when I went to take a look...

What do you think I saw?

... Dinner.

He was eating dinner.

That Ladd guy was eating dinner, from his own plate, right at the scheduled time.

The sight scared the living bejeebers out of me.

What was scary about it?

Well, because... Because.

Because he was eating dinner.

Ladd was all by himself, *surrounded by dozens of groaning prisoners laid out on the floor*!

In the hall that led to the prisoners' cells, the jailbirds who weren't out cold were trembling, packed into the entrance.

The guards who'd been watching were staring at Ladd as if a guy like him couldn't exist, and nobody was moving a muscle.

"Hey! What happened?!" I yelled. At my fellow guards, I mean.

It's pathetic, but I sort of didn't want to talk to Ladd directly. It was just too creepy somehow... The way he was sitting there, silently eating his dinner in the middle of a situation like that, was too eerie for words.

Guards who'd heard the ruckus and come running, the way I had, were already standing in the gun ports up at the top of the dining hall, rifles at the ready ... but the morons were all just looking at one another. After all, there was nobody to shoot.

If you thought about it normally, there'd been a big fight among prisoners, and the group that had done the thrashing had made tracks back to their own cells and were cooking up alibis right about now. Ladd had come along later, decided to stay out of the mess, and was calmly eating his dinner... Yeah, I wanted that to be what had happened.

Except, since they'd managed to flatten a group of several dozen guys, you'd think the other group would have been a big one, too. From the atmosphere, it really didn't seem like they'd all managed to take one another out, either...

......

Yeah, I know. I know what you're trying to say.

That's what I thought, too, the second I saw it.

I figured Ladd, who was eating his dinner without a care in the world, had shellacked the circle of hoods all by himself.

As a matter of fact, when you looked at him... you couldn't think anything else.

I told myself over and over, *That ain't possible*, but what I was seeing just wouldn't let me acknowledge it. It wasn't just what I was looking at then. The smile the guy had shown me that afternoon made me imagine something that shouldn't even have been doable: him, massacring the other prisoners all by himself.

And then—a scene that backed up that idea played out right in front of me.

All of a sudden, a big shape sprang up from among the downed prisoners.

"Gaaaaaaaaaaaaaaah! You little shit!"

I didn't even have to check. Nobody but Gustavo was that big.

Big and fast and tough.

And that charge! There's nothing I can say about it; it was beautiful.

*The guy's just like a bear*, I thought.

He grabbed a nearby table and picked it up one-handed.

Can you believe that?!

A table, pal! A table!

Swinging a chair around one-handed is enough to make you a

monster, and he just grabbed a long table that sat four to a side and brandished it like it was a piece of lumber!

"I'll crushyaaaaargh!"

With a bellow whose pronunciation had gone screwy, he brought the table down on Ladd, who'd just finished drinking the last of his soup.

That would splatter Ladd's brain and end him. Then the guards with guns would give a warning, and if the guy listened, we'd surround him and thrash him with our saps. If he ignored them, they'd fill him with daylight—The End.

…According to the manual, that was how things should have played out, but no matter what I did, I just couldn't see it happening.

And well, it definitely didn't.


There was this weird, messy *crunch*. Gustavo's table had splintered and snapped like a pencil. Busted right in two in the blink of an eye, like somebody had ripped it apart.

But, see…Ladd wasn't there anymore.

In between Gustavo's burly body and the table he'd brought down…he'd literally gotten right up in his face. That attack had seemed more liable to kill somebody than a lead bullet, but he'd slipped through it, wearing the same smile he'd worn that afternoon!

And then…he smiled.

What did you say? He was already smiling earlier? Well, yeah, but…

I mean… *He smiled even wider.*

Ladd had just appeared out of the blue, right in front of him, and Gustavo froze, like he was flustered.

Ladd had a perfect opportunity—but he didn't slug him.

He just shrugged, turned both of his hands palm up, and spoke to us.


"That makes this justified self-defense, yeah?"


And after that, well… To be blunt, it was over in an instant.

He must have thought the guy was making a monkey out of him.

Gustavo's veins popped out even farther, and he raised his other hand, and in that instant—Ladd's fist sank into his solar plexus...

And he *decked him across the room.*

The guy was big. He had to weigh more than twice what Ladd did, but he slugged this guy in the stomach and sort of ...punched right on through, like he was pushing him.

He rose up into the air, like he was floating. Gustavo did.

Then he flew backward several yards, and when he hit the ground, he coughed up blood and stopped moving.

The guy *stopped moving.*

A bear of a fella like that... Sure, he'd already gone down once at that point, but ...this was just one punch.

I figured he'd slugged him with that iron prosthetic of his. If he had, we would've confiscated that hand on the double.

But... But dammit...

He'd slugged Gustavo not with the prosthetic but with his flesh-and-blood right hand. Of course, now that I'm thinking about it, there's no way he could've punched that well with a prosthetic; it woulda dislocated his shoulder.

Yeah... And then...

As I stood there, stunned, he slowly walked up to me, and he said: "Life is long."

That's what he said. You'd have thought he was talking to a good friend he'd spent years with.

I was actually real close to yelling "Stop!" and raising my sap. If I'd had a gun, I might have had it out by then. Yeah—even though the guy was just walking toward me.

"Life is long, ain't it! You think so, too, don't you, Mr. Guard-Man?" He was all worked up, but I had no idea what he meant.

I did wonder, *What's this guy talking about?* but more than that, I was just scared out of my skull. What's the word...? If instinct exists, I think the fear I felt then was my instincts, sounding a warning.

*Run,* they were saying. *Runrunrunrunrunrunrunrunrunrun.*

"I've seen tons and tons of guards before now, but...in this pen, you're the one who's furthest from dying."

He spoke slowly, and his words sort of crept up on me.

As that voice slid into my ears, an alarm bell in my head clanged away.

*Runrunrunrunrunrunrunrunrunrunrunrunrunrunrunrunrunrunrunrun—do it, or you're gonna die!* it told me.

The guards around me looked like they were waiting for me to give him some sort of warning. Dammit, I obviously couldn't handle that right now! *And, you, the fellas with guns, just shoot!* —Right then, that's what I thought, but, well, he was only talking to me, after all. If they'd shot him for that, we would've gotten an earful about human rights later.

Only, after thinking it over real well…I think it would've been better if somebody actually had shot him dead back then.

…Uh, keep that bit off the record for me.

Let's see, where was I…? Oh right. He got up close to me, and he started "analyzing" me right out loud.

"Don't get me wrong; I don't mean your life is actually long… It's about spirit. Deep down, you are hilariously oblivious to death. I bet this is what you're thinking, yeah?—'In this jail, I'm part of the ruling class. You could say the prisoners' lives are in my hands. I'm safe. I'll never die.' The other guards are all obviously braced for the worst. They think, 'The prisoners could revolt and kill us at any time,' but you're awfully carefree, fella. You deserve a medal for that!"

There was no hostility there. There wasn't, but dammit… I still picked up on his intent to kill.

Back then, there was murder in the air. I definitely felt it.

"See, Mr. Guard-Man, my hobby—is teaching guys like that a lesson."

*He's gonna kill me. This guy is gonna kill me.* That feeling dominated my entire body, but even so, I couldn't do a thing, not one thing! The fear! Froze! My feet!

I was completely petrified—and he spoke to me, smiling.

He said this to me, bold as brass, right to me—right in my ears!

"I show 'em that death…is a whole lot closer than they think…"

*     *     *

…Haah. Sorry—I shouldn't have lost it like that.

When I remember that stuff, even now, I just can't stop shaking.

From an outsider's perspective, what he said was just a hood's threats. Only, when you heard it from him… How do I put this? It was real… Yeah. It felt real.

It was like he wasn't saying it to threaten me. It was just something he thought, plain and simple, like a little kid…

Huh? What happened then?

Well, they stuck Ladd in solitary after that, of course. It was more of a punishment cell than solitary: Except for a john and the door, there was nothing in it. Not even a bed. It did have a light, so it was nicer than the ones at some other prisons, but even so, a week in one of those was bound to knock the stuffing out of you.

They put Ladd in there for ten days.

But see, while he was in there, I quit my guard job.

I was pretty much running… Normally, they don't let guards quit that easy, but I was already half-sick, and I made them let me go.

I wanted to bolt before Ladd got out of solitary, no matter what.

…Him? In the end, I hear they did decide to send him to Alcatraz. You know Al Capone, right? They put him in just about that early. I think he's probably one of the old-timers there… I mean, it's still only been a few months, but anyway.

I dunno how much more time he has to serve. If he's not in for murder, he might be out again in a year or two…!

And so, y-y'know…

I'm scared.

Say, do I—I… D-do I look a little frightened to you?

Do I look like I—I know that I'll d-d-die?

I—I—I, I feel l-like he's, aaaah, aaaaaaaaah, aaaaaaaaaiiiee, heee's—he's coming! Coming! C-coming!

C'mon, answer the question!

I am! I am afraid, like I should be, right?!

My eyes look scared, like I could die tomorrow! Or even right now! Right?!

If they don't, he'll come. He's coming. Even in my dreams, that vicious grin crushes my right eye! And my left! Dammit! My legs, too! My arms! My body! My brain! Even when there's nothing left, he won't let me off; he'll keep crushing something about me, even though there's nothing left of me—what the hell is he crushing?! Forgive me; I'm scared. I swear, dying is scary… I'm scared, okay, I'm scared—but even if I scream and scream and scream, I can't get that guy's voice and eyes out of my hea——————— AaaaaaAAAh! AAaaaaah! Aaaaah! AAAAAAAaaaaaaAaaaAaaaa-aaaaAa-aaaaah! Aaaah! Aaaah! AaaaAAAaaah! Aaaaaaaaaaaaah! Aaaaaaaah! AAA-AAAAAAAH! Aaaaaaaaaaaaaaaaah! Aaaaaaaaaaaaaaaaaaaaaaaaaaaa aaaaaaaaaaaah…!

…I'm calm. Yeah, I'm okay.

A drink—gimme a drink.

Booze, c'mon, booze, boozeboozeboozebooze…booze… Too much drinking's bad for my health? It ain't that easy, genius. Something like liquor could never…

……

No, I might die, huh? I mean, I will die, won't I?

Okay, you're right. Dying is scary. I'm scared of dying, scared, scared… Right? C-c'mon; I am, right? Say it…

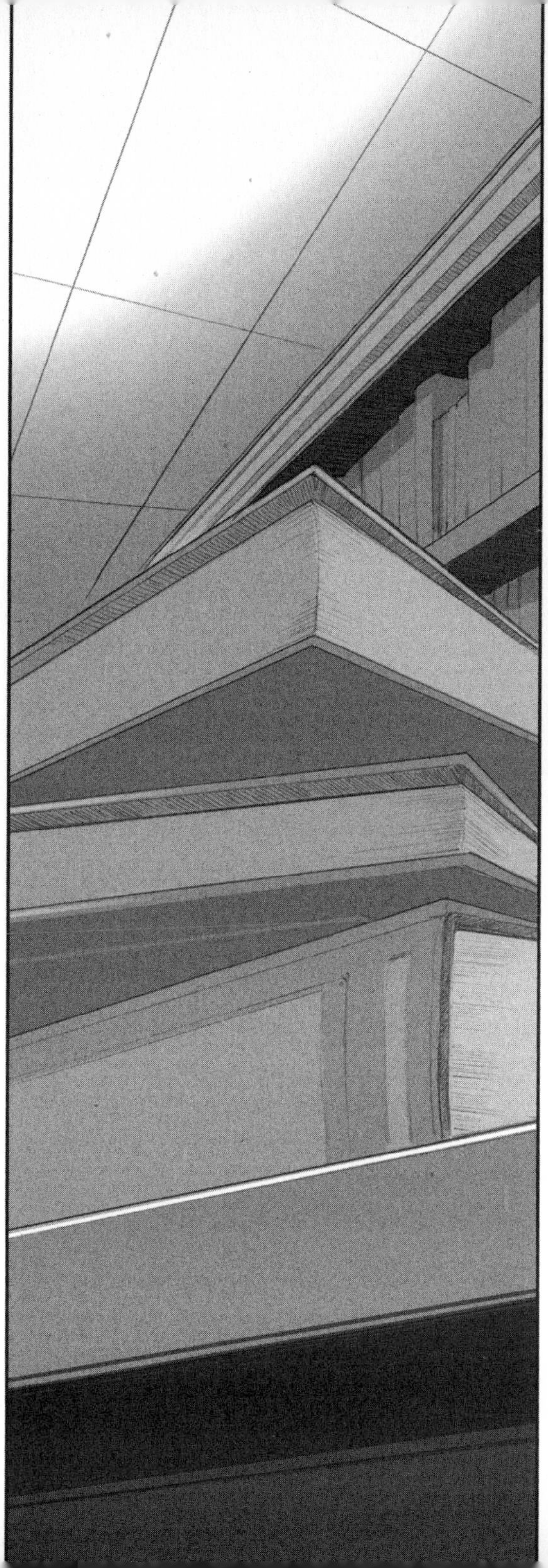

# PROLOGUE III

# ASSASSIN

Chicago    Nebula headquarters    Basement

It was an odd room, though it might have been more accurate to call it a facility of some sort.

Score upon score of books and documents lined the walls, were strewn messily across several wooden work desks—and a few were even scattered across the floor.

Microscopes and strange implements sat here and there among the documents, and the room felt like a combined laboratory and reference room.

Were that all it was, the place could easily have been mistaken for an abandoned building, but several people were bustling around inside, performing trivial tasks, jotting things down on the documents, and answering the ringing telephones.

"Aaaaaaaah, ummm… What'll I do, what'll I do…?"

The words had come from a bespectacled woman. As she dashed around, she tripped on a book that had been lying near her feet, and she took a spectacular tumble.

"Yeek!"

Documents flew everywhere. Her colleagues looked disgusted.

As this scene played out, like something from a university laboratory—

—in a corner of the room, on the other side of a thin dividing wall, the mood was completely different.

A young man in a suit sat in a chair.

He was resting his clasped hands on the desk, and his gaze was focused on a corner of the room, where a hanging curtain cast deep shadows.

A figure stood there, breathing quietly, erasing its presence in the gloom.

It wasn't even possible to make out the figure's features clearly, and the man in the suit sighed as he spoke to it.

"I don't think there's any real need to hide your face here. Is the ambience really so important?"

However, the figure stayed silent, holding absolutely still.

Seeing this, the man in the suit sighed again. Then, as if he'd given up, he broached the subject of work.

"Regarding our request today… While it is an important job, it is simultaneously one that would ordinarily be impossible. However, for that very reason, we believe there is value in requesting it."

The shadowy figure's only response to the man in the suit was more silence.

Even so, the man decided that his audience was listening, and he continued.

"Well… About the target's name…"

"……"

"It's Huey Laforet."

As before, the shape in the shadows showed no reaction.

"He's inside the notorious Alcatraz prison, and in a rather unique spot, on top of that. In addition, well… Frankly, he doesn't die."

At the man's words, the expression of the figure in the shadows contorted slightly.

However, the man in the suit didn't let that bother him. He kept speaking in a matter-of-fact voice.

"…I'm sure you understand that isn't a joke. Since you've worked with this division for a long time, you've seen several experimental cases, haven't you?"

Silently, with a glance, the shadow prompted the man in the suit to continue.

"Thanks. Well, the thing is…this man is different from those guinea pigs. He's a true immortal, and he's been alive for more than two hundred years. He's also a rather enigmatic fellow: He controls hordes of hand-raised followers, and he's currently issuing a variety of orders from jail."

"……"

"Yes, well, we do have a reason for sending you after someone who doesn't die. But no, we aren't asking you to dispose of him, not in this case."

Just as he'd finished his roundabout preamble and was about to get to the heart of the matter—

"Excuse me, I've brought tea… Eep?!"

—a woman in a white lab coat who'd carried in a tea set struck her little finger on the edge of the dividing wall, shrieked, and fell over dramatically, throwing tea and dishes into the air.

"?!"

"!"

The man in the suit and the figure in the shadows registered the situation at the exact same moment—and thus, the suited man took a direct strike to the temple from the corner of the flying tea tray while the figure in the shadows swiftly retreated out of range of the incoming hot water.

"Gwaaaaagh!"

"Aaah! I—I…I-I'm sorry! Are you all right?"

Eyes tearing up, the woman in the lab coat apologized, bowing repeatedly.

Above the lab coat, she wore black-rimmed glasses and a distracted expression, and long bangs hung loosely over her forehead. In contrast, the white coat encased a figure whose curves were rather too extreme; the sort that should have earned her the label of "model" or—in a different era—"Playmate."

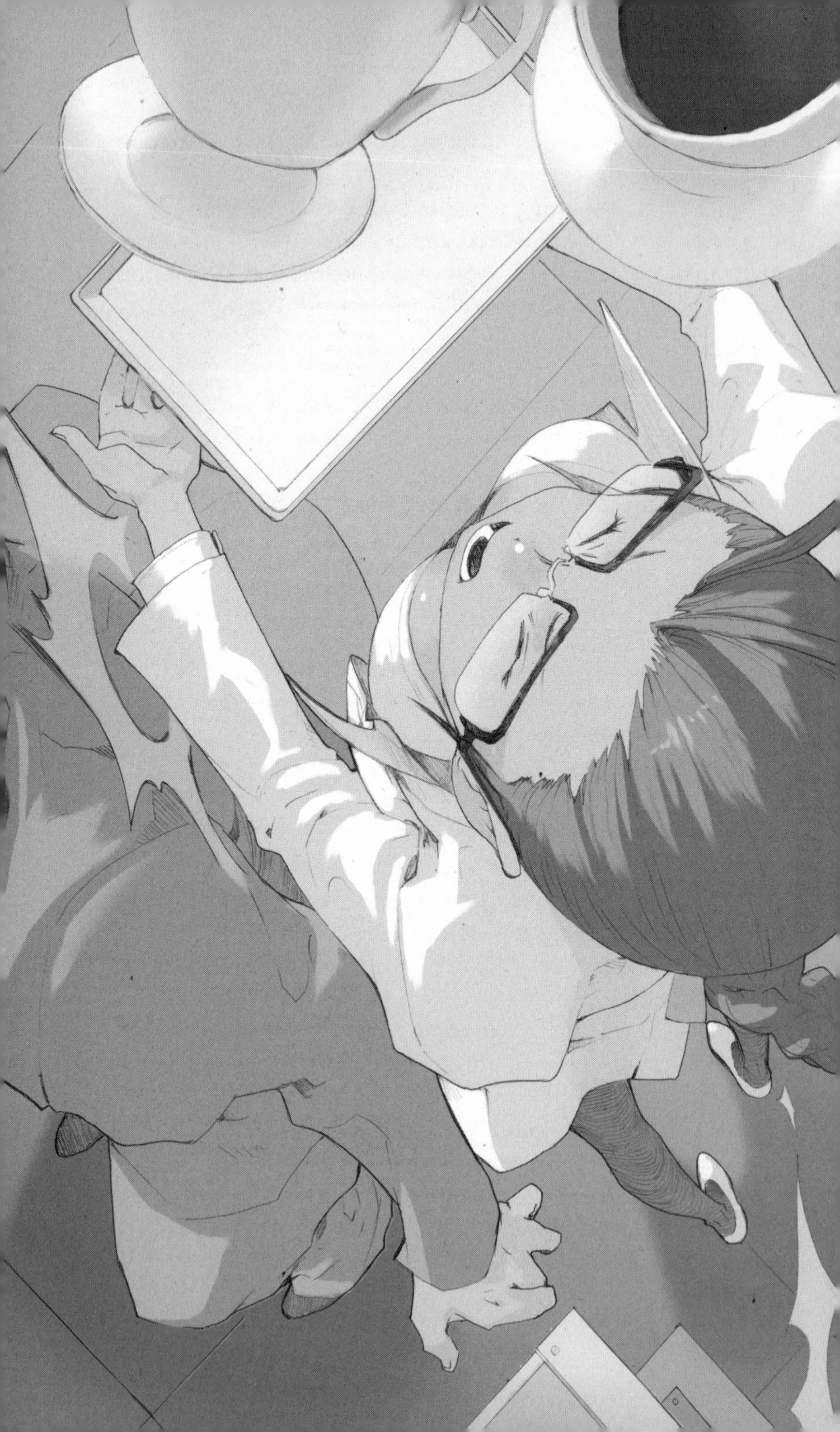

Every time she bowed her head, her bosom—which was empha-
sized in spite of her plain clothing—came into view, and the sight
would have probably improved the mood of an ordinary man, but…

…the man in the suit sent a nasty glare at the woman in the lab
coat. Then, resuming his seat as though nothing had happened, he
spoke to the figure in the shadows.

"…Ask her about the rest."

"Hmm? The rest of what?"

The curious question had come from the woman who'd spilled
the tea.

Showing clear irritation at her attitude—

"Of the request you spoke about this morning, *Director* Renee!"

—her *subordinate's* voice was prickly, and the woman clapped her
hands lightly in realization.

Although you never would have guessed it from her appearance, the woman—Renee Parmedes Branvillier—was apparently in
charge of the room. She turned to face the shadowy figure and, rec-
ognizing it, bowed respectfully.

"My! Imagine that! I haven't seen you in ages! If only you'd said
something, I would have made sure we had some nicer sweets to
offer you!"

The woman in the lab coat had suddenly begun to speak like some
sort of noblewoman, and her subordinate, the man in the suit, completely lost the composure he'd had up to that point. He shouted,
and the temple that had been struck by the tea tray twitched.

"You're the one who said to call him this morning!"

"Eek! I-I'm sorry. I just didn't think he'd be here so soon…"

The scientist shrank into herself, the man in the suit heaved a sigh,
and the shadowy figure stayed silent.

Renee checked to make sure her subordinate was finished repri-
manding her, then raised her head and spoke to him in an easygoing
tone.

"Um, how much have you told him?"

"That we want him to go to Alcatraz and do something about
Huey."

The man in the suit replied sullenly, and Renee clapped her hands again, then addressed the shadow.

"Oh, I see! Um, yes, well! What I'd like you to do is go to Huey Laforet, and…"

In a carefree, honest voice, without the slightest change in attitude…

…the woman murmured:

"Gouge out one of his eyes for me!"

⟺

"All right, thank you for your help, Mr. *Felix Walken*!"

In an attempt to restrain Renee, who was waving and seeing the visitor off, the man in the suit spoke sharply.

"Don't call his name out loud!"

"Aaaaaaah, I-I'm sorry!"

The bespectacled woman hastily covered her mouth. In response, the shadow sighed once—then finally managed to open its heavy, reluctant lips.

"Don't make me repeat myself—I sold that name to someone else a long time ago."

That was all the figure said. Then it started briskly down the corridor, as if it wasn't interested.

"Oh my, my, that's right, you're so right! I—I beg your pardon, Mr. Hitman!"

"Don't say his occupation out loud!"

"Eep?! I-I'm sorry!"

Although this was the ninth job the figure had taken from these people, he'd never asked what sort of work was being conducted in that paper-filled space.

The Nebula Corporation was one of America's leading conglomerates, and its operations were diversified. What was the purpose of

Renee's division, and why was the room located in an isolated area of the building? An ordinary person would have been curious about these things, but the shadow asked no questions.

Today as well, with the lady researcher and company kicking up the usual ruckus behind him, the shadow didn't ask any questions—he simply, quietly, *read* Renee.

Renee was certainly not subjectively evil.

She didn't have the faintest idea that she was bad, but viewed objectively, she was an undeniable villain.

Of course, there probably weren't many people who thought *I am evil!* while they did evil deeds, but hers was a particularly unique case.

She was a perfectly *innocent* person, the shadow decided.

A being who could strike others into the depths of hell without any malice whatsoever.

Once, he'd happened to walk in on her while she was conducting human experimentation.

When he asked where she'd kidnapped her subject from, she'd responded immediately:

"Oh, no, no, I didn't kidnap her!"

As she injected something into the little girl's arm with no hesitation—

"I bought her!"

—her smile hadn't even faltered.

The white-coated "researcher" merely said what was in front of her, with no hesitation, confusion, or doubt.

Hearing her voice at his back...

The man she'd called Felix disappeared into the depths of the corridor, and there were no doubts in his expression, either.

It was as if the lunacy he'd just felt in this world was common sense.

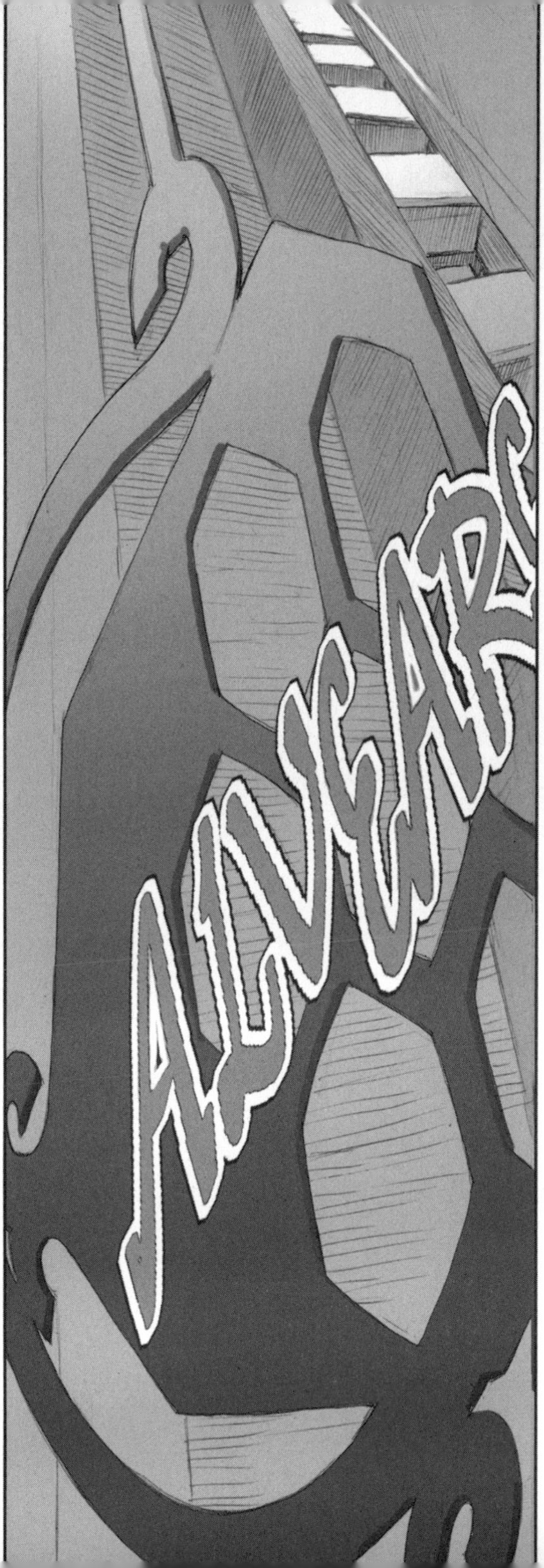

# PROLOGUE IV

# THE USUAL

New York    Inside Alveare, the honey tavern

In an establishment whose air was thick with the scent of honey, a man and woman were talking loudly.

"And so I said, 'O Romeo! Wherefore art thou, Romeo!'"
"Yes, my Romeo and his Hamlet!"
"And then the security fella said, 'Uh, my name's John,' and I said, 'Apologies, I mistook you for somebody else,' and we just turned on our heels and walked away."
"Yes, it was much ado about nothing!"
As the pair boasted proudly, the surrounding audience laughed and heckled them.
"C'mon, that was seriously all it took?!"
"Was that guard already gaga or something?"
Despite the teasing jeers, the indefinable something that shone between the couple didn't so much as flicker.
"Heh-heh! He came after us the second we started to run, but we were faster!"
"Yes, a victory for youth!"
As the two related their story, their eyes full of confidence, the drunks kept up with the verbal jabs.
"Don't that mean you just ran away…?"

"I see! You could put it that way, couldn't you! All we did was run, and we got away … Isn't that amazing?!"

"Yes, it's a natural gift! Beginner's luck!"

"…Nah, never mind. My bad. You guys are amazing in all kinds of ways."

Smiling with mild chagrin, the customers ordered more drinks. The stories this pair told just left ordinary people confused, and they knew that the best way to enjoy them was to listen with a glass of booze.

It had already been close to a year since Prohibition had been repealed nationwide.

In 1929, when the Great Depression began on Wall Street, opposition to the Prohibition Act had cropped up all across the nation. The United States teemed with people claiming the government stole work from their country and demanding the return of liquor brewing and sales jobs.

In addition, the Prohibition Act had ended up creating a hotbed for mafia growth in the form of bootleg liquor, and at the time, the government was beginning to take another look at all sorts of laws, hoping to weaken the enemies of the state.

On top of that, a variety of other doctrines and arguments had accumulated and overlapped. As a result, in 1933, the Prohibition Act was repealed, and the speakeasies—taverns that had gone underground—confidently appeared in the public eye again.

That said, naturally, many of these taverns had prospered precisely because of bootleg liquor, and speakeasies disappeared one after another when the light struck them.

This place, Alveare, was a venerable old establishment that had survived the harsh struggle, and it had continued to expand its sales as a restaurant that offered unique, popular dishes made with honey, in addition to liquor. The restaurant had new tables, and it was even grander than it was during its speakeasy days. It had more employees now, and five waitresses—including Lia, who'd been there for years—bustled around among the tables.

In the midst of this was a singularity: a couple who were regular customers—who practically lived here.

Isaac Dian and Miria Harvent.

Everyone at the tavern knew their names, but aside from their names and current behavior, people knew surprisingly little about them.

Almost no one knew the details of their backgrounds, and even among the restaurant's proprietress and the camorristas who hung out there, not many knew about their pasts. However, no one was suspicious of them or disappointed by this. Contrary to the intentions of the people in question, the daily tales of their heroic exploits were treated as hilarious anecdotes and were oft discussed at the restaurant.

"Well, that's really something. Tell me more about the capers you youngsters have pulled off."

The couple had given a general account of their story and had started drinking honeyed juice when an unfamiliar voice spoke to them.

The speaker was a whiskered man in late middle age, and he was smiling at them mildly.

"You know, every day, you two talk as if you've committed robberies all over the country… You wouldn't be somebody famous, would you?"

The tavern customer teased them as if they were children, but Isaac and Miria responded without seeming the least bit annoyed.

"No, no! Our disguises were excellent! I'm sure nobody knows it was us!"

"Yes, they were perfect crimes! Edgar Allan Poe!"

Cryptic words, cryptic interjections. It would have been hard for anyone who wasn't used to talking with them to even follow what they were saying, but the elderly man actively joined their conversation, still beaming.

"Ha-ha! Disguises, eh? That's really something, son. Say, just between you and me…a few years back, there was something in the papers. 'Bizarre Mummy Robbers!' they said. That wasn't you two, was it? You know…there was a man wrapped in bandages from head to toe, and a woman who wore a wedding dress over her bandages, and they robbed a bank. Got away with an absolute mountain of tissue packets."

The man's description had been detailed, and Isaac's and Miria's eyes widened.

"Huh? Did we get into the papers that time?!"

"Come to think of it, that strange person did take our picture!"

"Wow… They made us think they were just a photographer when they were actually a journalist—this is big, Miria. There's a master of disguise who's better than us out there!"

"Yes, a phantom thief! Arsène Lupin!"

Ignoring Isaac, who'd started being impressed over something dumb, the older man asked more questions about their heroic exploits.

"Then what about that other time? The ones who got into the Geno-ard house in Newark and stole a whole safe's worth of money…?"

"Heh-heh-heh… We can't tell you that!"

"Yes, we're taking the Fifth! We could even call a lawyer!"

"Hmm… Setting aside the question of whether you stole it or not, then, what were you wearing at the time?"

The man was smiling as he spoke, and Isaac abruptly frowned.

Then, looking grave, he spoke to Miria, who was next to him.

"Say, Miria. What were we that time?"

"Indians! Native Americans!"

"Oh, right, that's right! Indians, Indians!"

"Yes, the will of the great land!"

Seeing Isaac's and Miria's smiles as they continued their carefree conversation, the elderly man also smiled comfortably.

However, his smile was more of a smirk.

"Then what about when you scattered money around New York?"

"Oh, I remember that time real clearly! I was a priest then."

"Yes, and I was a nun!"

"Ha-ha-ha… Is that right? I see…"

The elderly man went on listening to Isaac and Miria's opaque conversation while asking about this and that. The story about stealing the doors off a museum. The one about pilfering a sack full of chocolate. The one about filching all the men's underwear they could find and the one about hitting home runs with the heads of some mafiosi in Chicago—

The elderly man listened to all this with a genuine smile on his face.

It really was more of a smirk.

"Well, that's amazing. You two really are something."

The man applauded, and in response, Isaac and Miria flushed red.

"Ha-ha-ha! You'll make me blush, mister. This is embarrassing; don't let us do all the talking. You say something, too!"

"Yes, it's only fair! It's equivalent exchange! It's depreciation!"

Isaac and Miria smiled as they spoke to him, and when the elderly man responded, his expression and tone were as mild as if he was talking to good friends he'd known for a decade.

"True. Well then, I'll tell you about me, so c'mon down to my place."

"Huh? You run some kind of a shop, too, mister?"

"Wooooow!"

"Yes, but it's nothing impressive."

The conversation had taken a rather odd turn.

With a dazed air that brought that characterization to mind, the customers who'd been sitting nearby—particularly the ones who stood out less than the Alveare's regulars—watched the elderly man, keeping their gestures natural.

However, Isaac and Miria, the intended recipients of those words, didn't seem bothered by them in the least.

Isaac patted at his jacket, then looked troubled and spoke to Miria, who was sitting beside him.

"Drat. I went and left my wallet in the storehouse when we were helping them clean this afternoon."

"Eek! We're penniless?!"

"I think it's probably still there. Could you run out real quick and get it for me?"

"Okay! Hang on just a minute, Isaac!"

Miria jumped from her chair and ran off lightly, disappearing into the back of the restaurant. As he watched her go, the older man smiled a bit wryly.

"You could have just gone to get it yourself. That was pretty lazy."

"Was it?"

Isaac's response was unexpectedly short. He was gazing after Miria.

About ten seconds passed—and then Isaac said something odd to the elderly man.

"So, erm, well, let's go to your place, mister."

"Hmm...? What's this? Don't we need to wait for the young lady?"

The man looked dubious. Isaac grinned and thumped him on the shoulder.

"Well, mister, *you're a cop, right*?"

"!"

")

"!"     "!"     "?!"     "?!"     "!"     "?!"          "?!"     "!"     "!"
     "!"     "!"     "!"     "?!"          "?!"               "!"     "!"     "?!"
"?!"     "!"          "!"     "!"     "!"     "!"     "?!"     "!"     "!"     "!"

The moment Isaac said that, startled looks and gasps went up all over the restaurant, sending a grim ripple through the air. The elderly man was reacting to the fact that his cover had been blown. The people in the restaurant—particularly the camorristas—were genuinely startled: *We had him pegged already, but, man, who'd have thought Isaac would figure it out?!*

"...You knew?"

"Well, I'm used to being questioned by policemen, see. Usually I just throw pepper bombs at them and skip out, but I would've felt bad about, you know, causing trouble for this place..."

"I see... Apparently, you haven't gotten away this long on luck alone. But what did you send the young lady to get? Those pepper bomb things? Or it wouldn't be some kind of pistol, would it?"

The elderly man sounded suspicious. Isaac looked around uneasily, seeming to be at a loss—but as if to throw him a rope, an extraordinarily fat man and an extraordinarily thin one walked over from the back of the restaurant, calling to him.

"Hey, Isaac. Did you fight with Miria or something?"

"She just went tearing hell-for-leather out the back door."

"!"

The young man who responded to those words was sitting a little ways off from the elderly man and had looked as if he'd come to the restaurant by himself. He was probably another cop. Hastily, he tried to dash outside, but the older man stopped him. "Don't bother," he said sourly.

Still looking irritated, the elderly man handcuffed Isaac.

He'd probably assumed that Isaac was just an idiot, too. He'd had a fast one pulled on him by somebody he'd completely underestimated, thinking he'd be an easy mark. The camorristas, the people on the gangsters' side of the law, guessed what was going through his head, thought *Serves you right*, and smiled.

Smirking, of course.

"I see... You let the young lady escape on her own. That's real admirable. But—"

Possibly because he'd picked up on the mood now pervading the establishment, the elderly man briskly put the scene of the arrest behind him.

As he went, he spat a warped parting shot at the man he was hauling away with his right hand.

"...We'll make you want to cough up her hiding place soon enough."


A few minutes after Isaac had been marched away by the two men and left the restaurant...

...Miria returned through the back door, looking perplexed.

"Say, Isaac? I can't find your wallet anywhere. I wonder if somebody stole it... Hmm? Isaac?"

Miria looked around the room. Her expression was calm, and

upon seeing her, everyone from the camorristas who'd put on an act to the waitresses and customers who'd seen the whole thing looked uncomfortable and said nothing.

"H-hello? … What happened? Where's Isaac? The bathroom?"

Miria must have felt the energy of the place and realized that something big had happened. Uneasy, she gazed around the room—and her expression gradually clouded.

"Isaac…? Um… Where is he? Where…?"

On that day—Isaac Dian was taken in.

He'd been arrested by a plainclothes policeman who'd been hearing rumors about the couple, who'd been telling tales of their larcenous exploits, for a while. He had been near retirement and wasn't given much work and, as a result, had had too much time on his hands—but, strangely, the incident wasn't reported in the papers, and nothing about trial arrangements ever leaked out. Time simply flowed on.

This happened about a month before Firo Prochainezo was brought in for questioning concerning property damage.

And thus, quietly, everything began.

**CHAPTER 1: FRONT**

# LET'S GO TO PRISON

Once, the island had been a fortress.

It was small, with an area of about half a square mile, and it sat just off the coast of San Francisco Bay.

Most of the island was bare rock, and its coast was made of steep cliffs all the way around. At the top were rough buildings made of concrete.

The island's name, Alcatraz, came from a word for *pelican*, but the atmosphere that hung over it was solemn and didn't suit the name.

Long ago, the place had been completely wild, but during the Gold Rush, construction had begun on a fort meant to protect the town of San Francisco. It was subsequently strengthened during the Civil War, ultimately becoming a maritime fort equipped with a total of 111 long cannons and Rodman guns, which were cutting-edge technology at the time.

Since the Civil War, Alcatraz Island had been used to detain military criminals.

Even after its role as a fortress ended, the island's buildings were used to jail soldiers who had committed crimes, war criminals, and Native Americans who'd been captured during internal disputes.

The fortress that had been built to guard against external enemies became a facility to keep others from escaping. By the beginning of the twentieth century, the island was a full-fledged military prison.

In 1933, the prison on Alcatraz Island passed from the military into the hands of the Department of Justice and was reborn as the nation's strongest federal penitentiary.

*Escape-proof.*

That simple, powerful catchphrase made criminals shudder, and at the same time, it gave the world new creativity. A place that was in the world yet completely isolated from its laws.

For many long years, the prison would be at the center of a variety of movies, depicted in many different ways.

But the Alcatraz Island of people's fantasies drew notice throughout America with one absolute certainty: the word *escape-proof*.

As if to strike an additional chord in its symphony of infamy, in August of this year, Al Capone—a man made more colorful by fear, dread, and a kind of adoration from all across the country—was incarcerated there. Thus, the legend of the prison continued to dominate San Francisco Bay, passively accepting embellishment.

And on one particular day, another boat set sail for the island.

It carried many types of despair and a few ambitions as it sailed under blue skies toward an island that made for a beautiful view.

⇔

One day in December 1934     San Francisco Bay          Prison boat

"...This is the pits."

"Quiet."

Firo had murmured to himself, and the expressionless guard muttered back.

Once he was on the boat, like it or not, he was forced to acknowledge where he was.

He was headed for a place buzzing with rumors like something out of a run-of-the-mill adventure story: not only "It's impregnable" and "No one can escape" but also "Every guy they put in there goes crazy" and "They do military experiments on the prisoners."

When he'd heard those rumors, Firo had always laughed them off as baloney, but once he was actually standing on the wharf and seeing the island rising from the bay, the rumors resurfaced in his mind.

It wasn't because the place looked creepy. It was the opposite, in fact.

From the sunny wharf, the prison on Alcatraz Island towered on top of its natural cliffs. Around it, there were several other buildings that seemed to be facilities of some sort.

The natural hues of the cliffs and the man-made colors of the facilities harmonized perfectly with one another, and between the blue of the sky and the blue of the sea, it looked like an artist's painting.

For that very reason, the place was like something out of a dream, and it seemed as though anything could happen there.

Firo could hardly escape that feeling.

After all, he was already living in the fairy-tale world of immortality. When he looked at that island from where he was, he would have even believed a rumor that a dragon slept on Alcatraz.

All the more so since he was bound for that island himself.

*This is the pits.*

As the boat pitched and tossed violently, Firo silently murmured the words to himself again.

The vessel wasn't moving all that fast. Even so, it rolled irregularly, forward and backward, left and right. The rumors about the strong currents in this part of the ocean seemed to be true.

*If it came down to it, could I steel myself to take a few bullets, jump into the ocean, and escape that way?*

Because of his immortal body, the idea had crossed his mind briefly… But what if he was unconscious when he hit those currents, sank to the bottom of the ocean, and never came up again? It wouldn't be at all odd for things to play out that way. The distance seemed swimmable, but in fact, the prison was separated from the outside world by a wall that was far thicker than distance.

\*      \*      \*

*Why the hell did I have to come here?*

Remembering the men from the Bureau of Investigation with an expression of clear loathing, Firo thought over the events that had brought him to his current situation.

⟺

One week ago

"Ha! I bet you're happy, huh?! I leveraged all my authority to get you special treatment. Nobody who's jailed goes directly into Alcatraz, generally. It's where the troublemakers from other prisons end up. Thanks to my snazzy arrangements, though, you've got an express ticket, no transfers. Just this once, I'll make an exception and let even a petty gangster like you be grateful to me."

"No, no, wait, hang on. Hold the phone. Just—hold it."

In the interrogation room, Firo waved his cuffed hands.

"I'll split what I wanna say into three pieces and say 'em real slow so that even your ridiculous mind will understand. One: Why. Two: Do I. Three: Have to go *there*?"

Firo's words had been the result of an extremely natural train of thought, and Victor answered promptly.

"Bragging rights."

"Huh?"

"Just coming back from Alcatraz is enough to boost your rep. In our world, previous offenses are cause for pure humiliation, but they're practically a medal to you people."

"…That depends on the time and place. As far as I'm concerned, getting threatened and shoved into jail without so much as a trial is definitely an embarrassment, and it's an embarrassment for my family, too."

Firo was gradually beginning to sharpen the blade of his emotions, but Victor shrugged his words off with an easy smile.

"Then what about getting popular in prison? With that girly baby face of yours, you'll be a favorite there in no time. That said, that place has a warden who's worth his salt. To set a good example, he takes real good care of things to ensure that none of *that stuff* goes on, so relax."

"…Edward? Mind if I kill this guy?"

"Sorry. He's immortal, so you can't."

Victor was cackling, and Firo was so irritated he could hardly stand it. Before, at this point, he'd probably have jumped him without giving it a second thought. He would have had the other guy's head pinned down with his right hand, would have made him beg for his life.

At that thought, Firo suddenly began thinking about who he was now. *"Before," huh?*

It was true that he was softer than he used to be.

Before he'd joined the Camorra, the only people he'd trusted enough to open up to had been the three Gandor brothers and Claire Stanfield, childhood friends who were practically family.

Then one day, a Japanese immigrant named Yaguruma had knocked him flat. That was when he'd encountered the organization known as the Martillo Family.

The syndicate had been part of a web of gangs known as the Camorra, and to Firo, it had become where he felt truly comfortable. At the time, he hadn't bothered to hide his hostility toward the world, but before he knew it, that place seemed to have broken the thorns off his heart.

And he'd mellowed out completely when—

*When I met Ennis, or maybe Isaac and Miria.*

You couldn't call them honest citizens, but you couldn't state categorically that they belonged to the underworld, either. He considered them family, and he was smiling wryly at the memory of their faces, when Victor abruptly brought up a strange subject.

"This is a plea bargain."

"Hunh?"

"Remember that Ennis doll we were talking about earlier?"

"…What about her?"

He'd just been thinking about her, and the mention of her name made his heart speed up.

"That woman ate an alchemist once. You knew that, right?"

"......"

It did ring a bell.

He'd heard about it from Ennis, and inside him, Szilard's memories also confirmed that it was true.

Once, back when Ennis was just an emotionless tool, she'd eaten an alchemist who'd come to eat Szilard.

However, as a result, all sorts of knowledge had flooded into her. It had given her emotions, guilt, and endless regret. It had also made her who she was today.

By now, he'd completely forgotten about it, but it was possible that Ennis herself was still plagued by guilt.

What was this guy trying to pull, poking at an old wound like that?

As Firo glared at him, Victor spoke, lowering his eyes slightly.

"That alchemist was a good friend of mine."

"......"

Firo looked away in spite of himself, accepting the weight of that statement. At the same time, a new doubt surfaced, and it was out of his mouth before he could think.

"So, what, you're planning to avenge him by killing Ennis?"

There was clear tension and determination in his voice.

Depending on the answer, he'd let the rage he'd swallowed blaze up again, and this time he was probably prepared to eat the man in front of him.

Firo waited quietly for the man's next words, calming his breathing so that he'd be ready to leap immediately.

Fielding that question, Victor gestured as if he was thinking about something for a little while. Then he responded slowly, choosing his words as he went.

"I don't wanna do that, either. If I thought it would solve everything, I would have eaten you back there, and Huey, too, ages ago... I don't plan to imitate Szilard, the old bastard."

"...I see."

"That doesn't mean I've got nothing against a broad who ate my friend, though. I get she was Szilard's puppet at the time, but I'm not at peace with it—plus, it's possible to pin suspicion for other murders on her, too."

"…What?"

Firo was scowling, and Victor responded quietly.

"Immortals aren't the only ones she killed on the old geezer's orders. As proof, several skeletons turned up in one of Szilard's old hideouts. We dunno who killed them, but it might have been her, and if so— Well, what do you think we'd have to do to bring a broad who doesn't officially exist to trial?"

"You asshole…"

Victor was smiling nastily, and Firo's reply was filled with loathing as he ground his teeth.

Victor watched him, as if enjoying the show, then calmly hit him with a "solution."

"So on that note: Ennis's current master—her main body—is you. As a result, I'm offering you a plea bargain."

"…You're what?"

"I'm saying, if you do the job we tell you to do…we'll treat that Ennis broad's crimes as 'unsolved.'"

"For someone throwing around insults like 'dirty' and 'low-life scum,' that's a pretty cheap move."

Firo had put everything he had into that counterattack, but Victor shut him down with a high-pressure look.

"Hey, I'm not telling you to sell out your buddies or anything. I just want you to check into the activities of a guy who could turn out to be our…common enemy, that's all. I'll fill you in on the details after you say you'll take the job."

"…You hate gangsters. What guarantee do I have that you'll keep a promise made to one of us?"

"I'll swear it. Swearing's all I can do. Whether you believe it or not."

Then, for the first time, Victor's smile vanished, and he leaned in closer to the other immortal.

Even if he was handcuffed, if he'd put out his right hand, he could have touched him easily.

But Firo couldn't move.

In the family he belonged to, the upper-level executives—Maiza, Ronny, Yaguruma, and the boss, Molsa Martillo—sometimes radiated intimidation. This was a lot like that.

Firo had just about put his anger away, and when he was confronted with that intimidating aura, which was supported by long years of practice and experience, he was unable to move.

He'd broken out in a thin sheen of cold sweat, and the agent who'd lived for more than two centuries hit him with a single, corrupt comment.

"I'll hush up Ennis's business for you.

"I swear it, on all the justice in this country."

⇐⇒

After thinking it over for three days or so, Firo chose to accept the proposal.

He was irritated with himself for not being able to make an immediate decision for Ennis's sake, but he'd thought that, while he let those three days go by, someone from his family might take action for him.

However, in the end, during those days, the situation hadn't changed at all.

The Bureau goons were probably being very careful and acting in isolation within a department that was independent to begin with.

It felt as if Ronny—who was sometimes abnormally competent—might do something about this, but it wasn't in Firo's nature to cling to a hope like that.

Even now, with every single moment that passed, he was making his family and Ennis worry.

*Even though this isn't the time for that.*

Finally, in order to break out of the situation on his own, Firo had accepted Victor's proposal—

And so, he now found himself on a boat.

\*      \*      \*

However, he wasn't muttering *This is the pits* over and over, because he was cursing himself for folding to Victor.

*"Monitor Huey Laforet."*

That was the mission the Bureau had given Firo.

If he called it a mission, it was likely that people would think he'd sunk to being the Fed's loyal hound dog, which was humiliating all on its own. His position was certainly no better than a government dog's—but it wasn't as though Firo had no personal interest in this man.

In an incident one year ago, a mysterious group called Lamia had messed with Ennis.

They'd called her their little sister and named Huey Laforet as the alchemist who'd created them.

The man had been on Firo's mind ever since.

Even in Szilard's memories, he was constantly shrouded in mystery. Only one person, an eccentric named Elmer C. Albatross, had been close to him; apart from that, the memories held almost nothing. Unlike Victor, with whom he simply hadn't interacted, it felt as though this man had intentionally behaved such that he wouldn't be remembered.

Firo didn't much like going into Szilard's memories, and he gave up searching further, choosing to simply go into his encounter with Huey as himself.

"C'mon, the guy's in jail. He can't have any dirt on you. You'll have way more intel than he does. You've got the advantage; believe in yourself."

"There's a guard who's in on this. He's supposed to make like he's taking you to your cell, but then he'll either take you to Huey Laforet or fill you in on the details of the situation."

That was what Victor had said to him at the end. It could have been taken as encouragement. He was a nasty guy, and he couldn't be trusted, but that comment had naturally raised Firo's morale.

As a result, he'd gone into this all-too-short voyage in fairly high spirits, but—

—when they were just about to board the police boat, one of the guards had murmured in Firo's ear:

"We've been waiting for you, Mr. Firo Prochainezo."

"Oh, so you're..."

*...the guy with the Bureau of Investigation?*

Firo was just about to ask the question, when the guard cut him off, speaking indifferently.

*"Master Huey is eagerly awaiting you."*

Firo shuddered.

The moment he heard that flat voice, he broke into a cold sweat all over his body.

"He says that *he will be terribly happy to have a fellow immortal so near...*"

"...Hey..."

"From this point on, there will be no talking."

The second Firo spoke to him, the man went back to being an ordinary guard.

It felt as if he'd been daydreaming for a moment; the sudden change in the guard seemed to imply that nothing had happened at all. It was as Firo were being compelled not to question the recent situation.

*What was that about him not having any dirt on me? That lousy excuse for an agent...*

Thus, on the boat, Firo was repeating the same words again and again.

A single phrase that described his current situation with blistering accuracy.

Over and over.

In his mouth. In his heart:

*"This is the pits..."*

## CHAPTER 1: BACK

# FIRST, LET'S TRY PICKING A FIGHT

New York    The bar Alveare

The bar and restaurant hadn't opened yet.

In the midst of the sweet, lingering scent of honey, a woman sat in a chair, looking sad.

There were several figures around her: the waitresses, who were getting the restaurant ready, the restaurant's middle-aged proprietress, and a few members of the Martillo Family, which treated the establishment as its stronghold.

However, a heavy air hung over the woman that set her apart from the surrounding mood.

There was still something girlish in her features, but her clothes were strange for this era: a rather masculine-looking suit and slacks.

The woman's name was Ennis. She had no family name.

She was an imperfect homunculus who had been created by an alchemist named Szilard.

When she'd betrayed him, her master and main body, she'd been prepared to die, but—

—a young immortal had eaten the ancient alchemist, and Ennis's life had been left in his care.

"Firo…"

He was good at looking after others. She'd been his enemy, but he'd taken her in and had even given her a room in his apartment.

He was the first family she'd ever had.

At first, she hadn't known how to act around him, but as time passed, he'd gradually become an integral part of Ennis's new life.

Now he was gone.

About a week ago, men who'd seemed to be agents from the Department of Justice had taken him away.

When Ennis heard that Firo had been hauled in, she realized she felt more ill at ease than she'd ever felt before.

It was true that he was an executive in the Martillo Family, a criminal syndicate, and that he toed the line of crime, or maybe even walked on the other side of it. Ennis knew this.

However, with her, Firo had been an oddly generous, agreeable young man, and she'd almost never seen his darker face. That said, he hadn't kept secrets from her, either.

He was precious family who'd given her a definite place to belong when she hadn't even known the meaning of her own existence.

Once she was no longer able to see him, Ennis realized just how important he'd become to her.

However, she couldn't just stay depressed all by herself.

Firo wasn't the only one who'd disappeared.

Isaac Dian had also been marched out of this restaurant about a month ago by some plainclothes policemen, and he hadn't come back. They hadn't heard a thing after that, but he'd probably been put in prison somewhere.

When his partner, Miria Harvent, had learned about it, everyone had thought she'd either cry and wail or become frantic and start rampaging around.

However, when Miria had understood everything, she'd closed her mouth and left Alveare without a word, and she still hadn't returned.

Ennis hadn't been there at the time, so she hadn't seen it herself. Even so, at the idea of what Miria must have been feeling, she was seized by thoughts that made her chest constrict.

Like Firo, Isaac and Miria had changed Ennis's life. They had saved her, and she also thought of them as precious friends.

And yet there was nothing she could do.

Ennis was terribly frustrated by her own helplessness, and yet she knew that just staying depressed wouldn't get anyone anywhere, so she'd decided to keep thinking about what she should be doing now.

Today as well, she'd meant to spend the afternoon driving herself into a corner, but—

"Ennis, are you okay?"

Ennis had been discouraged for the past few days, and seeing her that way must have worried him. Czeslaw Meyer—Ennis's roommate, a boy she treated like her little brother—spoke to her, looking concerned.

"Czes… I'm all right. I've just been feeling a little blue, that's all."

"If it's about Firo, you shouldn't worry too much."

"I'm sorry. I know I need to pull myself together…"

"Oh, that's fine. It's just… It really is okay not to worry… It sounds funny to say this, but you two *have time*. Even if Firo's in prison, *he won't die from sickness or an accident or anything.*"

The boy spoke frankly, and Ennis responded naturally, giving him a soft smile.

"You're right… After all, you managed to reunite with Maiza after more than a hundred years, Czes."

"Y-yeah…"

For some reason, Czes's answer sounded evasive, and Ennis grew uneasy, wondering if she'd said something wrong.

However, before she could ask, they heard the voice of the proprietress from the entrance to the restaurant.

"Sorry, mister. We're not open yet."

"The thing is, I've got business with the Martillos."

The voice that had answered Seina was low and male, with a sharp edge to it.

"…Well, well… Are they expecting you, sir?"

"Heh-heh, quit talking like city hall, all right? Is Maiza here? He's an old friend of mine."

When the man said that name, Ennis, Czes, and the stern-faced men around them all looked at the door.

Maiza Avaro was the Martillo Family's *contaiuolo* and one of the top executives. Outwardly, he looked good-natured, but he was actually pretty sharp, and he was one of the keys to the Martillo Family's continued existence on its small territory.

In addition, he had one other important significance for Ennis, Czes, and the others like them…

"Anyway, I'm coming in."

"Uh— Hey, mister, hold your horses!"

While Ennis and Czes were looking at each other and keeping an eye on the situation, the man stepped into the restaurant, ignoring Seina's attempt to stop him.

The individual who appeared wore glasses and a thin coat. His sharp eyes were filled with a light that could have been taken as either hostility or wariness, and the atmosphere in the restaurant, which had been filled with friendly chatter up until that point, abruptly turned tense.

After the incident with Isaac the other day, the family's men suspected that the guy might be with some sort of judicial organization, and the aura that clung to him actually did make him seem like that, in the extreme.

However—there was one person who was several times more apprehensive than those around him, but for a completely different reason from theirs.

"…Czes?"

When he saw the face of the man who'd walked in, Czes's expression had instantly stiffened.

On seeing it, Ennis realized that something serious was happening. She looked at the restaurant's visitor—

And when she saw his face, she realized who he was.

She'd never met him directly. However, she definitely remembered his face.

Ironically, although she had no way of knowing, it was the same reaction Firo had had when he'd met this same man.

*This man is… Oh, he's—*

She'd learned something she couldn't afford to know. That sensation, regret, and an immense feeling of guilt surged through Ennis.

The pain of that guilt was something she must never forget.

On top of that, the people who would have softened that pain… weren't here now.


Ennis's emotions were faintly visible in her expression, but the newcomer didn't even see her. He was looking around at each of the men in the restaurant in turn.

Then he spotted the boy with the stiff face beside Ennis.

"Hey, Czes."

The man's expression softened just a little, and he spoke quietly.

"I haven't seen you in a while. What's it been, *two hundred and thirty-three years* or so?"

The man spread his arms, waxing nostalgic, but Czes's guard stayed firmly in place, and he said only one word: the other man's name.

"Victor…"

⟺

"Sorry to barge in on you before you open. Don't worry about me, young lady."

The Asian waitress had been about to get him some water, but he stopped her with a gesture. With no reservations, the bespectacled man—Victor—walked up to Czes's table, pulled out a nearby chair, and sat down in an agile motion.

"It's been ages. You look good; that's great."

"Uh, uh-huh… You too, Victor."

Victor's tone was persistently cheerful, but Czes was clearly wary and frightened.

He sat on the edge of his chair, obviously putting distance between the other man and himself.

In other words, he was staying out of reach of his right hand.

Czeslaw—Czes—was an immortal as well, and he had a stark terror of getting eaten. Naturally, most immortals feared the one "death" that was open to them, but Czes was conscious of it more frequently than most.

In addition, he'd been betrayed by someone he'd trusted in the past, so he was also more skeptical than necessary. To this boy, an immortal who'd appeared here suddenly after a gap of several centuries was unnerving in the extreme.

"…Why are you here…?"

"I had a little something to discuss with Maiza."

"You weren't very startled to see me… Does that mean you knew? Did you know I was here?"

"Hmm? Yeah, of course I did."

His existence was known.

The fact made him feel a faint chill, and Czes's wariness toward the other man grew stronger.

"Did you hear about it from the information broker? Or from Maiza?"

"The information broker? You mean the DD newspaper? Nah, they don't say much to us Department of Justice types. Ah, but don't go thinking I heard it from Maiza. I haven't seen the guy in six or seven years."

"Then why…?"

"Well, I've had my men watching you all this time."

Victor spoke frankly, and as Czes kept asking questions, his eyebrows came together.

"Your men…?"

"Ha-ha. All you've been doing is grilling me. Let's enjoy this reunion a bit more, hmm?"

"…Is the question so hard to answer?"

"Good grief, Czes, what am I gonna do with you? All right then, lemme answer your question with a question… Let's trade. I had something I wanted to ask you, too."

Victor's expression was abruptly serious, and the boy felt deeply nervous. Every muscle in his body tightened.

"Wh-what?"

"Czes… *Where's Fermet?*"

"…!"

The change was dramatic.

Up until that point, although he was afraid, Czes had been trying to act brave. However, the moment he heard the name Fermet, he went so pale that even Ennis could tell from her seat beside him. He dropped his gaze to the center of the table, white-faced.

Naturally, Victor had registered the change, too, but he delivered the next blow with cold words.

"Fermet. The guy who left the ship with you. You two headed west after that. If you're living here by yourself, that means—"

"S-stop it…"

"…See? Everybody's got questions that are hard to answer. That's your dark side, and I don't plan to intrude. So when you poke your nose into my business, I'd be careful if I were you."

Victor suddenly smiled as he spoke, but the color didn't return to Czes's face.

When she saw how the boy looked, Ennis tried to protest—but every time she glanced at Victor's face, her heart failed her.

That face was still a solid part of the memories of the alchemist she'd eaten long ago.

Not as a mere companion but as someone who'd been a particularly close friend.

In other words, the man in front of Ennis having been a good friend of the man she'd eaten confounded her completely.

She wondered if he'd come to kill her in order to avenge his friend.

Or maybe in order to retrieve his friend's memories…

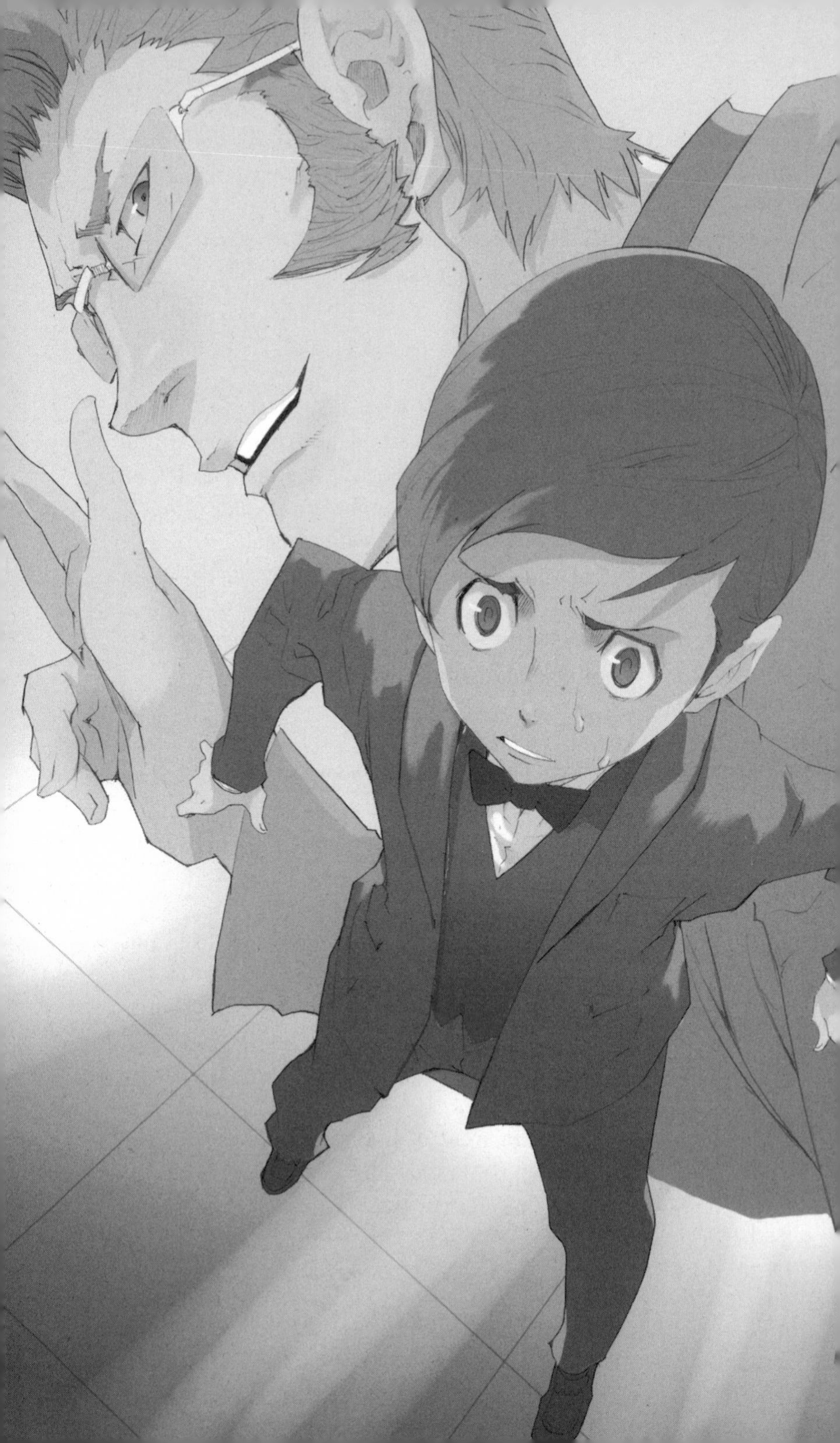

As she waited for the man's next words, Ennis tensed up as badly as Czes.

The man glanced at her and opened his mouth, beginning to say something, but—

Just then, a voice echoed in the restaurant:

"Victor."

It was a young man's voice, and it held a mixture of surprise, delight, and a little reproach.

"What's the occasion? Why come all the way over here?"

The newcomer was tall, and he looked as if he was in his mid-twenties.

Like Victor, he wore glasses, but the impression he made was completely different.

In the case of the tall man, his glasses topped a mild expression created by his threadlike eyes, and the aura he exuded made him seem like a good-natured scholarly type.

In contrast, Victor looked like a hard-boiled carnivore. Relaxing his expression somewhat, he raised his right hand in a friendly way and hailed him.

"Hey, Maiza! Enjoying life? Reunions are great, really great. When you see your friend, and he looks completely different from when you last saw him, sometimes it affects you more than your first meeting. Is it the other guy who changed, or was it you? I was just trying to teach Czes about that, but he's no fun at all. What do you think?"

"Have you converted all the blood in your body to liquor to celebrate the end of Prohibition? It's best to get drunk on yourself in moderation. The intoxication may induce nausea—for us, at least."

"Heh… That doesn't sound very welcoming. Should I not have come here?"

"Do you understand your own position and where you are right now?"

With a mildly disgusted sigh, Maiza spoke, sounding troubled.

"What business does a Bureau of Investigation executive have with a mere 'mafia' syndicate?"

*Clatter*

The faint vibrations became a single sound and ran through the restaurant, which hadn't yet opened.

At present, almost everyone in the restaurant had ties to the Martillo Family, and their relationship with members of the Bureau of Investigation bore a remarkable resemblance to the relationship between cats and dogs.

Even if that hadn't been the case, there were the recent incidents with Isaac and Firo, and every eye in the restaurant turned on the man from the Bureau of Investigation with more than the usual enmity.

"Ha! If you're so hostile at the name of the Bureau, you're practically advertising something underhanded here that doesn't dare show its face in broad daylight. Ain't that right, Maiza?"

Victor didn't look the least bit disconcerted, and Maiza gave a sigh that was half-resigned. "Did you come here to pick a fight? Or do you have some sort of urgent business with me?"

"Hey, keep your shirt on. Whether it turns out to be urgent or not is up to Huey."

"Huey?"

He'd abruptly mentioned the name of an old companion: an alchemist who had become an immortal on the ship, like Maiza, Czes, and Victor.

Eyeing the other man quizzically, Maiza openly asked him exactly what he was thinking.

"Didn't you capture him?"

"We got him, but apparently the bastard has swarms of minions... They've been real busy lately. I wouldn't be surprised if we ended up with another Flying Pussyfoot incident on our hands."

The Flying Pussyfoot.

Maiza and the others had heard the rumors as well: About three years ago, a train by that name had been occupied by terrorists. They'd heard about it because they'd had acquaintances on board; the incident hadn't been publicly reported.

Some sort of political pressure seemed to have been at work, and none of the papers had covered the affair. Even though the incident was believed to have left many people dead, for all practical purposes, it had been consigned to oblivion.

The sight of that far-too-skillful cover-up gave denizens of the underworld like Maiza and the others an eerie, nagging feeling.

From routine experience, they knew how hard it was to cover up any sort of incident.

Even mundane incidents were difficult. Keeping a train hijack under wraps would be nearly impossible, no matter how you looked at it, and the mere idea of trying sounded completely lunatic.

"Don't tell me keeping that matter out of the press was your doing as well."

"No, Maiza. Don't give us too much credit. We don't have that kind of power, either. Apparently, there's some other group that doesn't want business involving immortals to go public."

Victor denied his own group's power in a matter-of-fact way, then looked just a little displeased and muttered, as if talking to himself, "Among the guys at the top anyway... Dammit, we've got the same goal, but they get so hostile over every little thing... Goddamn assholes..."

"And? What about Huey?"

"Hmm? Oh yeah, sorry. Well, here's the thing: It seems like Huey has to be issuing orders from the inside... but we don't know how."

Prompted by Maiza, Victor began elaborating their situation in a loud, clear voice.

At the end, he added a comment that sent a jolt through Maiza and the others:

"To help with that, I have your sworn kid brother as our mole, see."

*Clatter    clack    rattle    clatter    skreek*
The next moment, all the men in the restaurant suddenly began shifting their chairs, and the resulting noise was louder than the stir when they'd discovered that Victor was from the Bureau itself.

Behind his glasses, Maiza's narrow eyes grew pointed and sharp, and he spoke to his former comrade coldly. "What have you done with Firo? Depending on your answer … we may decide that you are an enemy of our state."

Under that freezing gaze, Victor averted his eyes slightly and raised both hands, as if to say he surrendered. "Okay, okay, hang on, Maiza. It's true that I can't stand you gangsters—but I don't want to end up triggering one of those bloody purges, so I came here to clear up any misunderstandings. I'm no enemy of yours."

With a shameless reply, Victor got up from his chair with a muttered *Yeesh*.

"He hasn't spilled a thing about your family, and he didn't sell you people out to become my mole."

Then, sending Ennis a look that was full of complicated emotions, he began to speak, seeming to hide his own feelings somehow.

"You've got this doll Ennis here, right? He voluntarily took on some dirty work to get her crime struck off the books."

"Huh …?"

Abruptly hearing her name, Ennis gazed back at Victor, bewildered.

Victor didn't sneer, and he didn't give her an in-control smile. He just began to describe his exchange with Firo, looking brusque and cross.

Indifferently. Dispassionately.

Even when he saw Ennis growing paler, he didn't hesitate at all.

It was as if he was venting some sort of resentment at her.


"Victor …"

"Don't glower like that, Maiza. Miss Ennis and the mobster shits around here look like they've got something to say, but I don't have that kind of time, and I'm heading out for today."

Having told them everything, Victor spread his hands casually, then started toward the restaurant's exit.

Behind him, Maiza spoke, sounding a bit tense.

"When it comes down to it, what would you say Huey is planning?

I suppose it's all an experiment to him, but...especially since Elmer isn't with him...do you think he's gone out of control?"

"Hell, that's what I'd like to know."

After this exchange, which only they understood, Victor dusted off his coat and, looking as if he thought it was a pain, spat out a warning:

"Anyway...according to the intel I've got, Huey's planning to send up some kinda fireworks here in New York in the next few days... You get what I'm sayin', Maiza? If that research fiend approaches you somehow—*don't join that party*. Neither you nor your family stands to gain a single thing by it."

"...Is that warning the real reason you came here today?"

"I still think of you as a friend. Just don't pull anything that would make you my enemy. And while I'm at it...hurry up and cut ties with this gang already."

At that point, for the first time, the Bureau of Investigation executive gave an uncharacteristic smile, then murmured as though he was thinking about something he missed.

"Then we can go drinking together again."

After that, as if to cancel out those mild words, he loudly rattled on without even looking back at the Martillo *contaiuolo*, "Listen up, Maiza! I do still consider you a friend, but I hate you mob types—mafia, Camorra, 'Ndrangheta, whatever the hell you call yourselves—with a burning passion. Go ahead and bite the big one! Suffer! Writhe! Regret the fact that you were ever born! If you're smeared in shit long enough, you'll turn into shit yourself! Just remember that!"

Without bothering to calm his ragged panting, Victor marched briskly toward the exit.

But right then, an elderly man poked his face in through the restaurant's door.

"Whoops, 'scuse me."

As the old man spoke, he passed by Victor, who was on his way out.

"...Hmph."

Victor kept walking without pausing, but—

—abruptly, he noticed that something about his legs felt off.

*What's going on?*

Had he tripped on a chair leg or something?

Victor bent his head to look down at his feet and was struck by a strange feeling.

His feet weren't caught on anything in particular.

He couldn't even see the floor down there.

*?*

The moment he started to wonder about that—a dull impact enveloped his body, and a violent shudder ran through the air in his lungs.

Since the floor was right in front of him, he understood that he'd apparently made a dramatic fall.

*Why…did I fall down… just now?*

Had he tripped on something and fallen? Neither the feel of the experience nor the momentum he'd had matched that possibility.

A wrinkled hand reached out to Victor, who didn't know what had happened to him. It belonged to the old man who'd just passed him.

"What's the matter, son?"

Victor looked up into the old man's face, then realized he was Asian.

*Kanshichirou Yaguruma, huh?!*

"Hey, oldster. Did you do that?"

All he'd heard was that he had an interest in Eastern martial arts, but that fall couldn't have been anyone else's doing.

Irritated, he struck away the offered hand and tried to get up.

However, although he'd swung his arm with some force, Yaguruma's hand caught it firmly.

The wrinkled hand was as hard as tire rubber, and Victor felt as if his wrist had been trapped in a vise.

Then, using the momentum of his attempt to get up, his body rose lightly into the air—

—and the next moment, a light shock ran through his lower back.

He realized that he was sitting in a chair at the counter, and the momentum slammed his head down onto that counter face-first.

Before he had time to understand his situation, he heard the light sound of something shattering right next to him.

"Be careful."

When he looked in the direction of the noise, he saw the fine, shining shards of a broken liquor bottle and a man who was slowly scraping them into a pile.

"Even if you're with the Bureau of Investigation, or one of its top brass, or even the president of the nation—you could still fall onto a broken bottle and die."

The sharp-eyed man glared at him, and Victor understood what was going on perfectly.

The Martillo Family was probably getting a little revenge for the provocation he'd hit them with earlier.

Even though he knew that, he hadn't been able to do a thing about it, and he was irritated with himself. Pretending to be calm, he spoke to the man who sat next to him.

"…Is that supposed to be a threat? That crap won't work on m…"

As he spoke, Victor had his own constitution in mind, but the man in the seat beside him put his face right up next to his ear, whispering in a voice only he could hear:

"While that bottle's stuck in your face, *someone could put their right hand on your head, too.*"

"…?!"

*"Just like in 1711 on the* Advena Avis…*when Szilard did it."*

*Who…is this?*

Victor hastily took another look at the guy's face, but he wasn't one of his alchemist companions from the ship. That said, he couldn't imagine Maiza blabbing about the incident on the ship to other people.

*Who is this guy?!*

Victor was confused, and the man smiled quietly, wrapped his hands around the glass fragments—

—and as he gently lifted his hands, a perfectly undamaged liquor bottle peeked out from below them. It was as if it was being reborn from the man's fingers.

"...?!"

"What do you think? It's unexpectedly terrifying when a mystery presents itself in a place you thought you knew like the back of your hand, isn't it?"

"......"

Victor slowly shifted his gaze to Maiza, but Maiza was only watching him sternly from a distance, and he wasn't about to explain this phenomenon or the man who sat next to him.

"A magician, huh? Well, I'll check around and find out who you are."

The agent had abruptly fallen from his position of superiority, and he gritted his teeth hard, leaving the counter behind him.

"Just don't forget... Even so... Even so, we don't bend over for threats."

The murderous gazes of all the gangsters in the restaurant stabbed into Victor's receding back.

However, he didn't stop walking.

He absorbed that hostility with his whole body, as if to say that looks would never kill him.


"Yaguruma. Ronny. You both threatened him too much."

After Victor had gone, Maiza reprimanded the two upper-level executives who sat at the counter.

"Did I? If I'd really been trying to threaten him, I would've dislocated his arms."

In contrast to Yaguruma, who was cackling, the sharp-eyed man—Ronny Schiatto—was gazing at the liquor bottle and frowning.

"Ronny? What's the matter?"

"Nothing... It just seemed as though he had no memory of my face."

"That bothers you?"

Maiza sounded a little appalled, and Ronny's expression grew more complex.

"Well, never mind… Maiza, I've made a resolution."

The man who'd once been called a demon murmured in a voice that held mysterious power.

"Next time I'm summoned, I'll put more effort into making an impression."

⟺

Victor got into a waiting car outside the building and quickly put the place behind him.

Bill, who was driving, spoke to his boss in an unconcerned voice.

"Uh… How did it go?"

"Harrumph! Terrifying! Frankly, I thought I was gonna get bumped off! I've never felt so sure Maiza's glare was gonna kill me before, and the other executives, too… Dammit… The place is just lousy with things I don't get. That Maiza… He's completely devolved into a gangster!"

"Erm… I, uh, I'm not sure I should say this, but, um…"

"What? Spit it out."

Bill was being inarticulate, and Victor was short on patience.

However, the words Bill used to parry his supervisor's anger were still easygoing, and his response was mildly teasing.

"Hmm… You said, 'As his friend, I'm going to go persuade him not to let Huey tempt him,' so…if they directed so much hostility at you that your legs are still shaking even now, I'm wondering how exactly you delivered the message."

"Oho. What do you think, Agent Sullivan?"

He spoke as if he was ducking the question, but the response he got came in the form of an additional blow.

"Uh… you did something stupid, would be my guess."

"……"

He had no comeback for that, and yet he felt as though pulling rank here and lecturing him would be the same as admitting he'd lost, so Victor just closed his eyes, looking cranky.

Then, as he thought back over the recent scene, he remembered something with a jolt and opened his eyes.

"Damn. I was going to tell them one other thing, and I forgot."

"Mm… What was it?"

"Nah… Just a little something about that screwball immortal Isaac.

"We weren't expecting him to be involved at all, see…"

## CHAPTER 2: FRONT

# LET'S SAVOR SUPPER WITH A PSYCHO

San Francisco Bay     Alcatraz Island       The wharf

"Get out."

The guard's flat voice called him, and Firo quietly opened his eyes.

The quality of the waves had changed from what it had been a minute ago, and it was clear that the boat had come alongside a pier somewhere.

In the boat's hold, where the naked bulbs were unnecessarily bright, the young man took another look at his surroundings.

Aside from him, there were three other people being transported.

Since the guards were right there watching them, they hadn't been able to talk, but all three men were memorable.

One was an Asian man with dragons tattooed down both arms.

He was wearing a long-sleeved shirt, but it was possible to imagine the bright colors under the sleeves from the dragon mouths inked on the backs of his hands and the tail designs that reached his neck. His face still looked young; he was probably somewhere in his late twenties.

The second was a big black man.

From his salt-and-pepper hair and his features, Firo thought the man was around forty. His face looked tranquil, but the scars all over his body spoke eloquently of the man's true nature. Firo's experience told him that those weren't the sorts of scars he could have picked up in the course of labor or through an attempted KKK lynching. They were, plain and simple, the sort of scars picked up in fistfights, knife fights, and fights to the death.

The last one was a drooping white man.

He sighed constantly; he kept muttering as though he was frightened of something, and every time his voice grew loud, the guard gave him a warning. He seemed to be in his mid-thirties, but the man's worn-down look made him appear unnecessarily old, and so Firo wouldn't have been surprised to hear he was over fifty.

Looking at his diverse traveling companions, Firo sighed again.

Sinister-looking convicts. He'd be thrown in with them to walk into history's best—or, to its inmates, worst—prison.

Even though he'd come to terms with the idea, every time he accepted that fact, his spirits sank lower.

In this odd company, Firo stepped down onto a pier that was lit by the setting sun.

The first thing he saw was the looming guard tower.

It wasn't actually all that high, but under these conditions, with no tall buildings around, it exerted a pressure of the absolute—an inescapable symbol that looked down upon its convicts. At the top of the tower, a guard with a sniper rifle stared down at them, amplifying the tension. His presence bespoke that no matter how high it was, it wouldn't be high enough to run from.

*This place is pretty big.*

As Firo looked around, that was his honest impression.

A lot of bare rock was visible on the island. It was far larger than it had looked when he'd seen it from the wharf in San Francisco, and the many sheer, rough-hewn cliffs created a feeling of being closed in that was also greater than it had seemed from the outside.

When he looked back, he could see San Francisco's rows of skyscrapers. It looked as if he'd be able to touch them if he reached out, but the cluster of buildings, shrunk down like miniatures in a box garden, also seemed like the scenery of some far distant country.

"Walk."

Obeying the order, the four convicts left the wharf and started up the path that led to the upper part of the island.

The island was like a slightly elevated crag, and eyeballing it, Firo estimated that its highest point was about fifty yards above the ocean.

Even though the land that the prison was built on might be over five hundred yards in length, it probably wasn't even two hundred yards wide.

*Seriously… What is this? I wouldn't be surprised if Lupin or Moriarty had a hideout here.*

Firo had known extremely little about this place going in, and he regretted his lack of education: If he'd known this was going to happen, he would have skimmed the newspapers and gossip rags more regularly.

The white structure in the center of the island, the one they were walking toward, was probably the main prison building.

However, several other buildings stood around it, and the atmosphere it exuded was imposing, as if it really was a fortress.

Rust, grime, and a unique dullness could be seen on the boat dock and the pier, as if they prided themselves on having been used for a long time. Only the building at the center of the island looked new, so much so that it seemed like a type of distortion, and there was an oddly warped beauty to it.

*Yeah, you couldn't break out of a place like this.*

It was said to have been originally used as a military fortress, and its location lived up to that reputation. In addition, the guard tower and other facilities were perfectly situated to handle not just jailbreaks from inside but external attacks as well. People said the cold, swift currents would be too much for you and you'd drown, but the movements of the rifle-toting guards were also uniform and hyperalert, and the sight compelled you to imagine getting shot dead before you even reached the water. That was how solid the security was.

*Forget "security." These are full-scale military-grade defenses.*

As Firo walked on, breaking out in a cold sweat, new sights presented themselves one after another.

The blue ocean, the enormous red-orange bridge over San Francisco Bay, and the clusters of buildings at both ends of it seemed even prettier than they had earlier, giving off an air of vivid liveliness.

*Actually, this is a fairly long walk. If this were a stairwell, we'd be about ten floors up already.*

The slope was steeper than he'd expected, and climbing the road that zigzagged up it while handcuffed made for a rather rough trip.

About the time the sea wind had begun to cool Firo's sweat, the main prison building, which had been visible for a while now, finally barred his way.

When the guards who were escorting them sent a signal from the entrance, a bell sounded in the interior, and a door set in the stone wall opened.

Inside, there was an abrupt iron grill with a room that looked like a control post behind it. Several guards were watching them through a glass window.

With Firo in the lead, the four prisoners looked at one another as they followed the guards down the corridor, but—

"You're over here."

—abruptly, Firo was stripped out of the line and taken down a different hallway from the others.

The other convicts looked at Firo's face curiously, but the guards promptly pulled them away, and they disappeared around a corner.

"Why just me…?"

"I don't remember giving you permission to ask questions."

As the impassive guard marched him along, Firo looked at his face.

He'd thought it might be Huey Laforet's underling, the man who'd spoken to him before they boarded the boat, but he didn't recognize this guy's face at all, and he felt just a little relieved.

They entered a room deep within the depths of the corridor. Inside, a man at a desk was waiting for them.

The desk and the room's decor were plain; it seemed to be some sort of office. The man looked at Firo, then signaled with his eyes to the guard who'd brought him.

The guard immediately nodded, said "Excuse me, sir," and promptly left the room.

It was just one-on-one now, and Firo took another look at the man in front of him.

Unlike the uniformed guards, this man was wearing a sharp, neat suit. He was getting on in years, and his hair was thinning. He had stern features, but as he walked over to Firo, his expression was mild.

Was this the prison's warden?

Firo suspected he might be, but the man in question told him he'd guessed wrong.

"Welcome, Firo Prochainezo. I'm Misery, the special administrator here."

"Special administrator?"

"On paper, I'm the deputy warden's assistant, but my position is rather unique. You are a special case; rather than Warden Johnston, I and a few of the guards will be in charge of managing you. I'd like you to keep that in mind."

"You're Victor's friend, then?"

He was on the other guy's turf, so Firo kept his question basic but respectful.

Misery nodded, as if to say that would speed the conversation along, and calmly began to explain the situation in which Firo had been placed.

"Hmm, yes. Victor's told me about you. Personally, I was against using someone like you, an outsider...and an immortal like him, besides."

"I would have really appreciated it if you'd stopped him, even if you had to slug him to do it."

"Yes, I slugged, stabbed, and kicked him, but he's surprisingly obstinate. My only remaining option seemed to be to take his family hostage, but unfortunately, he's a bachelor."

*I see. Apparently, this guy's got a sense of humor.*

Relaxing just a little, Firo eased up on his hostility and listened to what Misery had to say.

"Now then...Huey Laforet. Victor's told you about him?"

"Yes, sir. Briefly."

"Right… He has multiple organizations he's trained personally, and according to Victor's information network, several of them are on the move. They seem to be planning some sort of large-scale maneuver in New York very soon."

"In New York?"

"Yes… Victor said that since you're an immortal, and since Huey doesn't know of your existence yet, we should send you in."

It was a pretty unappealing story.

The Mist Wall incident, which was the excuse they'd used to haul Firo in to begin with, had been something he'd gotten dragged into by Huey's henchmen.

*Besides…those guys said some stuff about Ennis.*

Remembering the saw-toothed monster who'd been one of Huey's men, Firo audibly ground his molars. Even if they told him this stuff now, he couldn't turn around and go straight back to New York. The thought that Victor had probably neglected to tell him earlier on purpose deeply nettled him.

Still, striking out in anger here would be pointless. In that case, all he could do was stop Huey from the inside.

"…I'm going to ask you a really blunt question."

"Go ahead."

"Are you saying I should assume that, if I want to save my friends in New York, I may be…compelled to 'eat' Huey? He'd be on his guard around Victor, but you think I could take care of him easily, since he doesn't know I'm an immortal."

There was a moment of silence.

However, after giving it a little thought, Misery shook his head.

"…No, Victor's not that much of an ogre."

"I dunno about that."

"Hmm… Well, I'd rather you didn't let it come to that. I'll contact you with specific instructions through the guards who work for me. As a rule, until you do have instructions, you're to behave just like the other convicts. No matter what, avoid doing anything that would unmask you as an immortal."

Misery spoke emphatically, but Firo responded with a bitter smile.

"Well, either way … It looks like I've been outed already."

"… What?"

"He already knows. He knew I was coming and that I'm immortal."

Then, in a matter-of-fact way, Firo reported what had happened to him.

Half-resigned and cursing his fate with a passion…

"I see…"

After he'd heard Firo's story, Misery shook his head. Clear fatigue showed in his expression.

"You look like you saw that one coming."

"Yes… That's the greatest mystery about him."

According to Misery, Huey was able to obtain information from the outside, and transmit information to the outside world, through some unknown method.

"As you say, there are guards who are under his influence as well. A mere handful, mind you. That said, we have no proof, interrogating them yields no information, and there are no problems with their past records. When I talk it over with the warden and have them transferred … before we know it, he's influenced another guard."

"What a great work ethic."

"Refrain from sarcasm, if you would. That said, even if he *is* winning over the guards somehow … that alone can't begin to explain his information-gathering capabilities."

"True."

There were very few people who knew Firo was an immortal. The DD newspaper—the information broker—was another story, but he really didn't think it would be possible to contact an establishment in New York from this prison.

So was Misery, the man here with him, actually Huey's underling?

Firo had considered that possibility as well, but it was only a guess, and if it had been true, he felt like the man would have simply revealed that fact right here, right now.

*Either way, whatever happens is gonna happen.*

The mission he'd been given from the start was uncovering Huey's information network. Reaffirming that he was far from being in a position of superiority and that he'd lost the advantage entirely, Firo heaved an immense sigh.

Misery watched the young man sympathetically, but abruptly, he inquired about something odd:

"There's one final thing I'd like to ask you."

"What is it?"

"Those three prisoners who were brought in with you… What do you think of them?"

"…?"

The Asian guy, the black guy, and the white guy? He didn't think anything of them. He hadn't even talked to them, so all he could say was what he'd thought of their appearances.

Determining this was the case, Firo responded to the question with one of his own.

"Why do you ask that?"

"Well…technically, you were the only one who was supposed to be admitted today."

"?"

"However, over the past few days, there was an abrupt burst of activity in our contact system… Prisoners who were supposed to be jailed next week were hastily rescheduled to come to the island with you."

That was truly weird. It didn't sound particularly unsettling to Firo, but something about the story did seem strange. He'd just assumed that he'd been admitted on the same day as other prisoners to camouflage his arrival, but from the sound of things, it had been the other way around.

"Did any of those three men strike you as being abnormal in some way?"

"No… If I had to say, I was a little worried about the white guy muttering constantly, but that's it."

"I see… Well, forget I asked. We plan to put them in cells on either side of yours, so get along as well as you can. Ah, although private conversation is against the rules."

*Are you telling us to be pals through sign language?*
As he bit back that sarcastic remark, Firo underwent a health exam in another room.

A young gangster stripped of his clothes, naked as the day he was born. The doctor was bad enough; being seen by the guards was frankly humiliating. With incredibly practiced motions, working thoroughly and quickly, the doctor checked the insides of his nose, mouth, and ears, going from basic physical tests, such as making sure his hair was the real thing, all the way to a rectal exam.

Ordinarily, if he'd been subjected to a rectal exam in front of other people, he would have gone bright red and sworn revenge, but it was over before he could even work up those emotions.

*Ah, geez...*
Looking worn-out, Firo reached for the clothes he'd removed, but a guard rebuked him.

"Hey. Don't get dressed."

"?"

"The latest fashions are waiting in your cell. You're in the buff until you get there."

⇔

Firo, stark naked, was escorted between two men in trim uniforms.

His anger had no place to go, and looking sour, he turned it on himself.

They rounded a corner, entering a long corridor.

Although there was nothing that would have qualified as noise, the sounds of people living their lives seemed to come from everywhere, and Firo knew immediately.

*So this is our hive, huh?*
As far as he could see, the walls were *made entirely of iron bars.*

Both sides of the long corridor were lined with cells, with no gaps in between, and there was an incredibly clear sense of people moving around in the narrow rooms.

*Two floors… No, three?*

The cells were lined up not just horizontally but vertically as well, like an apartment complex. They reminded Firo of a two-dimensional beehive…although, unlike bees, they weren't able to come and go freely.

*Just being on this island is enough of a handicap, and then they stick you in cramped cells like these?*

However, right now, he couldn't think past that point.

From behind the bars, several of the prisoners gave him the up-and-down, checking out the newbie walking naked down the corridor.

Most of the men just glanced at his face, then looked away, but a few of them scrutinized every inch of him.

"Welcome to Broadway, *sweetheart.*"

Firo glanced in the direction of the quiet murmur.

A little man with sagging flesh was leering at him, baring a mouthful of bad teeth.

*I'll remember your mug.*

As he was about to take the next step, planning what he'd do to that guy later—

—one of the guards glared at the little man and spoke in a flat voice.

"Shut up."

That was all.

The guard hadn't raised his voice, but it echoed in the corridor, turning into a feeling of stark power that bore down on the surrounding cells.

"The next guy who says anything liable to start a fight goes to the Dungeon."

The next moment, a frozen silence enveloped the long hallway.

As he walked on, startled by the dramatic, almost magical effect of the guard's voice, Firo was stopped about halfway down the first floor, then pushed toward a cell on the left.

A guard farther down the hall worked the cellblock's switchboard, then opened the heavy barred door.

"A word of advice."

The guard pushed Firo into the cell, gave a simple sign, and then his fellows closed the door.

Then, making sure he was understood, he gave Firo a kindly warning.

"I know what that guy said to you back there was an insult. If you try to work him over for it, though, don't expect any sympathy from us. We'll throw you in the Dungeon—into solitary.

"Revenge is a *splendid thing*, and it's not for the birds who end up on this rock."

⟺

"The latest fashions, huh?"

Muttering savagely to himself, Firo picked up the clothes that had been set on the bed.

Work clothes in a dull blue color. Around here, these were probably the most common rags to be seen.

Released from the humiliation of being naked, Firo looked over the items that had been set out on the bed and realized that he'd been provided with an unexpected number of accessories.

Two undershirts, two pairs of underwear.

They'd given him six pairs of socks.

One cap, one handkerchief, one belt. Surprisingly, there were even two different types of shoes, one for work and one for days off.

He was even happier to see a wool coat on a hanger.

*Well, I guess I won't be freezing to death, anyway.*

Completely forgetting that he was immortal for the space of that thought, Firo looked around, seeing what else was in the room.

The bed was a folding type that was secured to one of the cell's sidewalls with chains. In the back, there was a toilet without a seat. A sink sat beside the toilet, and when he gave the knob a twist, clear water gushed out with greater force than he'd anticipated.

On the side opposite the bed, two shelves—also folding—were fixed to the wall, one above the other.

Even more surprising, a variety of prison-issue items sat on the open shelves and the sink.

A razor.

A metal cup.

An eye mask.

A comb.

Soap.

A toothbrush and tooth powder.

Toilet paper.

Shoe polish.

A broom for indoor cleaning stood in a corner of the cell.

A thick sheaf of documents with *Prison Regulations* written on it sat proudly on the shelf, and Firo casually skimmed through it as he continued looking around the cell.

The cramped room held so many things that for a moment, he thought, *Huh. They treat you pretty well here.*

However, as soon as he looked up at the ceiling, his spirits sank.

The abnormally low ceiling made him feel as if he were on the verge of being crushed, and the single light bulb set into that ceiling seemed to sizzle his eyes and sensitive skin.

When he glanced into the cell across the way, its inmate was doing his business on the toilet behind the bed.

He averted his eyes, clicking his tongue in irritation. Realizing that if he could see that from here, the other guy would be able to see everything he did as well, Firo found himself wanting to break out already.

$$\Longleftrightarrow$$

When the first post-admission headcount ended, Firo was able to confirm that the occupants of the cells on either side of his were the two men of color who'd come in with him. Three men must have been released from the prison recently, either by coincidence or...

some other method of removal. The white guy was probably somewhere farther away, under similar conditions.

*All right, so...what should I do?*

Growing tired of being pessimistic about his situation, Firo told himself that at least the walls were sturdier than they had been during the poverty of his childhood.

The problem was the meals.

He'd been told that prison food was nasty.

According to what he'd heard from Pezzo and Randy, who'd messed up and landed in the clink temporarily, the meals had been so unappealing that they'd started to miss liquor made from diluted industrial alcohol, and they'd sworn in their hearts that they'd never mess up again. The fact that they hadn't sworn "never to do bad things again" had been very like those two, but although they'd always laughed about that story, remembering it dampened Firo's mood.

That was what it was like even in ordinary prisons.

What kind of leftover slop was waiting for him in a place people feared as its own brand of hell?

Since he'd been thinking exclusively about things like that, as Firo headed for the dining hall for his first meal, his footsteps naturally grew heavy.

When he entered the dining hall, he saw that the space had an atmosphere that was different from the cells.

Broadway—the cell-lined corridor—had given him a sense of mild claustrophobia. In contrast, even though it was surrounded by institutional walls and a ceiling, this place was one of the most spacious rooms in the prison.

It was a momentary feeling of freedom.

Firo wanted to pause briefly and draw a deep breath, but he was part of a moving line, and he couldn't actually stop.

They picked up their dishes and utensils in order, had their meals dished out in order, then left the line in order and sat wherever they wanted to.

He looked around. The mess hall was overflowing with convicts, and the sense of liberation he'd felt a moment ago was already gone.

As a rule, the seats farther back were filled before the ones in front, but even so, there were several loose groups.

Black guys sat with black guys, while white guys stuck with other white guys.

It wasn't clear whether they'd been invited or they'd just gone over of their own accord, but... the black man who'd been admitted along with Firo had already joined one of the groups, while the Asian man was already part of another small group and was silently eating his supper.

The white man was sitting in a corner of the dining hall, shivering hard. However, thinking that it would be a pain to go all the way over there now, Firo decided to eat right where he was.

From what Misery had said, it was possible that one of those three had infiltrated the prison with a goal in mind.

He'd assumed the diagram here was simple—"the Bureau of Investigation versus Huey"—but there might have been some other intention or organization at work, too.

Or had the guy simply been summoned to help Huey break out?

Either way, he really couldn't see them being in the same position as himself. If that was the case, Misery would have known about it, and he couldn't think of why they'd need to fool their allies that way.

*Well, that's fine. Regardless, everything here is the enemy.*

In this situation, there was no telling when someone might try to kill him in his sleep. Everyone around him was a stranger. There was no one he could trust.

Steeling himself, his expression tense, Firo began to flip the mental switch that would let him be thoroughly heartless.

Just then—

"Whaaaaaaa—?!"

—a dopey-sounding cry echoed through the dining hall, and all the prisoners' eyes darted to one spot.

At the same time, a thrill of frank astonishment raced through Firo—

"Heeey! Firo! If it isn't Firo!"

—and the next moment, his energy drained out of him.

*No, no, no, no, wait, wait, wait, wait.*

He knew that voice.

This time, the memories weren't Szilard's. This was a voice Firo Prochainezo had heard in his own lifetime.

*Why?! Why is he here?*

Fearfully, he raised his head, and there—

—he saw a man whose face was far too familiar, enthusiastically waving his arms at him and wearing a smile that was completely inappropriate for where he was.

*Isaac!*

His friend had been arrested a full month before he had, and Firo checked several times, making sure it wasn't an illusion.

*Come to think of it, after we heard he'd been nabbed by the cops, we really didn't hear anything else… I never thought he'd end up here…*

*…Huh?*

All the prisoners had glared at Isaac and his flailing. However, when they registered that it was him, their eyes went back to their own meals, as if this happened all the time.

*Meaning…what? Why?*

The guards also looked at one another. Then, sighing wearily, they jogged over to Isaac. They surrounded him from all sides, their footsteps completely in sync.

An excessively perfect formation.

Their skill was captivating.

"You again, huh?"

"Huh? Me again?"

The hands Isaac had been waving at Firo were caught firmly, and they locked down both of his legs while they were at it.

"Yeah, you."

"Oh, listen to you! You're such a kidder!"

"Too bad openly breaking the 'no conversation' rule isn't a joke…

Congrats: This is your tenth trip to the Dungeon. To commemorate it, we'll hook you up with two chains today."

Then the guards carried Isaac out as if he were a statue, heading toward the corner of the dining hall so dynamically that it seemed as if they might start tossing him into the air.

......

As he watched them go, Firo had nothing to say. All he could do was fidget with the spoon in his hand, turning it around and around.

Isaac protested after being dumped on the ground, kicking and struggling against the guards who surrounded him.

"Waugh! What do you think you're doing? That wasn't conversation; I was exulting in a reunion, and that was a New York–style greeting—"

In response, the guards picked Isaac up as if they were used to this.

"Yeah, yeah, we get it, we know."

"We get it, so c'mon down with us quietly."

"Too bad. See, this ain't New York."

"Hurry up and learn Alcatraz-style already, birdbrain."

"Yeah, yeah, this way—there's a good boy. You'll be able to have a nice, long nap in that dark, dark basement. Boy, am I jealous."

With the same skill you'd use to pitch a mutinous child into a storage shed, the guards carried Isaac, bound hand and foot, out of the dining hall on their shoulders.

*Um… What am I supposed to do here?*

Firo wondered whether he should throw him a lifeline and whether that would even do any good. However, when he heard Isaac, who was being carted away by the guards like so much luggage, his thoughts broke off temporarily.

"Huh? You're jealous? But listen, you don't get as much food down there as you do up here, and you're chained up and can't move!"

"If there's less food, you'll slim down, and if you try to break the chains by hauling on them, you'll slim down even more."

"I—I see! Well, I guess that's fine, then. Do I really have that much fat on me, though?"

"Nerve, buddy. The only thing you've got a lot of is nerve. Just shut up, all right?"

......

*Uh... Erm... I, uh...*

*Well, never mind, I guess?*

He sighed, thoroughly disgusted with himself for not being able to do anything but accept the situation.

*At least I can trust him...*

The idea that he had a friend here brought him just a little relief, but—

"Hey, are you friends with that mor—?"

"Dunno."

Firo answered before the guard even finished his sentence, then sighed one more time, smiling wryly.

*...Not that I can count on him.*

⟺

For just a moment, the mood in the dining hall had changed.

Watching Isaac disappear from the corner of his eye, Firo turned his gaze to the food he'd brought over, deciding to get his meal out of the way instead of thinking.

*Hmm?*

He'd been anticipating something like cold leftovers, and the sight that waited for him on his tray was unexpected.

Firo had been distracted when he'd carried it over, so he hadn't really looked at it, but the contents of the plate bore a startling resemblance to actual food. Not only that, but it was still hot enough to steam, and the portion sizes were no different from what he would have gotten outside prison.

A creamy soup ornamented with red and green vegetables. Garlic rice that seemed to have been fried carefully so that it wouldn't scorch. Beside them, there was a green salad that was still fresh and juicy, a substantial meat pâté, and a main dish smothered in a sauce whose color and fragrance reminded him of beef stew.

*Why?*

It might only look good.

However, he couldn't think of any reason for just making it appear ritzy.

Puzzled, Firo pressed the back of his fork into the meat on his plate.

Naturally, it wasn't as good as restaurant hamburger, but a little juice welled up between the fine iron tines, and the aroma woke up his stomach.

When he tried a bite, just to see, a flavor that was more pleasant than he'd imagined spread over his tongue.

The fact that he'd been envisioning awful slop up to that point made this a total bolt from the blue.

The soup was richly flavorful, far better than what he usually cooked for himself.

When he bit into the vegetables, there was a light, juicy crunch, and for that one moment, he forgot he was surrounded by rough concrete.

*Whoa. Geez, what is this? This is actually pretty…*

"Tasty, ain't it?"

Just as he finished off the greens, the prisoner next to him spoke up cheerfully.

"I was pretty startled the first time I ate here, too."

*Huh? Is it okay to respond to this?*

He'd just seen the business with Isaac.

Here, in this prison where private conversation was banned, Firo wasn't sure whether he should answer the question—but the con next to him kept speaking, his tone casual.

"Yeah, when this place was just getting started, talking like this was enough to bring the guards tearing over to toss you into solitary. Now, though, as long as we're in the cafeteria, it's okay to speak quietly."

"Huh. Why's that?"

"The warden knows real well, see. If he comes down on 'em too hard, the inmates will get desperate and start a riot, and they'll just be harder to manage. The guard fellas don't actually want to cause a revolt and massacre all of us. The American public would roast 'em for it."

"I see…"

He responded casually, testing the waters, but the guy was right. The nearby guard didn't say anything to them. If he listened closely, his ears picked up the static of whispered conversation from his surroundings, too.

"Well, that doesn't keep the place from being boring as hell. Look at these other guys. Most of 'em look apathetic, like flies, and they look like they're wondering if they'll get to die soon."

"That's real rough."

"You're new, right? How'd you get here?"

"? They brought me over by train, and then I took a boat from the pier."

The con next to Firo responded to his comments with a ready nod, then spoke with a sunny smile.

"They brought me over with several dozen other fellas, back when this prison was first set up. They had us in leg irons, and we spent three days and three nights on a train… And get this: They never let us off that train."

"Huh?"

How had they gotten across to the island without getting off the train? As Firo was wondering about that, the inmate told him, chuckling deep in his throat.

"They just loaded the train cars onto a ferry."

"…Is that for real?"

"Yeah, for real. When it comes to stuff like that, this country pulls out all the stops, or maybe they're logical about it… Frankly, I think it's real impressive."

Firo was genuinely intrigued by this story, and he realized that he seemed markedly different from the inmates around him. "You don't look like you're wondering if you'll get to die soon, to use your term."

"Hmm…? Oh yeah. That's because I've got a goal."

Firo took that answer to mean that he had something he needed to do as soon as he got out of jail. He didn't know how long the other guy was in for, but he thought the fact that he was able to smile so optimistically on this hopeless island was really something.

The man thumped Firo lightly on the shoulder, speaking firmly.

"Well, I bet we'll be seeing a lot of each other for a while. If there's anything you don't get, just ask me."

"Sure. My name's Firo. You?"

As he spoke, Firo put out his left hand—but then he realized that his new acquaintance's left arm had hardly moved at all this whole time, and he hastily retracted it.

"Your left arm…"

"Oh, this?"

The man used his right arm to lift his left one, shifting it to rest on the table.

There was a dull *clunk*, and a solid vibration ran through the tabletop.

"It's a prosthetic. It's real well made, ain't it?"

"Huh… Is it steel? Hey, you're lucky they let you wear that thing in here."

"Well, it's special. See, this hand… It's bolted directly to my bones. Even I dunno what'll happen if I take it off. I might even die, maybe."

At first, Firo thought the man was joking.

Was there any other reason for the guards to have left this false iron arm alone, though? Firo thought about it, and he couldn't come up with an answer. For now, he decided not to worry about it.

At the same time, the man with the prosthetic arm flashed him a brilliant smile and held out his artificial left hand.

"I'm Ladd… Ladd Russo. It's great to meet you."

There was something ferocious in that smile. If a wolf smiled, it would probably look something like this, it seemed.

For some reason, that was what was on Firo's mind as he gripped the cold prosthetic hand.

He was completely unaware of the peculiar connection between himself and the other man—

## CHAPTER 2: BACK

# FOR NOW, LET'S TALK

New York     Millionaires' Row

It had started with Carnegie.

In 1901, Fifth Avenue was no more than a Manhattan backwater. Then Andrew Carnegie—the "Steel King," a man who'd made a huge success of himself through vertical integration of railways and steel mills—had built his mansion in a corner of it. In that moment, the avenue's destiny had leaped into motion with a roar.

At present, the street was known as Millionaires' Row. Many other winners had been drawn to it, following Carnegie, and like magic, the rural landscape had transformed into a city where grand mansions jostled one another.

Most of the people who built mansions here had amassed great wealth in the space of a generation.

The road itself changed shape like the American dream at the hands of those who had managed to achieve that very dream, and as "a dream made real," it became an object of adoration for those who fantasized about success.

Even those who said money wasn't everything couldn't deny the fact that there were people who'd managed to succeed with it.

In a corner of that dazzling avenue, where it felt as if you could hear voices like those—

—someone was crying.

A young man, whose expression seemed as far removed from the word *winner* as it was possible to be, was crying.

On and on. Wailing and sobbing.

"Uu, waAAaaaaAAaaaah...*hic*...*hic*..."

"Come on, Jacuzzi, don't cry. You're going to make me sad, too."

"Ugh... Eep... I-I'm sor— *Hic*... I'm sor...ry... Eep... Niiiice..."

In the hallway of a residence that was fairly opulent even for the ranks of splendid mansions, the young man had buried his face in a marble pillar and was making tearstains on the red carpet.

There was a large tattoo in the shape of a sword on his face, and at first glance, he seemed like someone who wouldn't be caught dead crying. However, a closer look at his face revealed that his features were still quite childish, and tears did seem to suit his timid-looking eyes.

The individual who was comforting that young man was a woman who also wasn't a typical resident of this neighborhood.

She was probably about the same age as him. She had symmetrical features, technically, but a huge scar ran across her face, covering her right eye, which was hidden by a jet-black eye patch. Over the eye patch, she wore a smart pair of glasses that gave her an intellectual air. You could say she was an unbalanced girl in several ways.

The pair weren't the only ones in the hall. People who were obviously urban delinquents had taken up positions all through the magnificent hues of the interior, surrounding the odd couple as if they were watching over them.

"Uu...*hic*... B-b-but, Niiice... Graham... Graaaaaham..."

"Don't be sad, Jacuzzi. If you cry, Graham won't be able to cross over in peace. You see?"

On hearing that conversation, the delinquents around them muttered to one another.

("Hey, what's up?")

("Huhn?")

("No, I mean, what? Did somebody die?")

("Dunno. Jacuzzi was crying when I got back.")

*("Y'know, I think that crybaby streak of his is getting worse as he gets older.")*

*("He might actually dry up soon.")*

*("By the way, do tears come out of your brain?")*

*("Oh, crap. Brain juice. Freaky.")*

*("Mrrg... Dying sad... Jacuzzi cry... Die. Nnnngh... Who dead?")*

*("Hya-haah.") ("Ki-hyaah.")*

*("Dammit, you people are useless. Hey, Jon, what's that idiot Jacuzzi crying about today?")*

*("Oh, see... You remember Graham, right? Graham Specter.")*

*("Whozzat?")*

*("Huh? Didn't you know him? ...Well, he was sort of the boss of the thugs around here. Back when we first came to New York, we tussled with him over this and that, and he took care of us sometimes, too... After that, he turned into our supporter. He looked out for Jacuzzi and stuff; we owe him a lot.")*

*("Huh. I didn't know there was a guy like that.")*

*("Yeah, look, you know that warehouse on the wharf that we use as a hangout? Graham's letting us use that place, too... Well, nobody's got the property owner's permission, but anyway.")*

*("Oho... So, what—did that Graham fella die?")*

*("Hya-haah.")*

*("No. If he had, Nice would be giving Jacuzzi his space for a while.")*

*("Huh? He's alive? I mean, just now, Nice said something about how he couldn't cross over...")*

*("Yeah, 'over' ain't heaven. She meant Chicago. Chicago.")*

*("Chicago?")*

The moment Jon said the name of that city, the eyes of the surrounding delinquents lit up, and the word began to appear in their conversations. They were originally from Chicago; after picking a fight with the local mafia, they'd fled here, to New York.

*("What? Chicago?") ("Glamorous Chicago, huh?") ("Uh, that's our hometown, remember?") ("Man, that takes me back.") ("Think things are still too hot for us there?") ("Think the Russo Family fellas are still alive?") ("I wonder when we'll get to go home.") ("I say we just stay*

*here. We get to live in this huge house and everything.") ("Geh-heeeh.") ("Hya-haah.")*

Ignoring the people around them, who were engaged in that sort of rambling conversation—

"Ngh... But, Niiiice...Graham and the rest said that since we came to town, their territory got smaller...and so they stole turf from a big gang, remember? And so...that's why they got ch-chased like that... What should I do...?"

"Listen, they ran to Chicago, so there's nothing to worry about now."

"But... But Graham said something about going to go help out a mafia group he knew... *Hic*... And that he might die, so take care and all... *Hic*... I, I, I couldn't stop him, but I can't go back to Chicago to save him, either... Aaaah, aaaaaaah, but what should I do...?"

Jacuzzi's sorrowful expression didn't falter in the slightest. Every word that came out of his mouth was pessimistic, and he was driving himself into a corner.

Nice continued to comfort him patiently, and everyone thought this was probably going to turn out to be a long struggle, but—

*Bonk!*

—something struck Jacuzzi's head lightly, and he turned to look back with round, tear-filled eyes.

A girl with blond hair stood there with her cheeks puffed out, gripping a thick book.

"Honestly, Jacuzzi, you mustn't do that! If you cry that hard, you'll wash that pretty design right off your face."

"M-Miria."

At Miria's unexpected words, Jacuzzi involuntarily held his breath and put a hand to his face.

After checking to make sure there was no color in the tears he wiped away, he turned to Nice, who was standing beside him, and asked an uneasy question.

"I-it's not gone, is it?"

"It's fine, Jacuzzi. I've never heard of a tattoo washing off with tears."

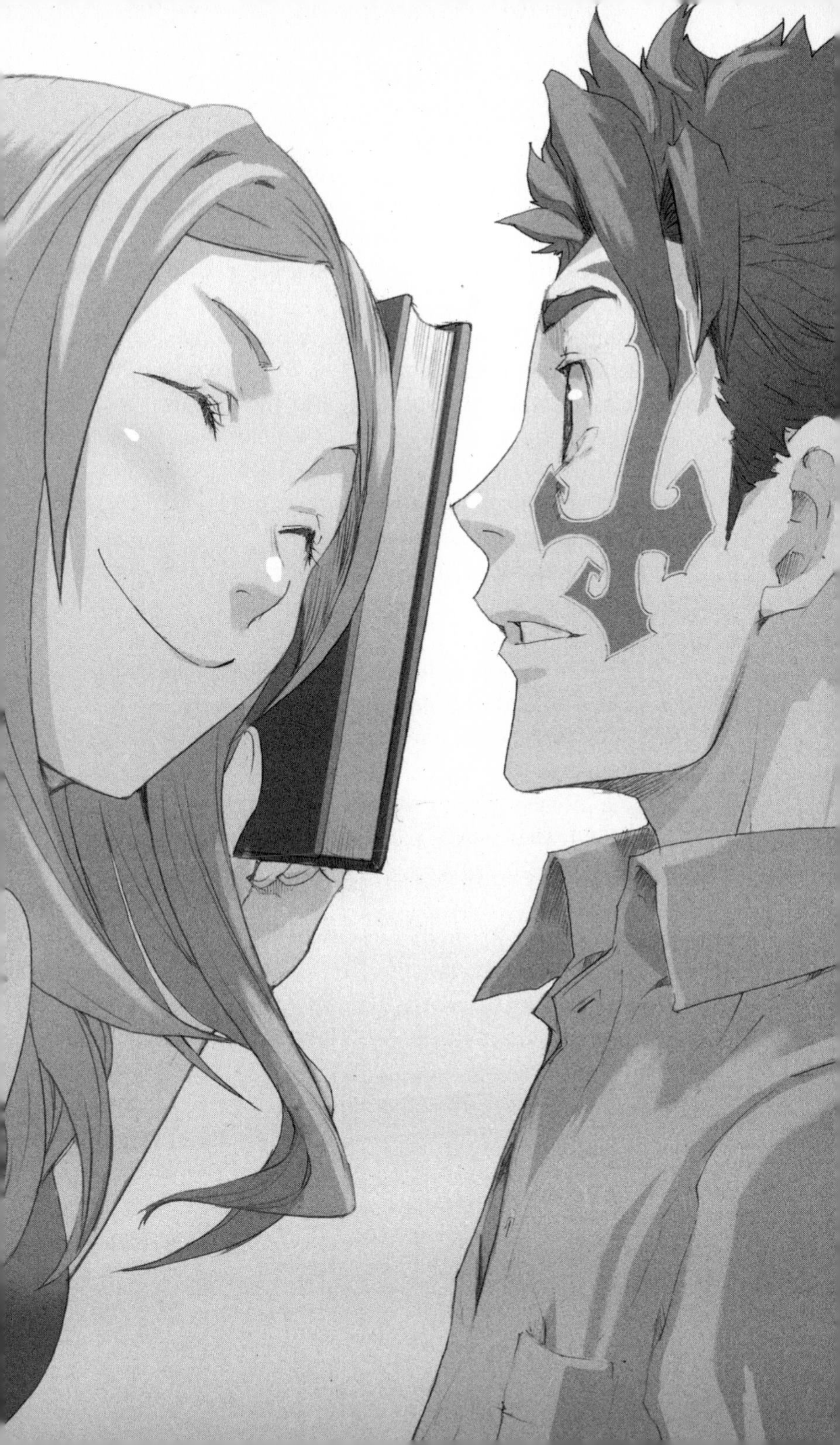

"O-oh, good…"

Jacuzzi seemed to be particularly attached to that tattoo, and on learning that it was safe, he sighed, relieved. When that faint relief showed in his expression, Miria smiled.

"There! It's much easier to see the big picture when you're not crying."

At the sight of Miria's carefree face, Jacuzzi stopped crying, as if her smile had been contagious.

Miria was, by appearance, a little older than Jacuzzi. Still, when you saw that innocent smile of hers, it was impossible to tell who was older, Miria or the delinquents around her.

Seeing her childlike expression, Jacuzzi wiped his tears away more thoroughly and smiled back at her.

"Y-you're right! You're hurting too, Miria, so I can't just cry on my own…"

The next moment—

—all of the surrounding delinquents shot sharp looks at Jacuzzi.

The looks seemed to be loaded with some sort of accusation. If it had been converted to sound, it would probably have been the simple, angry yell *"You moron!"*

For just a moment, Jacuzzi stood there looking dumb—and then he figured out what those gazes meant, and he hastily glanced at Miria's face.

"Uh, um, Miria…?"

Miria had bowed her head completely, and he couldn't see her expression.

However, her cheerful mood from a moment ago had disappeared in an instant, and she murmured a name in a voice so faint it seemed as if it might fade away.

"Isaac…"

She'd said the name only to herself, and naturally, there was no response.

Possibly because that immutable fact had saddened her, a rush of air escaped from the depths of Miria's throat.

"Waah…"

*Agh, she's going to cry.*

Sensing the helpless dreariness in that voice, the delinquents gulped, watching the situation unfold.

It wasn't hard to imagine her face crumpling and tears beginning to well up in her eyes.

However—swallowing the sob that was about to escape from her lungs at the very last second, Miria bit her lip and set her hand on a nearby door.

"…I won't cry."

"Miria…"

"No, I'm okay. I'm sorry for worrying you. My crying won't help anything, will it?!"

By the time she turned around, Miria's usual smile was back.

However, the fact that she was talking more than she normally did made it obvious that she was shaken.

"Isaac said he liked to see me smiling. I liked it when Isaac smiled, too… So I won't cry, no matter what!"

Miria shut the door with a *thunk*, disappearing from view. Jacuzzi and the others watched her go, then glanced at one another, looking uncomfortable.

"She won't cry…? Didn't she cry for three days straight when she first came here last month?"

"Yeah, and Jacuzzi caught it from her. That was rough."

"Please refrain from talking nonsense!"

A few of the hooligans were chatting and grinning foolishly, and Nice scolded them, looking stern.

"D-don't get all mad, Nice. We were just kidding…"

Ignoring his crew, who hastily ducked back from her, Jacuzzi's expression grew gloomy again.

"Aaaaaah, it's all because I said something that made her remember…"

"Don't you cry either, Jacuzzi! We're not going through this again!"

"Eep! I-I'm sorry… *hic*…"

＊　　＊　　＊

As he watched the conversation go around in circles, Jon, one of the delinquents, spoke to the Asian young man who was standing beside him.

"By the way, Fang, it was Chané who first got Miria to stop crying, wasn't it?"

"Right. I was surprised, honestly. I mean, they'd barely even seen each other before then."

"Yeah, well… By the way, where is Chané? I haven't seen her for a while."

"Oh, Chané's… She went out today."

Jon was about to ask *Out where?* but it hit him almost immediately, and he didn't ask after all.

However, as if to confirm Jon's thoughts, Fang spoke, smiling a little.

"On a date. With Mr. Felix."

⟺

New York　　Madison Square Park

In a park right next to Fifth Avenue, a young woman sat on a bench, lost in thought.

It was an unexpected green space in the center of the city.

The Empire State Building and other skyscrapers peeked through the leafless winter trees. The sight felt a little strange, and it enveloped everyone there in a dreamlike state.

This park was far smaller than Central Park, but it was an irregularity, like an oasis in the desert, and it caught people's attention. Once inside, they immediately found themselves in a peaceful haven.

Some of the snow that had fallen the other day still lingered. As she watched children playing baseball in the distance, the woman—Chané Laforet—quietly immersed herself in her own world.

\*　　\*　　\*

She was remembering something that had happened a month ago.

A woman who was friends with Jacuzzi's group had come to stay, and she had been crying constantly.

The woman's name had been Miria, and Chané hadn't known all that much about her. All she remembered was that her relationship with Jacuzzi's group was mutual and ongoing; she'd come to visit them from time to time, then either cause all sorts of trouble or help the others resolve the trouble they'd caused. She'd saved Jacuzzi's life, apparently, and Chané felt no particular aversion toward the carefree girl.

She was always with an oddly fatuous man, and so when she'd shown up all by herself at the house where the group lived, Chané had felt very strongly that something was wrong.

The man who was always with her wasn't there now. Even though Chané hadn't been in contact with them for long, she must have begun to see the two of them as a single, inseparable being before she'd even become aware of it.

Had they fought?

If so, it probably wasn't anything she should involve herself in.

On that thought, Chané had decided to just leave her alone, but…

…a few days later, she'd overheard Nice, who had heard about the situation from someone else, telling Jacuzzi about it.

"They say Isaac was arrested by the police…and they haven't heard anything since…"

That fact had startled Jacuzzi, and Chané had begun listening to the conversation in earnest.

After giving it a little thought, she made for the bedroom where Miria was resting.

"Oh. Chané…"

When Miria noticed her there and turned around, Chané saw her eyes were red and bloodshot, and her eyelids were puffy. She'd probably been crying until just a moment ago.

*"Are you all right?"*

Chané couldn't speak, so as a rule, she conversed by writing.

She held the paper out to Miria, and with a weak smile Miria answered:

"Yes... I'm sorry. I just barged in on you all of a sudden... Somebody told me the apartment where we lived wasn't safe so I should go somewhere else... I'm causing trouble for you, aren't I?"

Miria apologized meekly, and Chané slowly shook her head.

Personally, Chané didn't think the girl was unpleasant, and she was sure Jacuzzi and the others weren't inclined to be nasty to her, either. Jacuzzi seemed to have heard Miria crying and had begun to cry himself, and Nice was having a hard time calming him down—but she'd decided that was Jacuzzi's problem and had nothing to do with Miria.

When she saw that Miria was comparatively calm, Chané's pen raced across the notebook she held.

*"Someone important to me is in police custody, too."*

"Huh? Oh... Is it the person you like?"

*"He's my father."*

She'd never conversed with her through writing this way before, but Miria understood the mechanics far more easily than Jacuzzi and the others had, and she responded naturally, even as her expression was listless and wet with tears. In the end, even though Chané was out of the ordinary, Miria had accepted her readily, and that made Chané feel more than a little well-disposed toward her.

"...Then you haven't seen him for years and years?"

*"It's been about four years since I last saw him."*

"I see... Weren't you sad, Chané?"

At Miria's words, Chané's pen paused for a moment, and she pondered.

Saying that she hadn't been sad would have been a lie.

However, when her father had disappeared, all that had welled up inside her was pure anger.

Endless rage at the people who'd stolen her father.

Spurred into action by that anger, and by the feeling that it was her mission to protect her father, she'd helped terrorists who'd been his henchmen occupy a train.

Yet, the real sadness and loneliness had come…after she'd met Jacuzzi and his friends.

Jacuzzi's group had diluted her anger, and in exchange, the sadness it had hidden had welled up. However, at the same time, they'd banished her loneliness.

As a result, there had never been a time when she'd dampened her pillow with tears like the way Miria had—but what would it be like now? If she lost her father forever, or if Jacuzzi or the man who was her lover disappeared from right in front of her…

She didn't even want to imagine it.

Chané hesitated, not sure how to answer Miria's question. Finally, she wrote something that wasn't an answer at all.

*"Even if I'm sad, it won't bring my loved one back, so…"*

"Oh, I see… You're awfully strong, Chané!"

Chané wasn't able to simply agree with that assessment.

Was she really strong? She'd never thought about it, and actually, weren't people like Miria—who was able to be true to her feelings and cry when she lost someone special—stronger?

She didn't know how to respond. Miria's eyes were still filled with tears, but she smiled gently and asked her a question.

"You're waiting, too, aren't you, Chané? Waiting for him to come back home."

That was a statement Chané could agree with wholeheartedly.

"That makes us friends, then!"

The words had been spoken artlessly, and although Chané's face was still blank, her cheeks flushed slightly.

When she noticed the change in herself, she decided she wanted to talk with Miria for a bit.

After giving a little thought to what she wanted to talk about, she wrote the words down in her notebook in neat letters.

*"Would you tell me about your special person? What is he like?"*

"Sure!"

After that, Chané spent the whole night talking with Miria…and she found herself smiling as naturally as could be.

*    *    *

The next day, Miria stopped crying and appeared in front of Jacuzzi's group as her usual self.

Sometimes she'd remember Isaac and begin to tear up, but even so, compared to the way she'd been at first, she seemed to have calmed down significantly.

But even as she was relieved by the change in the other woman, Chané kept thinking.

True, there weren't many things Miria could do now. Since Isaac had been arrested by the police, waiting obediently for his release was probably the best choice. From what she'd heard, the crimes he'd committed didn't seem to be very serious, and he might be free again soon.

However—her father's situation was different.

He'd been arrested on the charge of plotting acts of terrorism against the country, but that was probably not the truth. The papers had reported "official" information regarding Huey and his career, but it was all false.

As an immortal, her father couldn't have falsified it himself, but it would have been possible for someone else to go against his will and forge his paperwork.

The goal of the people who'd captured her father probably had something to do with the immortals.

He might not be released for years and years.

Another immortal might even make him disappear.

However—the people who'd appeared during the Mist Wall incident the previous year…the ones who'd claimed to work for her father…

If she could believe what they said, he was still alive and in a situation that allowed him to issue orders to people outside. The knowledge had relieved her, but there was no guarantee that those circumstances would continue. In the first place, what was the objective of this "research" her father was conducting?

All alone, Chané looked up at the trees that spread overhead, the buildings that were visible between the branches and sparse foliage, and the wan blue sky that covered all of them, as she thought.

Now that she'd met Jacuzzi's group and her world had expanded, what should she do?

*Should I try talking it over with the others when I get the chance?*

With Miria.

With Jacuzzi and company.

And with the person she'd be meeting here—the lover who'd been the first one to expand her world...

There were still thirty minutes left until the time they'd said they'd meet.

Chané sat on the bench in a corner of the park, gazing absently at the scenery.

However, the next moment—

—her vision was filled with countless flapping birds.

It was a wild flock that had been milling around at the entrance to the park.

Was *he* here already?

She didn't think that was it. Even so, although her face was still blank, Chané's heart swelled with anticipation, and she looked toward the entrance—

But the moment she saw the individual who stood there, tension raced through her from head to toe.

The man was wearing a long black coat, and he clearly didn't belong.

He wore a jet-black eye mask; it had gunsights embroidered on it in white, and it covered his eyes entirely. He held a long staff in each hand, and he was walking in her direction, his steps slow.

He was probably blind, but his footsteps were steadier than she would have expected, and he was headed directly for the bench where she was sitting.

...?

She didn't know any men who wore eye masks, but she recognized his face from somewhere.

The old wound in her right shoulder ached, and as alarm bells rang in Chané's mind, she desperately retraced her memories.

Until she remembered the man's identity completely, she didn't dare take the initiative and slash at him.

However, obeying the danger signals her instincts were sending her, Chané carefully reached toward the small of her back, outwardly remaining calm.

The distance between them had closed to five yards. Even if the man pulled a gun, under these circumstances, she'd be able to deal with it.

Tensely, she watched the man—

—and then he stopped suddenly, warping his lips up unpleasantly. When he spoke, it was sneering:

"...You just went for a knife, didn't you?"

——!

"Hee-hee... Hee-hee-hee-hee-hee-hee-hya-ha-ha-ha-ha-ha!"

At the sound of that coarse laugh, Chané knew for sure who this man was.

*Why...? I thought he was dead!*

Stroking the thin beard on his chin, the man faced Chané, opened his mouth wide, and sent vulgar words at her: "Well, how about that! The fanatic bitch, in a park, surrounded by greenery and lost in thought. Is this some kinda joke?"

*...Spike!*

The Lemures had been an organization created by Huey Laforet.

Chané herself had once belonged to that organization, and there had also been a man who worked covertly as a sniper. That was Spike.

She didn't know whether that was his real name or not, and his past career was a complete mystery. As far as Spike was concerned, his sniping skills were the one solid thing by which he proved himself, and as a matter of fact, the only thing the group had needed was the results generated by the bullets he'd fired.

They'd worked together during the occupation of the Flying Pussyfoot, but in the end, the Lemures had betrayed Chané, and Spike had shot her in the shoulder with one of his vicious bullets.

"Well now… Just what sort of expression is Huey Laforet's young lady wearing as she glares at me, hmm? Maybe you've fallen for me, and you're gazing at me, blushing bright red, with tears running down your cheeks! Well, I'd never go for a frigid-looking little brat like you. I like broads who react violently in bed."

Holding her right shoulder tightly, Chané hesitated. With her past suddenly materializing before her, she wasn't sure what to do. He might have been sent by her father. If he had been, she couldn't just cut him down, even if he was exasperating.

"Whoa there. Take your hand off that knife already, wouldja? We've got a bit of a history, you and me, but I'm not here for a fight to the death today."

He was still holding the staffs in each hand, and he spread his arms wide to show that he didn't plan to resist, but his taunting words didn't stop.

Chané couldn't tell what he wanted. It was also possible that those staffs had guns built into them.

Keeping her guard up, she waited quietly for the other to make his move.

"Tch… You don't trust me, huh? Well, that's fine. I'm here today on an errand from my master. Find Huey's daughter—that'd be you—ask her a couple of questions and get the answers, he told me."

"……"

Chané narrowed her eyes.

*This man just…*

*He called me "Huey's daughter."*

*And then he said, "an errand from my master."*

Judging by the way he spoke, she thought that "master" couldn't be Huey.

—Meaning this man wasn't currently carrying out Huey's will.

*In that case, it doesn't matter.*

As she calmed her breathing, Chané decided that, for now, she'd slash the tendons in his arms and legs.

Having made a cruel resolution in an instant, she slowly brought the tension throughout her body under control, watching for an opportunity.

Whether or not he'd noticed how she looked, Spike gave a mean-tempered smile and continued spitting out words.

"Well, I can tell you to answer, but you can't talk and I can't see. How're we supposed to communicate in a situation like this?"

Chané was already through listening to him.

Spike drew a big breath, and the moment he began to say his next words—

"Well, there are probably ways to do it, braille and such, but the easiest thing would be…"

—Chané launched herself off the ground and charged at Spike with the momentum of a cannonball on a horizontal trajectory. On the first step, she drew a knife with her right hand; on the second, she grabbed a second knife with her left. On the third, she intended to carve Spike up with motions that hadn't dulled at all since she'd come to stay with Jacuzzi's group—

"…*to call an interpreter, right?* Hya-ha-ha-ha-ha!"

Chané flew through the air.

"——?!"

It had been abrupt.

Without even feeling an impact, she realized she was spinning through the air, and she hastily righted herself, slamming the soles of both feet into the ground.

Her balance and breathing had been shaken badly, but she had managed to avoid falling by the skin of her teeth.

When she whirled around, Spike was standing behind her. He hadn't moved a step from his original position, and it was as if nothing had happened.

However, one thing was different from before: A lone black figure stood beside him.

It was a man with blond hair who wore what looked like mourning clothes: a black coat, black shoes, and a pitch-black suit. He had a hunting cap pulled low over his eyes, and she couldn't see any part of his face above his nose.

Unlike Spike, she'd never seen this man before, but it seemed likely that he'd done something to her and had flung her to where she was now.

Chané's wariness jumped by several levels. Glancing at her, Spike whistled appreciatively and complimented the man.

"Yowza… Was that the sound of you throwing that unruly frail broad all the way behind me? That's just like you, all right. It's you all over, *Mr. Felix*."

*Felix…?*

She knew that name.

In a way, she heard it practically every day.

It was the name of the lover Chané was waiting for. Felix Walken was the name Claire Stanfield used for himself with everyone except her.

However, this man didn't look anything like Claire. He was a completely different person. If there was one thing about him that seemed similar, it was the aura of danger that seeped from his entire body.

The man in mourning clothes was silent for a while. Then he gave a weary sigh, turned to Spike, and corrected him.

"…How many times do I have to say it before you get it?"

"Hunh? Is this the 'I sold the Felix Walken name to somebody else' thing? Aw, who cares? There's nothing else to call you, and you sold that name because you wanted to ditch your past, but here you are still doing this job, so there's not much point to it, is there?"

Ignoring Spike, who was smiling as if he was having fun, the man soundlessly turned back to Chané. Then, in an indifferent tone, he said something that was very easy to understand.

"We want to ask you one thing, Chané Laforet. If you answer, we'll let you go right away—"

"And we'll let your precious little pals get away, too, see? Hya-ha-ha-ha-ha!"

———?!

"I tell ya… When I heard about it, I couldn't believe it. To think you fell right in with the tattooed brat who messed up our plan! Well, personally, I don't have beef with that guy. Thanks to him, I met up with a good employer who pays a lot better than Huey!"

"You talk too much."

The man in black shut Spike down, then asked Chané, who was shaken, the rest of his question.

"All right. We have one question for you, Chané Laforet.

"What exactly is your father, Huey, planning here in New York?"

**INTERLUDE I**

# IN THE
# DARKNESS

Alcatraz Island     Underground

On Alcatraz Island, there was a group of special segregation units that had been dubbed "the Dungeon."

These were dark, solitary cells that were unanimously feared by convicts who had been too much for prisons all across the country to handle.

In the depths of the jail, below the cellblock with the long corridor that would later be nicknamed Broadway, were cells for solitary confinement that had been created by remodeling storerooms.

This place was surrounded by brick, a relic of the building's days as a fortress, and there was absolutely no light. Prisoners who caused trouble were thrown into this darkness.

Because the brick walls crumbled more easily than concrete, raising the possibility that some intrepid prisoners would dig a tunnel and escape, the convicts' legs were completely restrained in the gloom.

Warden Johnston was against the custom of chaining up prisoners, and once the new block of segregation cells—D Block—was completed, the Dungeon would no longer be used.

However, that was still in the future, and at present, the Dungeon was the source of the darkness the convicts feared, along with various rumors.

*　　*　　*

Below that darkness, in the very heart of the prison, in a place that wasn't recorded on any layout drawings inside the facility—

—*he* was there.

A special cell built for just one man. There were rumors that it had originally been a hidden storeroom for the fortress, or a space to hide noncombatant VIPs, but no one really knew.

It was about the size of a hotel room, too spacious to really call a cell.

In exchange, the only facilities in the room were minimal—a bed and running water—and as with the other cells, the only small articles in sight were things like soap and a tin cup. Unlike in the Dungeon, however, an electric bulb shone brightly, somewhat staving off insanity.

In this area, to which even prison guards were admitted only rarely, a man spoke quietly.

"And? How does he look?"

The light of the electric bulb illuminated two men.

"The immortal named Isaac spotted him, and then he spoke with, um…with Ladd Russo, but he hasn't done anything particularly notable."

One of the men was inside the cell. The other was outside it.

The uniformed guard was bathed in the electric light that came through the sturdy glass of the window.

Their voices traveled through the service slot under the window that was used to deliver meals, and the conversation was going relatively smoothly with the man inside—Huey Laforet, who was sitting a small distance from the door.

"What about the three prisoners who came in with him?"

"I don't know any details. At this point, they haven't made any suspicious moves."

"…You mean even your network hasn't been able to locate them?"

"No, I mean I've been able to check into their past histories, and I didn't find anything particularly suspicious. It's just…the *selves* I've had infiltrate Washington and Chicago *are being erased one after another.* There are accidents and sudden deaths while I'm asleep…

From their methods, it's probably safe to assume our enemies understand beings like Hilton and myself."

For a while, the prisoner and guard continued their suspicious conversation. Then the prisoner inhaled lightly and temporarily put an end to their discussion.

"I see. Please continue your observations, then, Sham."

"Yes, Master Huey."

The guard bowed his head respectfully, turned in a gesture so mechanical it seemed faked, then disappeared down the hallway that led upstairs. All that remained in the corridor were the echoes of his footsteps.

Listening as the footsteps gradually disappeared, Huey quietly spoke to the figure that was curled up on the bed in the corner of the room. It was a built-in bed, just like the ones in the other cells.

"Leeza... Leeza, wake up, please."

"Ugh..."

The voice that issued from the bed belonged to a girl, one who sounded very young.

She rubbed at her tired eyes, but in the next moment, oddly, she spoke so clearly that she might as well have been awake all along.

"Oh, Father. Good morning!"

The girl, who'd woken instantly, bowed to her father with a bright smile that really didn't suit the gloomy room.

In contrast, Huey gave an artificial smile and spoke to the girl in an impassive voice.

"Good morning. How do things look over there?"

"They're taking the bait pretty nicely, and Sham seems to be doing well, too! The only thing is, there are some kinda strange guys."

"Strange guys?"

"Everybody else is checking into them, so I can't say much... But if they're enemies and we all work together, I think we'll be able to finish them off really fast, so don't worry!"

The black-haired, golden-eyed girl spoke like a child, but she was saying things that weren't childlike at all.

Huey thought for a little while, but his thin smile didn't fade. The girl came over to him, and he set his left hand lightly on her head.

"All right. If you learn anything, let me know, please."

"We'll do it just like we planned, then!"

The child nodded as if she was really and truly happy, then she trotted over to the corner of the room.

As he watched her back, Huey's expression tensed slightly, and he spoke the name of a certain immortal.

"I doubt *he'll be able to reach you* this time, but... do be careful of Victor."

At that, the girl did a precise about-face and said exactly what she felt, her face shifting through a kaleidoscope of expressions.

"Okay! I'll be careful! That Victor guy—he's super nasty, isn't he?!"

"Ha-ha... Yes, he is."

Responding with a smile, Huey remembered an earlier conversation with him.

It had been the last time they'd spoken alone together, right before he'd been pushed into this cellar.

⇔

*"Weep, rejoice, and lick my shoes, Huey. I got a special room at Alcatraz just for you."*

*Well, well. So you'll be dissecting me for research in there? Or is it torture? True, no one will hear the screams on such a remote island, and no information will get out, but...*

*"Neither of the above, you moron. Sure, some of the country's top brass want to mess around with your body, and it sounds like the folks at Nebula have a ton of questions for you. But don't worry. And abandon all hope. If you've got the leeway, be grateful to me. I'm not letting anybody pull crap like that. No matter what."*

*...By "abandon all hope," you mean...?*

*"Listen up, scumbag. You're an idiot who doesn't understand other people's feelings or pain, but you're also genius, dangerous, crazy, and damn easy on the eyes, too, which means everyone just flocks to*

*you. Not only that, but you're a skilled actor; plus, if it meant getting research results in a year's time, you'd be fine with spending the other three hundred sixty-four days killing yourself. Same goes for using other people."*

......

"Just try giving a guy like that to politicians or researchers. With your wiles and that silver tongue of yours, you'd make them your faithful servants inside of three days. First, you'd whisper sweet words, and when they start to listen, you'd pour in the poison, drop by painstaking drop. By the time one researcher starts thinking, 'He's a good person. If I talk to him directly, I might be able to get information out of him,' your venom will have already melted his brain so that it's dribbling out his nose. Then your restraints get loosened juuust a little bit, and the next day, whoops, everybody in the lab is dead. Oh hey, you've evaporated into thin air, too! And suddenly, everyone's yelling at *me* and it's 'Find him, find him, goddammit, what the hell, Talbot, what's wrong with you, this is all your fault...!' I'm not gonna mince words: No fucking thank you! I'll say it one more time! No fucking thank you! One more for the record! No! Fucking! Thank! You!"

*You give me too much credit. Your imagination's as robust as always, Victor.*

"Ha! Imagination? It's still nowhere near enough to help me understand the stuff you do! If there's anybody out there who can read your actions completely, then let's hear the guy's name! Well?!"

*Elmer. Or Denkurou...*

"Don't actually give me examples! You're making me look like a dunce! Seriously, what have you got against me anyway...?"

*I have no grudges. In any case, I don't have the ability to deceive people that way.*

"I doubt it. To folks who live and die in the usual way, our immortality alone makes us poison enough. I was good and bottled up my corrosion, but you're volatile, and you run around doing whatever you want like slime mold. You think I could leave you on the loose?"

*In that case, why haven't you eaten me?*

"This is you we're talking about. There's no telling what kind of trap *you've rigged your memories with. Say there's some kind of power-ful hypnotic suggestion in there, and after something triggers it, I'm brainwashed into thinking I'm you. One day, you'd just hijack every-thing I was. The memories are complete, so all you need to do is switch the perspective. Talk about a smooth takeover."*

......

"What's the matter? I nailed it so well you've got nothing to say?"

*No, no. That idea hadn't occurred to me, and I'm genuinely impressed. You may have the makings of a playwright, Victor. That's truly fascinating.*

"I see. In that case, just sit tight and let yourself be locked up."

*I'd like to request a more logical conversation.*

"Denied. I'm pretty sure I couldn't beat you at logical conversation. Fortunately, we're the ones who caught you, and I don't plan on trying to get you to understand anything or understanding anything about you. In other words—I'm putting you on ice, bold as brass, through an irrational action."

*You're as uncouth as always, aren't you?*

"Well, you won't be seeing the sun for a while, and to be honest, I feel sorry for you there. Don't worry. I dunno how many years it'll take, but… Once we do something about the lot from Nebula, I'll let you walk right out."

⇔

Remembering Victor's triumphant expression, Huey gazed nostalgically into empty space…

Then, continuing that conversation, he spoke.

"Being unable to see the sun isn't such a painful thing."

He kept murmuring to himself in a voice no one else could hear.

"However…I've begun to miss the stars at night, you see."

The man chuckled, smiling a little, and slowly got to his feet.

"I've made up my mind. I'll be leaving this place soon, Victor."

Then, in a commanding voice, he spoke to the little girl who was sitting on the bed, swinging her legs.

"Leeza, send a message to the twins."

"What is it, Father?!"

The girl happily jumped up from the bed. Huey murmured quietly.

"Starting now, the areas and people I previously designated ... are my *research subjects*."

There was no trace of delight or sadness, or even resolution, in those words.

They were simply indifferent.

The declaration had been made in the voice of someone carrying out a routine task.

Arbitrarily. Far too arbitrarily ...

## CHAPTER 3: FRONT

# LET'S RELISH LIFE IN THE HOOSEGOW

Alcatraz Federal Penitentiary     Broadway          Night

"Hey. Hey, neighbor."

The whisper came to him from the next cell over, through the thin wall.

Since there was nothing else to do, Firo had been lying in bed when a voice he'd never heard before called to him.

"Say, this afternoon...you came to the island with me, right?"

The voice wasn't reaching him directly through the wall. By coincidence, when Firo had lain down on the bed, his neighbor seemed to have gotten as close as possible to the wall, put his face up near the iron bars, and spoken to him from there.

Even under these circumstances, talking wasn't allowed, but when there were no guards nearby, conversing in whispers didn't cause problems. The guards did come by frequently, but the corridor echoed like crazy, so if one was approaching, they'd know right away. If they temporarily broke off their conversation and got into their beds, they could throw them off the track to a certain extent.

*The guy on the side with the bed was the inked-up Asian guy.*

"Yeah... Maybe I did."

There was what the deputy warden's assistant had told him when he'd arrived, too.

Since he didn't know who this guy really was, he couldn't afford to tell him any more than neçessary.

On that thought, Firo decided to listen carefully to what he said.

"They called you into another room. What happened, huh?"

"…They asked me all sorts of stuff about the fellas I left outside. Apparently, they got it into their skulls that I'm mafia. I just told them some random things and got through it."

"Huh… What did you do that landed you in here?"

"Hmm? Oh… I hit a guy a little too hard."

Being unable to see the other person put more pressure on the conversation than Firo had expected. Talking on the telephone wouldn't have given him trouble, but his interlocutor was right here.

On top of that, this was the first time they'd spoken.

The guy on the other side of that wall was a criminal dangerous enough to get thrown into this prison. What expression was he wearing as he listened? Firo was technically from *that side of things* as well, but in a situation like this, even he felt pretty tense.

At Firo's answer, the tattooed one gave a wheezing laugh.

"Not that, buddy. Not that."

"?"

"I meant afterward. If you don't do something after that, they don't transfer you in here."

*Oh, right.*

Nobody got sent straight from their trial to this jail. Special cases like Firo and Huey were extremely rare exceptions.

*Hmm? I wonder what Isaac did, then…*

Even as he thought about that, Firo responded to the question from the other side of the wall.

"Oh… I hit a guard a little too hard, too."

"……"

"What? You don't believe me? I don't look like I'd do that?"

He'd meant to just duck the question, but maybe he'd been a little too careless…

*Well, if he says, "With that kiddie face of yours?"—I'll knock him flat tomorrow.*

Firo was thinking stuff like that when the Asian gave a sly laugh.

"Ohhh! I see, yeah, sure, I see, I see. Huh. You're just like me, then."

"... You too?"

"Yeah. In my case, there was this guard who was bossy as hell, so I did a little number on his throat. 'Chomp.'"

*"Chomp"?*

Firo visualized what that sound effect meant, and a quiet shiver traveled down his spine.

"Heh-heh! Do you know about *odori-gui*? That's what they call it when you eat critters that are still moving. The second I latched on, he flinched, and I felt it in my tongue and teeth... It was a little salty, too, sent this indescribable thrill through my mouth!"

"All right, okay. That's enough. Stop."

"Well... Even when I remember it now, it's just... The sensation of ripping into him! The overflowing taste of iron! That flavor spiced with the guard's screams and the pain of the saps thrashing my head... Delicious! It tasted so good, I thought my brain was gonna melt!"

The man ignored the attempt to shut him down and kept rambling. He sounded thoroughly happy, so Firo hit him with his honest thoughts:

"You're nuts."

"You think? Appetite is human instinct, you know? I'm just obeying the will of Nature."

No sooner had the man finished talking than, on the other side of the wall, a light clicking noise started up. The eerie performance echoed in Firo's ears: *Click, click, click, click, click, click.*

*This guy's creepy. Are they all fangs or something? ...Oh.*

When he visualized all the man's teeth as the fangs of a ferocious animal, Firo remembered someone completely different.

*That* man's teeth had all been pointed, like a dolphin's. Along with his deep-red eyes, those teeth had branded his monstrous appearance into Firo's brain.

*Compared to him, this guy's way better, I guess... Or, well, maybe not...*

For now, if he was going to suss out his new neighbor, shrinking the distance between them to a certain extent would probably be the best move.

Making the call, Firo quietly asked his name through the bars.

"What's your name?"

"Huh? Ah... Right, these guards just use numbers, and they never say our names. Well, let's see... For now, call me Dragon, after my arms. It's actually Ryuujirou, but you're American, and you'd have a hard time with that one, yeah?"

"Okay, Dragon. My name's—"

Just as he was wondering whether he should give him a random alias, Firo remembered that he and the other immortals physically weren't able to introduce themselves by false names—and as if striking an additional blow, Dragon cut him off.

"I know. Firo, right? That dim-looking fella was yelling it."

"......"

"The guards ended up hauling him off somewhere. How do you know him? Were you together at the jail before this one?"

"...Uh, well, it's...sort of a long story."

Firo was racking his brain for a way to explain, and getting nowhere, when—

—suddenly, a distinctive sound echoed in his ears.

It was a sound he'd really rather not hear—but one with which he was far too familiar.

"Gunshots...?"

"Huh? ...Yeah."

A string of the dry sounds rang out, and Firo frowned, feeling an inexplicable eeriness, but...

...from the next cell over, the sticky voice went on, its tone unchanged.

"Maybe somebody tried to crush out and got shot... Or maybe your dumb pal did something even dumber and got himself drilled. Hee-hee!"

"Oh, the rifles? That happens every night. If you let it get to you, you'll go nuts."

"Is that right? What was that anyway?"

It was breakfast time, the next day.

Firo was sitting across from Ladd, and the first thing he'd done was ask about the gunshots from the night before.

However, Ladd didn't seem particularly surprised. As he answered Firo's question, he waggled the spoon he held in his right hand.

"It's the guards training. So that they'll be able to pick off attackers or cons without getting confused, even on a dark night."

"Oh, I see… Wait, attackers?"

"Well, yeah. There are tons of big-shot gangsters on this island. Several dozen gang members in boats, coming to take 'em back… It could happen, right?"

"Scary stuff."

Firo gave him a quick reply, trying to get off the subject, but Ladd paused the hand he'd been eating with and kept talking.

"Yeah, the guards on this rock are great, really great."

"…? What's great about them?"

"These guys are prepared. They know they could die anytime."

A ferocious, carnivorous smile came, the same one he'd shown at dinner the night before.

Exhaling aggressively, Ladd began—calmly, as far as his words went—to state an opinion.

"What I mean is, when they work, they're braced to kill escaping convicts, and at the same time, they're fully aware that they could get killed themselves. I'm drawn to folks like that. I even feel a camaraderie with 'em. Just like with you."

"Me?"

"Yeah, when I first saw you here in the mess hall, you were glaring every which way. I could see it in your eyes; you had no clue when somebody might bump you off. You looked like you thought everybody but you was the enemy."

"I—I did?"

*Did I let it show in my face that much?*

If so, had he put other inmates—or Huey, who might be watching from somewhere—on their guard?

As Firo's uneasiness grew, Ladd kept murmuring, as if he was talking to himself.

"On the other hand, I hate soft types... I hate, hate, hate the ones who live with easygoing mugs, like they're never gonna die. Can't stand 'em. D'you feel me?"

"...I getcha."

"So I teach those softies. I show 'em just how thin the tightrope they're walking through life really is, and I carve that knowledge into their bodies, their hearts, and their lives. It's fun. Although that's what landed me in here."

"Ah..."

*I see. So this guy's a hitman or something, huh? He does seem a little like Claire.*

Just as he was remembering the face of a hatchet man in New York who was his childhood pal...

...the one who'd been sitting next to him finished his breakfast, rubbed his lean belly, and added his two cents to their conversation.

"Ahhhhh! Boy, did I ever eat! Thanks for the feast indeed! Oh, Firo, you can get seconds as often as you want here. Isn't that incredible? I did think the work pay was low; I guess they sink the difference into food costs!"

Isaac made that declaration with a smile that was no different from what it had been outside prison, and Firo sighed, smiling wryly.

*He's pretty chipper for a guy who spent yesterday in solitary...*

"Hey, were you okay last night?"

"Hmm? Oh, they bawled me out, put me in leg irons, and locked me up again, but I'm used to that by now!"

"Used to it...?"

Firo frowned, and Ladd, who was across from them, laughed and broke in.

"That fella talks loud or does dumb, weird things, like yesterday, so he gets carted off to the Dungeon regularly. Well, he only does little stuff, so he's always back after a night... Normal guys would settle down after getting sent to those cells even once, though."

Even as Firo felt convinced by Ladd's explanation, another question welled up, and he asked it.

"You've been in, too?"

"The most I've been in for is ten days. That place is awful. It's pitch-black in there—no light bulb. You lose all sense of time. Every now and then, they don't bring meals, so I didn't know ten days had passed until they let me out and I asked another guy. It's underground, so you can't hear those gunshots we were talking about... That actually makes it harder. Your legs are chained up, you're in the dark, and there's no sound. Just imagine it. You'd be sick of it inside a minute... I heard about this afterward, but a guy who was in for about two weeks at around the same time as me went cuckoo and got put in the island's hospital. He still ain't back."

Coming from a guy who'd actually been through that, the words carried weight. When he heard them, Firo swallowed hard and looked at the seat next to him, bewildered.

"Isaac... even if it was just for a night, I'm impressed you lasted through that."

"Huh? Ah... You think so? One night's not so bad, is it?"

"No, I think that was really something."

"Really? *A fairy dropped by* yesterday, so I wasn't even bored."

"......"

A fairy.

At the abrupt appearance of that word, there was a short silence. Then Firo shook his head, looking exhausted. "...There you go, talking bushwa again."

"No, it's true, I tell you! There was a little girl's voice, and we talked for quite a while!"

"Isaac... You poor guy. Now that you can't see Miria, you've finally gone around the bend..."

"No, no... Being unable to see Miria is the loneliest thing in the world, but...I really did hear a voice! It was there, in the darkness, asking about you! I'm positive it was Tinker Bell."

"C'mon, fella, gimme a break." At the idea that he'd been dragged into Isaac's delusions, Firo sighed, looking troubled, but—

"Let's see… Something about, how did I know that new guy, and *did I drink the liquor, too.* All the questions that Tinker Bell asked were funny."

"…?!"

The moment he heard Isaac's words, Firo's entire body froze up.

*"Did you drink the liquor, too?"*

As Isaac had said, to someone who knew nothing, it would probably have passed for something funny.

However, to Firo, the question held important significance.

*Was that…the liquor of immortality?*

At the same time, it vividly showed that the "fairy" actually existed. Isaac didn't know about the liquor of immortality, and he couldn't think of any reason he'd tell such a strange lie.

*Does this have something to do with Huey…?*

It worried him, but Ladd—a stranger—was here, and it would seem odd if he latched on to the topic.

Deciding to watch for a chance to get the details out of him later, Firo determined to push Isaac away for now, the way he usually did.

"Yeah, yeah, all right, okay."

"Hey, you don't believe me!! Things happen to fellas who don't believe in fairies!"

"Things? …What things?"

"Huh?!"

Isaac had spoken vigorously, but when Firo responded with a question, he glared up at the ceiling, thinking hard.

"Well… Things. You know… I wonder what does happen. Hey, Firo, what do you think?"

"Like I'd know!"

Firo shut him down, but Ladd, who was sitting in front of him, joined the conversation in his place.

"Well, they end up happy, don't they? After all, these are fairies we're talking about."

"Oh, I see! You're right! Ah, well then. You'll be fine, Firo!"
"Pipe down!"

"Eat quietly."

The guard's voice rang out, and instantly, the dining hall was silent.

To avoid standing out, Firo looked down, pretending to spoon up soup from his empty bowl, and spoke to Ladd in a voice that was even quieter than before.

"What you said before, about those people you hated… Did you mean guys like him? The ones who don't give the slightest thought to the risks they run?"

Firo shot a glance at Isaac as he asked the question, and Ladd grinned as he answered.

"Nah. I've been watching that guy for several weeks now, and frankly, with a brain like his, that whole issue's moot. He doesn't even irritate me."

On seeing that Ladd held no particular dislike for the man, Firo responded, feeling vaguely relieved.

"…Well, that's true."

"What's this, what's this? What about my brain?" Isaac asked quietly, lowering his voice to a whisper.

Giving the wryest smile he could muster, Firo tapped Isaac's head with his spoon.

"It sounds like your brain managed to squeak by without ticking off Ladd over there."

"Huh? What's that about? …Um. I get it! In other words, you didn't get mad at me! Thanks, pal! You're a good guy!"

Isaac said something that was way off base, but—thinking that if he was satisfied, then that was fine—neither Firo nor Ladd bothered to correct him.


Mealtimes weren't all that long, but even so, they had enough leeway to make small talk.

"Oho… So you fellas live in New York, huh?"

"Yeah, well."

"I've been all over America! It's more as if I live in America than in New York!"

On hearing the toponym *New York* from Isaac, Ladd began to wax nostalgic.

"The city, huh…? I've got a sworn little brother over there. He's a weird fella who doesn't feel right unless he's constantly breaking stuff. He was always swinging around a wrench the size of my arm, and lot of the time, he'd take a car apart while he was talking to you. By the time I was done whaling on the driver, he'd have the car completely dismantled."

"That doesn't sound safe. Hmm…?"

"What's the matter, Firo? Aha. Ennis can drive, so you're afraid she could get worked over by this fella! Don't you worry—he's a good guy!"

"I'm not thinking that! …No, Ladd. Does that fella maybe wear a blue coverall? One that's a whole lot bluer than our work clothes?"

Possibly because he'd visualized what Firo had described, Isaac smacked his hands together lightly and leaned forward.

"Ah! I think I've seen that man with Miria! He talked with Jacuzzi once in a while, too!"

"Hey now, hey, hey, hey, what, what, what's this? You people know that kiddo? Graham, the wild child?"

"Yeah… Although recently, I heard he messed with the Runorata Family's turf, and now they're after him."

At Firo's words, Ladd briefly glanced into empty space and thought.

Then, his face turning a little serious, he muttered, "I see… Well, when I get outta here, maybe I'll go give him a hand. My fiancée's waiting for me in New York, too…"

On hearing that, Firo turned appalled eyes on Ladd and reproached him.

"Your fiancée…? You've got somebody like that, and you still got yourself sent here? What were you thinking?"

"I told you already. I've got a goal."

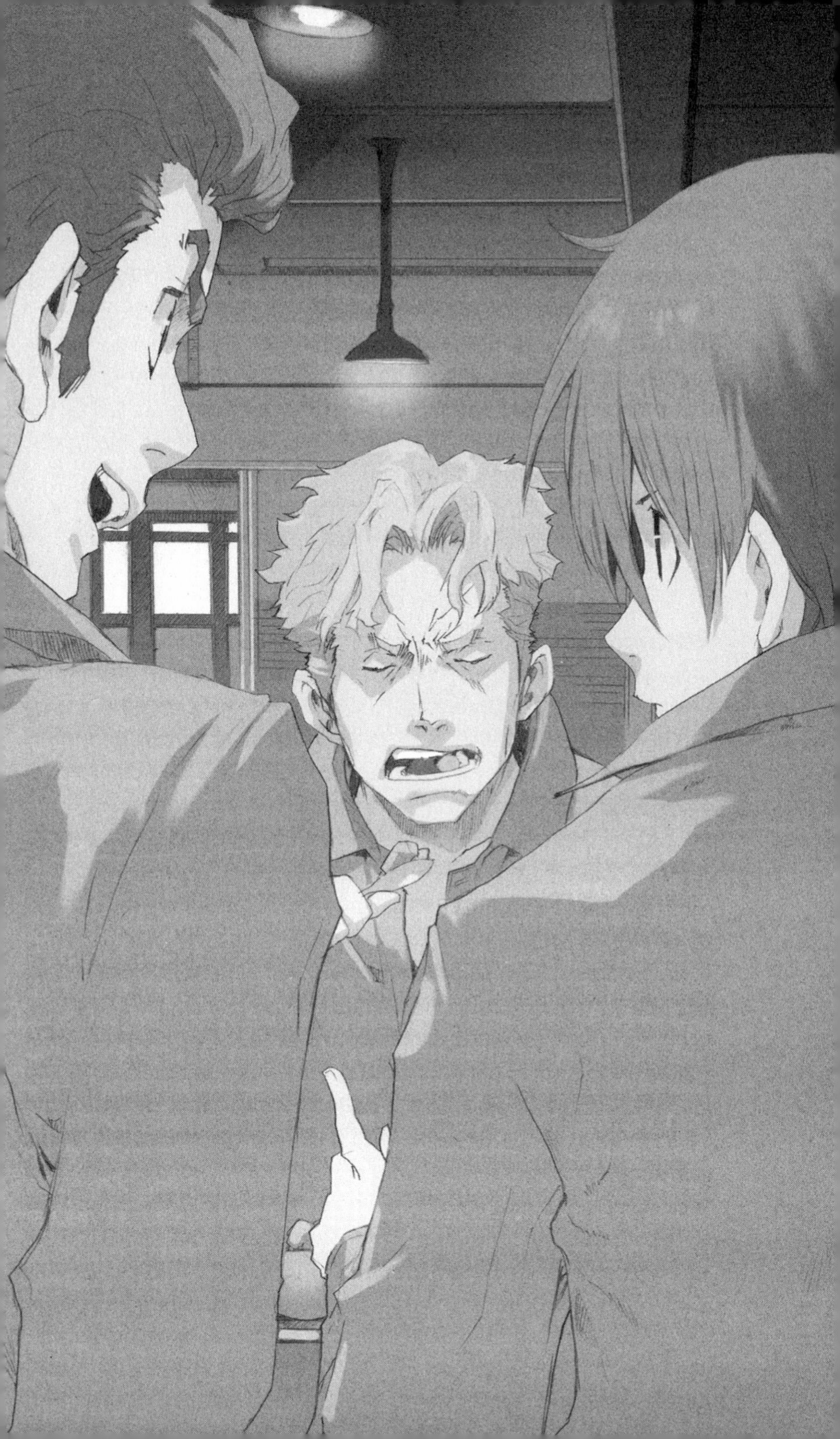

"? Oh, the one for when you get out… Is it meeting up with your girl? That's good."

"My goal is meeting up with Miria!"

Apparently having remembered Miria's face, Isaac made a declaration that completely failed to read the room, and his voice, which was louder than he'd tried for, caught the ear of a nearby guard.

"Fellas, you were told to eat quietly…"

As the stern-faced guard came closer, Firo and Isaac hastily looked down.

However, the next moment—
—an incident occurred.

⇔

"Don't screw with me, you runty bastard!"

The sound of scattering metal dishes rang out, and an abrupt din enveloped the dining hall.

When all the convicts and guards in the cafeteria turned to look that way, they saw a struggling white man hanging high in the air.

The man was kicking and flailing roughly two yards above the ground. There was a dark, scarred-up hand on his throat, and its enormous owner was keeping his prey suspended so steadily that he might as well have been a coatrack.

"Eep! EeEEEeee! Eeee…!"

The smaller one was screaming desperately and fighting to free himself from the massive hand, but it had a firm grip on his throat, and even when he hit and scratched at it, it didn't budge.

"Those guys…"

When Firo saw the scene, he remembered the pair's faces immediately.

Like Dragon, both the white man and the black man had come to the island with him.

The big black man's scarred face twisted into a grin, and he looked up at the white man he was holding in the air with his right hand, hitting him with violent words.

"You were grumbling about me on that boat yesterday, right, ya bastard? You looked at me and snorted just now, too. Is my scratched-up face that funny? Huh?"

"I—I—I—I didn't do a— Gah-gah-gah-gah-gah-aaaAAaah! Aah!" the white man cried.

Ignoring his victim, who seemed to be in pain, the man put more force into the hand that was clutching his neck.

"Hey, Gig. Knock it off."

Some of the other black men who were sitting nearby tried to talk their newcomer down, but Gig didn't listen. Instead, he kept compressing the white man's windpipe and carotids with one hand.

"What are you doing?!"

"Stop!"

The guards were on the scene almost immediately, and the sense of tension they brought with them was completely different from when they'd hauled Isaac off yesterday. What would happen to that big man, here in the dining hall, with all eyes trained on him? At this point, there was nothing Firo and the others could do but watch.

That was what Firo assumed, but—

"Ah… Perfect timing. Just perfect. Ain't that right, Firo?"

"Huh?"

—watching the figure slowly get up from the chair across from him, Firo sounded skeptical.

"'Perfect' is actually a real fuzzy concept, ain't it? What strikes a guy as 'best' changes all the time. The shape he's in, the weather, his mood, the special pals around him, the hated enemies he's squaring off with, the weak guys he should kill, the tough guys he should kiss up to—although, he'll kill 'em all in the end anyway. As my circumstances push me this way and that, I think that the best, the absolute best 'perfect' is something truly valuable, and so even if I risk my life over it, I'll have no regrets."

Ladd had turned abruptly eloquent, and when he saw his face, Firo was beset with a nebulous uneasiness.

"Okay then, *I'll be right back*."

"Hey, wait. Where are you going…?"

"Someplace good. The only thing I see in front of me is my path. On it, there are guys I need to kill, like that red monster and Huey Laforet."

"Hue... What?!"

"Huey Laforet" was the last name he'd expected to hear.

Wearing a ferocious smile, Ladd turned his eyes on the black man who was at the heart of the trouble.

He cracked his neck once. Then, as if he was genuinely enjoying himself, he said something very odd.

"I got a little curious about the fairy that guy over there was talking about. All this is perfect for giving my mood a shot in the arm, and for getting into the Dungeon."

However, as Ladd walked away, his attention wasn't on his tablemates any longer.

"I tell you what, this is ab-so-lute-ly ...*brilliant*."

Instead, all that was left were the dregs of a sharp murderous intent—the sort that froze anyone it focused upon.

"Freeze!"

"Settle down!"

Holding billy clubs, the guards surrounded the scarred black man.

Behind the gun ports in the walls, there was the sound of hasty, running footsteps.

Some of the convicts in the mess hall were watching the ruckus play out, while others were gazing up at the small holes in the ceiling.

The holes were there so that gas could be pumped in when riots broke out. It was actually tear gas, but the rumor that circulated among the prisoners said the gas would be lethal.

"Heeey, we are settled. Both of us, this guy and me."

No sooner had he said this than Gig squeezed the still-struggling man's neck even harder.

"G'on, they said settle down."

"...Ah...gkh..."

The white man had completely stopped breathing, and his face was turning a deep purplish red.

Faced with a situation in which it was anyone's guess which would happen first, suffocation or a broken neck, the guards braced to jump the two men at once, but just then—

—a moment sooner, a shape slipped in the middle of the group.

The guards saw the shadow out of the corners of their eyes, and the smile of a man who'd found his prey branded itself into their retinas.

However, it definitely wasn't the smile of a hunter.

At this point, it wasn't even the carnivore's smile that Firo had seen before.

It wasn't delight.

It wasn't instinct, either.

He'd completely warped it, voluntarily—

It was the smile of a cold-blooded murderer.


"Hey, pal."

"Hunh...?"

When the cheerful voice spoke to him abruptly, Gig looked down and to the side, sounding suspicious.

There was a man who was about a head shorter than he was, and just as Gig was about to register his face—

—an impact ran through his stomach, and he heard something inside him creak.

"——?! ?! ?!"

He'd been prepared to take blows from the guards' saps.

He'd thought that, compared to the pain he'd experienced up until now, pain on that level wouldn't bother him much.

However, the impact that had assaulted Gig's side, at the base of his ribs, was beyond any blow he'd ever felt.

In spite of himself, he let go of the white man he'd been holding in his right hand and curled in on himself reflexively.

His side was still numb, and he felt something hot seeping out, right next to his stomach.

He'd been shot by a guard's rifle.

For a moment, he was caught by that illusion. He was still surrounded by a crowd of people, though, and he'd assumed they wouldn't shoot him. His expectations had been roundly betrayed.

But what had assaulted him hadn't been a rifle bullet.

Right in front of Gig's agonized face, an amused voice spoke.

"Now we're the same height."

The voice was cheerfulness itself, and it was speaking as if its owner had just reunited with an old friend.

"You're a lot easier to hit now."

As Gig raised his eyes, he saw the man's limp, dangling left arm. It had misshapen fingers formed out of rough iron, and it was just a shade better than Captain Hook's false hand in *Peter Pan*.

Finally attempting to see the mystery man's face, Gig looked up, fighting the pain, and saw—

—a torso that was in the process of twisting dramatically and the back of a man's head.

"Actually, to take it further, this is *that*: You're massively, tremendously, truly, supremely, absolutely, ludicrously…"

"Uh………"

"Easy to hit."

His torso, which had twisted as far as it could go, rebounded like a spring, and before Gig could register the other man's face, a heavy right hand sank into his nose.

"_____"

At the moment of impact, he'd already lost consciousness. Gig's oversize body spun 180 degrees and flew—then, pulling in one of the guards and a table, slammed into the floor in grand style.

A roar echoed.

The mess hall went silent.

In the next moment, the glossy black tubes that were visible through the gun ports were pointed at Ladd, several more guards came running in to provide backup, and the dining hall went into a complete lockdown.

"You again…?"

The guard who'd spoken was wearing a stern expression, and Ladd shrugged as he responded:

"My, my. What's this, what's this, what's this? What's the gloomy mug for? What I just did was legit self-defense, see? As a matter of fact, I think you should gimme a letter of appreciation and cut my remaining time by half a year."

Ladd had abruptly started talking nonsense, and the guards looked at one another, then edged closer, tightening the perimeter. Something had probably happened in the past: Nobody tried to just walk up to him and pin him down. The guards treated Ladd, a lone convict, as carefully as they would have if he'd had a gun.

The skinny white man was slumped in front of Ladd, shaking hard. Pointing at him, Ladd calmly said his piece.

"See, that big lug tried to throw this little guy at me and kill me. I got scared and hit him first. If I'd been a second later, I'd have been dead."

"... You think anybody's going to buy that excuse?"

"Hell no! I don't believe this prison's accommodating enough to let an excuse like that get through, and as a matter of fact, last time I tried it, you chained me up hand and foot without even listening and sent me to the Dungeon. That's right! That's exactly why! I trust you fellas! You put your lives on the line and do your jobs seriously, and because you do—I can hold back this feeling that's welling up inside me, and hold it, and hold it... and focus it on one single guy."

Ladd spoke with a frank smile. The guards glared at him, but Ladd didn't let it bother him; he turned his gaze to Firo and Isaac, who were watching from a distance.

"See ya, New Yorkers. Let's meet up again, if we're all alive."


As he watched them march Ladd away, Isaac murmured, sounding impressed: "I see... So that big man was trying to kill Ladd?! That was a close one— Humff, mrgle."

"Quiet."

Isaac had been about to express his admiration of Ladd's opinion, and Firo covered his mouth with a hand. He was gazing tensely at the face of the man who'd been chatting with them just a moment ago.

*What the hell is that guy...?*

He'd reacted to Isaac's fairy story and headed to the scene. At that point, he'd already been nuts enough, but those moves, combined with a punch so forceful it was impossible to believe he'd hit with a bare hand, made Firo realize, belatedly, that the man he was looking at wasn't just any jailbird—

And, belatedly again, he remembered exactly where he was.

*Alcatraz.*

When, among groups of vicious criminals who'd snapped, individuals went past "snapped" to "crazy," this prison was where they all ended up. As he recalled the situation he'd been placed in, and thought about the future, Firo broke out in a cold, stealthy sweat.

"Hey, Isaac... Seriously, why did you come to this rock?"

Firo thought the thief was an idiot, but he'd decided that he wasn't crazy. He watched the man's face, asking his question as if he found the whole concept strange in the deepest depths of his heart.

Isaac looked back at him, clearly wondering why he'd ask a question like that this very moment. However, he didn't seem to have any doubts beyond that, and he spoke about his circumstances easily.

"Huh? They just told me, 'We can't put you in a regular prison, so go to Alcatraz, and in exchange, we'll make your term shorter.' They said I'm only in for fifty days!"

"What's with that nutty prison term? Who told you that stuff?"

"Uh, some big shot named Victor set it up."

Firo had half expected that answer, and it triggered a memory of an irritating, bespectacled face.

*So was Isaac insurance or a lure or something in case I didn't get nervous when Ennis's name came up?*

If Firo hadn't complied when they'd come for him the first time, or if any other uncertain elements had come into the picture, Victor might have been planning on using Isaac as a hostage to lure out Ennis, then using her as a hostage to control Firo.

Having reasoned out the agents' objectives, Firo clenched his fists tightly, an intensely bitter expression on his face. Blood dripped from the gaps between his fingers, but it ran up his legs immediately, slipping back into his fists as though nothing had happened.

*That damned agent...*

## CHAPTER 3: BACK

# LET'S ADMIT OUR MISTAKES GRACEFULLY

Somewhere in New York    The temporary offices of the Bureau of Investigation

"Okay, minions! Let's get a report on what you know to your capable supervisor, shall we?"

In an old office used only by a select few within the Bureau of Investigation, Victor, who'd just woken from a nap, clapped his hands together loudly, announcing that their work was starting again.

However, the only response he got back was delivered in a voice so lazy it seemed to beckon him back to slumber.

"Uh… Sorry to butt in, sir, but shouldn't the minions be capable in this case?"

"I won't lie to myself or my men. After all, that is what makes capable people capable. Or so I'd like to believe."

"Never mind, Assistant Director, just do your job, please. The reports are in document form already, and they're sitting right there."

In his cramped open-plan office, as his subordinates pelted him with criticism, Victor silently read through the reports.

As he scrutinized the information that had come from Alcatraz Island, Victor's expression turned serious. He sent some significant words at Bill and Edward, who were working at their own tasks in the same room.

"Well, all joking aside...if Huey's pawns are going to make a move, they'll do it soon. Don't be shocked if everybody in New York abruptly disappears today."

"What kind of nonsense is that?"

"Don't underestimate him."

Edward had tried to take the statement as a joke, but Victor cut him off short, then began to explain Huey to his men.

"Of all the immortals, that experimentation maniac is a weirdo of the first order. He doesn't give a flying fig for other people, nothing fazes him, and if it came down to it, he wouldn't hesitate to use himself up as a guinea pig, too. After all, like Maiza, he messed around with stuff you could call magic, not just with alchemy."

"Ah... In other words, you're saying Huey is a magician?"

"Nope. Nothing that romantic. In the end, he's a hopeless researcher and seeker and investigator. That's all! Once he gets what he's after, it's immediately just a stop on the way! He never gets the means and the end mixed up, because to him, they're the same thing right from the get-go! And so, even if you manage to figure out what he's thinking, you can't figure out the means at all! Even if you try to forestall him, he's the type who'll have worked the fact that someone forestalled him into his experiment! Dammit... The guy doesn't even make it clear whether he's stubborn or flexible."

"Mm... Please make it clear whether you're complimenting him or tearing him down."

From next to Bill, who'd put in the desultory comeback, Edward piped up, looking serious: "As long as we don't even know his objectives, there's no way for us to act. What does the report from Alcatraz say? Is Firo making any moves at all?"

"No, it doesn't look like he's made any contact to speak of yet..."

The name his subordinate had mentioned reminded Victor of what had happened at Alveare a short while ago, and as he spoke, he hid an irritated expression.

"Well, that Firo kid was always just a throwaway pawn. I don't expect much from him. If he figures out how Huey's contacting the outside, I couldn't ask for better, but... According to the call I got from Misery, it sounds like somebody else may have sent in special 'prisoners.'"

"Somebody else…?"

"Uh… Could that be Nebula's doing?"

In response to Bill's weary question, Victor nodded, looking even wearier.

"They probably want to ask Huey for some information, or maybe they're planning to take it by force. Either way, we'll just do all we can, but… Hmm? What is it, Agent Noah?"

Realizing that Edward was looking his way and glowering, Victor adjusted his glasses and asked him a question.

"You look like you've got something to say."

"Well… What you just said, about not expecting much from Firo—"

"What about it? Feeling conflicted over using him, since you know him real well?"

"No, that isn't it. It's just—"

Right as Edward was on the verge of saying something—

*Brrrrrrrrrrrrrrrriiiiiiiiiiiiing     brrrrrrrrrrrrrrrriiiiiiiiiiiiiiing*

The mechanical noise of the telephone bell echoed, interrupting the flow of events.

⟺

At the same time     Alveare

In the restaurant, it was just after noon.

The waitresses were bustling around busily, shuttling between customers of all ages and genders. At this time of day, when the number of respectable customers increased, out of consideration for the establishment, the members of the Martillo Family—who practically lived at the restaurant—holed up in the back.

In a corner, a man whose demeanor was very obviously different from that of an upstanding citizen sat lost in thought, nursing a glass of liquor in one hand.

"…Frankly, I didn't expect that, either. To think you'd noticed me among all the noise…

"This is what makes a life with unknowns in it so interesting.

"Don't mind me. I'm only talking to myself.

"…So you're asking me for assistance.

"Are you sure that's what you want?

"Fundamentally, there are no limits on the power I can wield.

"For that very reason, as much as possible, I use it only for the sake of my family.

"Even for the family, I've never committed such a foul to begin with.

"Splitting clouds and finding people is one thing, but that…

"Breaking someone out of prison, an extreme subversion of the law…

"That said, I did sneak in secretly to see an acquaintance.

"Well, never mind. In other words: If I use my power to save him—

"—it will put him completely on this side of things.

"Are you prepared to go that far?

"…You're hesitating. Hmm. Well, forget about it.

"You seem drawn to that man from the bottom of your heart…

"However, for that very reason, you're unsure whether it's all right for you to decide his fate, correct?

"I'll give you time to worry about it. I'm not that impatient.

"…What's the matter? Decided not to go through with it?

"I see; so that's your resolution. Believing in him and continuing to wait isn't a bad idea.

"Fate is something you carve open for yourself, and being tossed about by others is the natural human state.

"Finally, and this is simply a word of advice from a friend…

"…The police may have already gotten to your apartment.

"Go stay with friends.

"It's fine to cry your eyes out for a while.

"True, what he did may have been selfish…

*"But that's the side of him you were drawn to, isn't it?*

*"Don't nod so vigorously. You'll embarrass me."*

"Hmm…"

Remembering a scene from about a month ago, Ronny Schiatto smiled in spite of himself.

Maiza, who was sitting next to him, noticed, and he looked him over as if he was seeing something unusual.

"What is it, Ronny? When you smile during your reminiscing, it's unnerving."

"Mm? Ah well, it's nothing."

"No, no, no, I mind… What's the matter? You aren't usually this pensive."

"I was simply pondering human love."

That word—*love*—had sprung from a man it really and truly didn't seem to suit, and Maiza froze up for a bit. Multiple question marks rose in his narrowed eyes, and he broke out in a cold sweat, as if disturbed.

"Do I take your reaction to mean you're picking a fight with me?"

"Oh, no, no! Not at all!"

"Well, never mind. More importantly, you seem to be pretty worried about Firo."

"… Yes. I've heard the rumors about Alcatraz, after all."

Maiza glanced at their surroundings, then went on in a voice that was low enough to disappear under the ambient noise.

"He may be immortal, but that won't save him from dying inside."

"Don't worry. He'll be fine."

"I do believe that, but…"

Maiza was still unable to hide his unease, and Ronny spoke about Firo as he appeared to him, not as a demon or alchemist but as a lone gangster.

"He is an immortal, but more importantly, he's a Martillo Family camorrista. The *caposocietà* didn't acknowledge him for the sake of appearances or on a whim."

On hearing these words from a man who had been his close friend for many years, Maiza nodded, smiling wryly.

"I tell you, this is an unlucky business."

"Would you have rather stayed an alchemist?"

"…No. I have regretted summoning you on board that ship, but…I don't have the faintest regret that I'm here now."

"Hmm… Likewise."

After that, for a little while, they chatted about unrelated matters and drank together, but…

…about the time the lunch crowd was beginning to thin out—something unexpected happened.

Suddenly, the radio that sat on the restaurant counter began reporting a peculiar news item.

"……z…zZ…in……of ……are related…investigating …"

"…poli…think the incident is the work of a large-scale criminal organization…"

"…What's up?"

A few people in the restaurant began listening to the words they could catch in the static.

Possibly because the tense character of the broadcast had drawn her attention, one of the waitresses adjusted the tuner, improving the reception on the radio.

"…repeat. Mr. Placido Russo is believed to have been deeply involved with the kidnapping and serial bombing incidents that took place in Elleson Hill in Illinois. The authorities are currently—"

The sound was now coming through clearly, and when they heard it, Randy and Pezzo spoke to each other as they worked on their lunches.

"Elleson Hill. That's over by Chicago, right? Bombings and kidnappings? Dicey stuff …"

"And Placido… Ain't that the Russo Family's don? He's not

famous like Capone, and they're still running his name on the radio like that, bold as brass…"

"Yeah, even in Chicago, the Russo Family's about as down on its luck as you can get. By now, they probably don't need to be careful around 'em. Plus, officially, the guy's in car sales."

"Still, bombings and kidnappings, huh? What's that knucklehead doing?"

The pair had decided that the topic was one to be laughed off, but—

—the moment they heard the next words from the radio, the mood in the restaurant changed drastically.

*"Explosives were set in roughly three hundred locations. It isn't clear how many casualties have resulted, but the concurrent kidnappings occurred in neighboring Chicago as well, with more than two hundred people simultaneously disappearing from the surrounding areas. The situation has the residents of Illinois visibly uneasy—"*

"Three hundred?!"
"Two hundred people?!"

*"With regard to this incident, Senator Manfred Beriam, who is currently staying in Chicago—"*

The radio relayed more information, but no one in the restaurant was listening to it any longer.

The place had suddenly begun to buzz. Frowning, Maiza said frankly, "Some pretty unsettling things are happening in Chicago."

"Yes, they are."

"…Elleson Hill… That's where Nebula's based, isn't it?"

Nebula was a leading domestic conglomerate. It had its headquarters in an enormous building in Chicago, and many of its branch companies and plants were located in a neighboring town called Elleson Hill.

"It's an odd place. There are rumors that even the mayor is involved with Nebula."

"I hear sixty percent of the town's residents are Nebula personnel, in any case. I wonder what it could be... Did they start some sort of trouble with Placido? Although the matter seems to be beyond that level..."

The incident was an extraordinary one, and even if it was something on the other end of the radio, some tension was visible in Maiza's eyes. If this actually was the mafia's doing, the federal government might also begin working to stamp them out.

If that happened, it was bound to have a massive effect on even little organizations like the Martillo Family.

Beside Maiza, who was listening intently to the radio, Ronny put a hand to his mouth and began to lose himself in the world of his thoughts.

*Hmm... I figured it would be one or the other—New York or there. But...*

Inside his mind, he meshed the information from the radio with the information he "knew"—and, possibly because something had occurred to him, he knocked back his liquor, then murmured to himself:

"No, this incident is actually... Heh-heh. Well, never mind.

"Let's see what you've got, Huey Laforet. And all you mortal human beings."

⇔

Madison Square Park

"All right. That's how it is, young Miss Chané. It'd be a big help if you'd come with us quietly."

Spike was leering, and Chané ground her teeth lightly, reviewing the situation she'd found herself in.

If Spike had been alone, she would have had no trouble. She didn't think a blind sniper without a gun would be able to pin her down here.

However, that other man who had appeared from behind him—the man Spike had called Felix Walken—was clearly on a different level from ordinary people. She didn't know whether this was due to innate talent or the product of hard work, but the aura he'd directed at her, the fact that he'd flung her away in an instant, and—more than anything—his name were making Chané tense.

Felix Walken.

She'd heard about him from Claire.

He'd said he'd gotten the false name he was currently using from a certain hitman.

The hitman was rumored to be a top-class hired killer, even in New York, and had become a covert legend. She also remembered Claire himself saying something to the effect that the individual was "the strongest, after me, of all the people I've seen so far."

If the man in front of her was this "former" Felix, then her current situation was pretty serious.

However—although Chané had made that call, she didn't show the slightest trace of fear.

She had no intention of withdrawing, and if there was anything that scared her, it was the idea of letting these two get away and inflict damage on Jacuzzi's group. Before she let that happen, it would be easier to make them cough up their employer's name—and most of all, she couldn't overlook people who were trying to obstruct her father.

"…I see. Holding out to the bitter end, hmm?"

As the former Felix murmured quietly, he took his hands out of his coat pockets, rolled his head on his neck, and took a step toward her.

*He's coming.*

Chané's hands tensed on her knives. She was just about to launch into a run—as if to demonstrate that victory went to the swift—when, in the shadows of her field of vision, she registered several approaching figures.

"?!"

When she looked, about ten men were walking toward her from the park entrance. They were also dressed in black, as if they were in mourning. Half of them had powerful builds; at first glance, the other half looked normal, but their sharp eyes were all focused on Chané, too. In combination with those black clothes, the group reminded her vaguely of the Lemures.

"Heeey, over here, this way. It's this brat."

He must have heard their footsteps. Spike hailed the men, his lips twisting.

He'd already had the upper hand, and these new reinforcements had improved his mood. However, the black-clad newcomers muttered, and there was something vaguely tense about their expressions.

"Spike. There's a slight problem."

"What? What happened?"

"Just now, on the radio..."

"Hunh? Hang on a minute."

Spike checked the words of the approaching men in black, and his smile vanished completely. Frowning, his words were tinged with doubt.

"Those footsteps... There's one too many."

The former Felix picked up on what he meant, and he was the first one to run his eyes around the area.

His cold eyes spotted...a lone man.

That man seemed to have appeared out of thin air.

Just as the former Felix had seemed to do from Chané's perspective, by the time he noticed him, the man was already standing beside her.

Spike noticed him next, and he called to the sudden intruder irritably.

"Who're you? You're not one of us."

At that, the intruder spoke, and his eyes were perfectly clear.

"If you're asking who I am...I'll give you a real brief answer."

Hugging Chané's shoulders and pulling her close, the man introduced himself in a voice that brimmed over with confidence.

"I…am *me*."

Silence enveloped the park.

The answer had been so bold, and so nonsensical, that Spike and the men in black fell silent for a little while. Until—

"What're you, punk? Showing up in the nick of time… You think you're a movie hero or something?"

—recovering his leer, Spike lobbed a taunt at the intruder.

In response, with no hesitation—although he did look just a little bashful with regard to Chané, who stood beside him—the intruder spoke.

"Well, uh… I didn't show up in the nick of time… Actually…I've been watching for a while."

"Huh?"

"See…I couldn't quite curb my enthusiasm, and I'd been in the park for quite a long time already… But then I spotted Chané, lost in thought under the light filtering through the branches. And she was just way too cute, so…"

Those words had been said right by Chané's ear, and she flushed bright red, turning reproachful eyes on the man.

"Ha-ha, c'mon, don't act like that, Chané. I'd swear to it. You were incredibly cute."

"…! …!"

"This isn't the time for that? What are you talking about? As far as I'm concerned, your charms are a more important topic than these small-timers."

Spike strained his ears, but naturally, he couldn't hear Chané's voice. She didn't seem to have let go of her knives, so she probably wasn't using sign language. Spike felt as if he were being made fun of, and he yelled at the couple, venting his irritation:

"Yeah, this really ain't the time for that! Hold it, hold up, whatever, just hang on, people!"

Spike had been completely shut out of the pair's world, and he

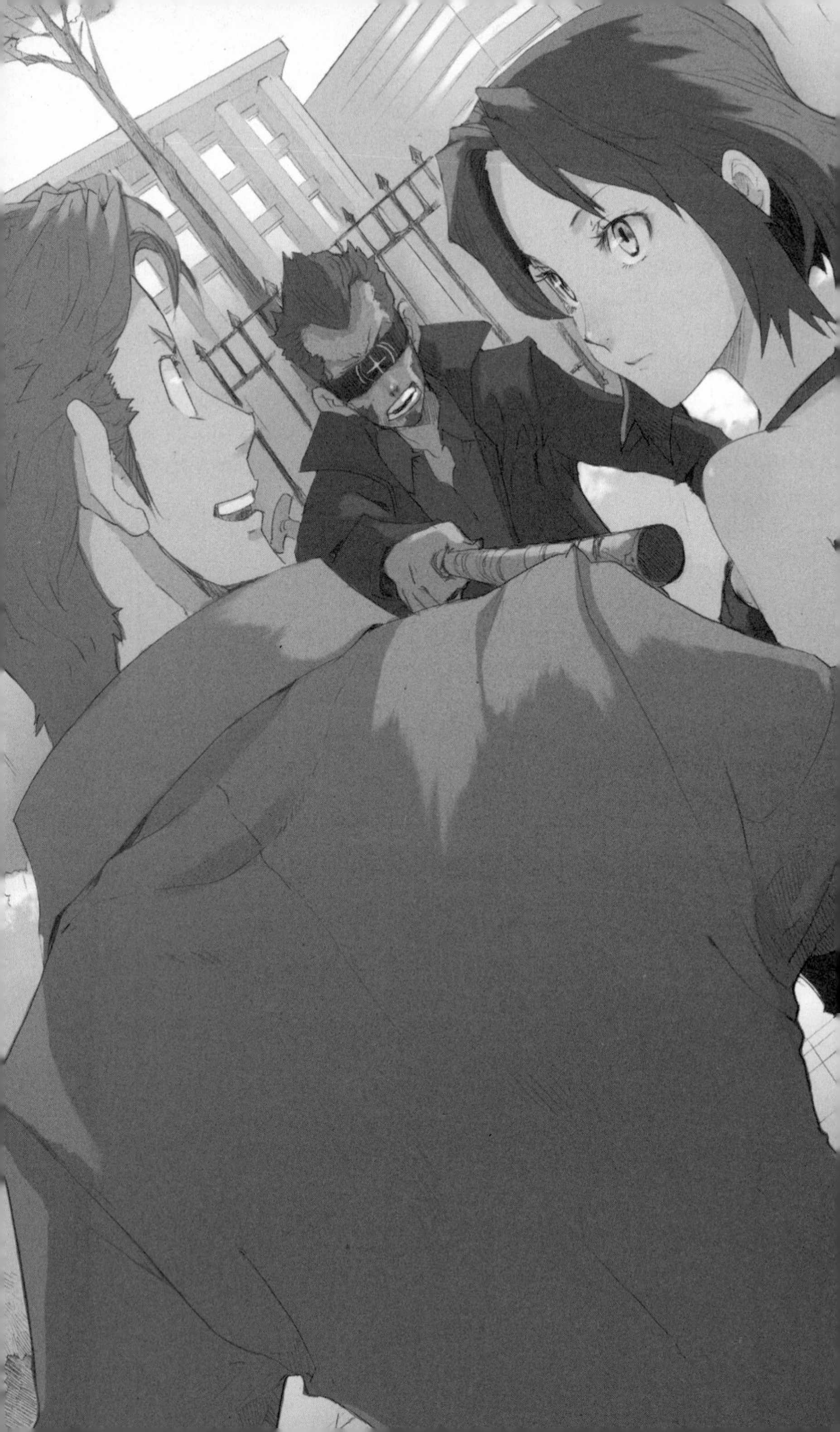

swung the staff in his right hand down at the ground. The skin over his temples was taut.

"So who are you?! If you're dumb enough to get involved in this, you'll get hurt, or, uh, you know. Die."

"*You* will, you mean?"

"Wha...?!"

*Dammit, what the hell is this bastard?*

At having his taunt answered with a taunt, Spike gnashed his teeth, glaring in the direction of the man's voice with his mind's eye.

*But... What is it? I dunno, but this guy... There's something nasty about him. Alarm bells are clanging away in my head like nobody's business.*

Spike broke out in a cold sweat, hoping that the people around him would make the first move, but...

...beside him, the former Felix's icy stare hadn't changed, and the surrounding men in black were waiting to get orders from *somebody.*

Deciding that if he didn't calm down, there was no point, Spike desperately held back his irritation and sent another question at the intruder.

"Okay—fine, but gimme a name, at least. This is going nowhere."

Spike wasn't fully expecting answer, but the man responded with unexpected ease.

However, what he said threw the situation into further confusion.

"I'm Felix. Felix Walken."

"...Huh?"

Nobody had seen that answer coming. Spike and the other men in black all turned to look at the former Felix. Felix looked away uncomfortably, refusing to make eye contact with them.

Not seeming to care about any of it, the intruder—Felix Walken, aka Claire Stanfield—spoke, indifferently and boldly.

"I'm Chané Laforet's... fiancé."

⟺

The Bureau of Investigation     Special offices

*Brrrrrrrrrrrrriiiiiiiiiing*     *brrrrrrrrrrrrrriiiiiiiiiing*

"...Is that from Donald?"

The call had come at an odd time, and for just a moment, Victor hesitated. Then, drawing a deep breath and resetting his mood, he put on his "coolheaded boss" face and picked up the receiver.

"Talbot speaking... Oh, so it is Donald, huh? What is it?"

Victor took his subordinate's report in a dignified manner, but then—

"What...?"

—as he listened to the voice on the other end of the line, his expression stiffened instantly.

Then, still listening to the report through the receiver, he turned to Edward and silently gestured for him to turn on the radio.

Edward caught the meaning of the signal immediately. He turned the radio on and was about to adjust the tuner—

—but he didn't even have to tune the station: Breaking news was already airing.

*"Explosives were set in roughly three hundred locations. It isn't clear how many casualties have resulted, but the concurrent kidnappings occurred in neighboring Chicago as well, with more than two hundred people simultaneously disappearing from the surrounding areas. The situation has the residents of Illinois visibly uneasy—"*

Hearing the content of the broadcast, Edward froze in astonishment, and even Bill stopped moving and opened his sleepy eyes wide.

"Why...didn't we get that information...before it was broadcast?"

Desperately forcing down his anger, which was on the verge of exploding, Victor kept listening to Donald's report, shoulders trembling.

"Ah... I see... Understood. Understood, Donald. I'll call you back as soon as we verify the situation with FBI headquarters."

Once he'd heard the full report, Victor set down the receiver with startling slowness. He'd probably decided that, if he put even a little force into the action, he'd break it. His expression, which had been calm and arrogant, was now filled with nothing but quiet anger.

"Those bastards at Nebula… Apparently, they're planning to keep the Bureau of Investigation out of the loop no matter what."

His voice was calmer than they'd expected, and it made Edward's and Bill's hearts shrivel up.

"Huey Laforet… So all the men he had in New York were decoys?!"

Just as he said that:

The door opened with a *click*, and a man poked his head in.

It was a face Victor and the others didn't know. From his clothes, he seemed to have been left homeless and unemployed by the Depression, which had been going on for several years. However, his face was filled with an intense energy, and he made a strange impression on the members of the Bureau.

For one thing, it was weird that a homeless man was in here at all.

"Who're you?"

They hadn't set a guard, but this wasn't the sort of place anybody would wander into by accident…

The man spoke to the confused investigators in a polite tone that didn't match his appearance.

"It's a pleasure to meet you, or perhaps I should say it's been a while, gentlemen of the Bureau of Investigation… Although I see there are only three of you here."

"…?! Who are you?"

"As you seem to have been properly notified by radio, allow me to deliver a message from Master Huey."

"?!"

At the name, tension flickered across the faces of the three men.

"Master Huey says, 'I'm afraid I'm going to cause trouble for you, Victor, and I'm sorry.'"

"…?!"

*A messenger?!*

From the fact that he was here at all, and from the words he was saying, there was no chance that this was just a prank. In which case—

A hint regarding the contact method—what Victor and the others had wanted more than anything—had appeared right in front of them with exquisite timing.

However, at the same time, Victor's instincts were sounding alarms.

*Why now?*

"I see… I don't really get it, but… Stay right where you are."

Victor's icy glare seemed to freeze everything, but the man met it with a perfectly calm expression, and he even smiled as he spoke.

"Master Huey also says this: 'I apologize for adding to that trouble, but…I can't afford to involve you in the relationship between myself and Nebula at this point, and so…'

"'…I'm going to tie you down just a bit longer.'"

The next instant—there was a light *clunk*, and they saw something fall at the man's feet.

It was a cylindrical, brass-colored object—and a little smoke was rising from the string that sprouted from one end, along with a crackling sound.

The instant he realized what the object was, Victor's face twisted in a yell.

"Get d—!"

Even before he could say it, Bill and Edward had dived into the shadow of their desks.

"Hey! That's not fair, you—"

Before he'd finished speaking, there was a flash at the feet of the man, who made no attempt to run—

—and the roaring flames of an explosion enveloped the office.

## CHAPTER 4: FRONT

# LET'S THINK WISTFULLY OF THE OUTSIDE

Alcatraz Federal Penitentiary    Broadway        Night

"Hey. Hey. Hey, neighbor."
The night Ladd had been hauled off to solitary, Firo woke to the sound of a voice beside him.
He'd had nothing in particular to do, so he'd doused the light in his cell before lights-out. He'd been curled up in his blanket half-asleep when an awfully excited voice reached him.
"...Dragon?" Firo murmured.
"Yeah. So hey, what was that?! This morning, that, uh... The guy!"
"Hmm...? Oh... You mean Ladd...?"
"That was murder! I'd never seen such a fantastic punch!"
"Haaaaah... Jack Dempsey's tougher'n that."
Yawning and responding carelessly, once again, Firo confirmed that the events of that morning hadn't been a dream. If possible, he would have liked the fact that he'd come to this island at all to be a dream, but reality was not so kind.
"Tch! I was startled, too... Not 'cause his punch was so powerful. That fella was way off the track."
As Firo answered, he was rubbing sleep gunk out of his eyes. In contrast, the one on the other side of the wall was apparently still feeling a lingering buzz of excitement and didn't seem overly concerned as he whispered eagerly:

"That guy's something else, all right! They say his left hand's a fake. What, did he fight a man-eating bear or something and lose it in exchange for a win? Or did the ticking croc from Neverland bite it off...? Hee-hee, I bet it tasted real good. I'm jealous."

Firo half expected to hear Dragon licking his chops, and he scowled, spitting out something that had just occurred to him.

"Then who's the Pan who cut off his hand?"

Thinking that had been a lame joke if he did say so himself, Firo gritted his teeth in irritation. Then, to divert his attention from it, he tossed something else across the wall at Dragon.

"And actually...I'm surprised you even know about that book," Firo remarked.

*Peter Pan* was a popular novel from England, and even in America, it had been released nationwide.

Firo remembered getting a copy from Claire, after the guy was done with it, and he'd read the whole thing a long time ago.

*The eternal boy, huh...? Come to think of it, Claire really admired that.*

In contrast, he himself had wanted to hurry and grow up to get stronger.

As he mused on the past, Firo gave a quiet, wry smile.

*Who'd have thought I'd be the one to end up as an eternal youth...?*

Firo was thinking that maybe he'd tease Czes by calling him Peter Pan later on, when abruptly, he realized that the response from the next cell was a long time in coming.

"? What's up?"

"Uh... No, well... I used it to practice reading and writing English."

"Huh. Come to think of it, your English is really good."

"Yeah. Well, it ain't bad. It's not like I lived in an immigrant community anyway."

*Hunh... For all that, he seemed to be talking fluently with those other Asians during meals.*

Dragon's words sparked a doubt in Firo, but he had no time to linger on it.

Just then, footsteps sounded on Broadway.

The sound echoed between the bars, clinging to the convicts' ears like a grim reaper's scythe.

Firo stopped talking, burrowed under the covers, and waited quietly for the footsteps to pass by, but—

The footsteps stopped in front of his cell.

"Hey, you… What did you just hide?"

*Huh?*

The voice was clearly directed at his own head.

He didn't know what it was talking about, though, so he stayed under the blanket for a little while, waiting to see what would happen.

After a pause, he heard the noise of the grate opening.

There was a scraping sound with no creaking right by his head, and Firo finally peered out from under the covers.

When he looked, there was a young guard standing there—and no sooner had the man stepped into the cell than, without giving Firo time to resist, he ripped the blanket off him.

"What? What gives?!"

Hastily, Firo sprang up, and the guard's cold voice rang out ostentatiously.

"That's what I want to know." As he spoke, the guard tilted his palm, making the knife that lay on it gleam.

It was small, the sort you could hide in one hand, and its bright silver color made it look brand new.

"…Huh?"

Naturally, Firo had never seen it before, but—

The guard smirked, then grabbed Firo's arm without letting him argue.

"Nice move, joker."

Firo was dragged out of his cell. He still wasn't fully awake.

He double-checked to make sure he wasn't dreaming, but the handcuffs that had been put on him were hopelessly real.

When he looked around, the denizens of the surrounding cells seemed to be watching them.

Dragon, who hadn't extinguished his light yet, was looking his way and smirking, and Firo finally understood that he'd been placed in a unique situation.

Once the knowledge of his position had sunk in, as if to strike an additional blow, the guard waggled the knife in warning.

"All right… Let's have a little talk about how you smuggled this in."

"…In the Dungeon. For a good long time."

⇔

"So you're the guy who works directly for Misery?"

They were down some stairs, through a door that was closed particularly tightly, then down the corridor beyond it.

Up until that point, they'd been surrounded by several guards, but now Firo and the guard who'd "discovered" the knife were walking by themselves.

When he'd heard the door shut behind them, Firo had told the guy what was on his mind, plain and simple.

Without even looking at him, the guard answered his question in an indifferent tone:

"That'll make this go faster."

"I didn't think I'd get called out on the second day."

"We've gotten backed into a bit of a corner."

The guard betrayed no emotion as he spoke, and Firo frowned.

"Backed into a corner? By what?"

"You're a con. You don't need to know about the outside world."

*Then don't bring it up!*

Firo wanted to complain, but he knew it wouldn't do him any good, so he let the remark slide.

"So what are we doing?"

"We hear Huey already knows about you. In that case, we'll just have the two of you meet. If there's something you want to ask him, go ahead and ask; he's probably got questions to ask you, too.

"...That's a pretty reckless maneuver. Misery looks kinda by the book; did he really order this?"

He'd meant the words to be mildly sarcastic. However, the guard smiled quietly, then spoke, still walking.

"As if."

That was all he said.

"...Huh?"

"I certainly am Mr. Misery's direct subordinate, and tonight, I was told to take you to the Dungeon and get your opinion on our future course of action."

"......"

Firo had a bad feeling about this.

A very specific bad feeling, as if nausea was working its way up from the depths of his stomach.

Remembering what had happened on the wharf when he was brought to the island, he reluctantly tested that premonition.

"So in other words...you're Misery's henchman *and* Huey's?"

Firo sounded half-resigned. The guard nodded, smiling.

"It's great that you're so quick on the uptake."

⟺

They were even deeper than the underground floor where the Dungeon was located.

On the other side of a hidden door, they descended a staircase that had been covered by a brick wall, and beyond its end, in the depths of the depths, far, far underground...

There was a room.

On the way down the stairs, Firo had felt as if he were journeying deeper and deeper into the island's history, traveling back to the past. However, the moment they reached the lowest level, that idea was magnificently pulverized.

What waited there was a series of three doors covered in concrete and steel plate—a space meant to seal people inside.

The intervals between those three doors were only a yard each, and every door was tightly locked.

When the final door was opened, it revealed a rather long passage—and at its end was another locked door.

Unlike the previous doors, this one had a window set into it. There was a small cover beside the door, probably so that meals could be sent inside.

*So they've sealed him in two or three times over?*

He probably couldn't grind his own body to a pulp, but if he rammed it desperately enough, he might be able to escape even through that little hole. The air vent might have been equipped with the same sort of double and triple measures.

*Couldn't they just cut off his oxygen and leave him like that forever?* For a moment, a cruel thought crossed Firo's mind. However, he realized, in the end, that would not be any different from encasing him in concrete and sinking him in the river, and he began to think—though it meant nothing—that Victor might be surprisingly humane.

*Well, either way… If some of the fellas who have access to this place are traitors, it's all pointless.*

The idea made Firo smile wryly, and as if he'd read his mind, the guard also gave an ironic smile.

"The man who spoke to you on the wharf was transferred to the mainland. Naturally, he gave nothing away, and they can't torture him. I hear they're letting him roam free, under strict surveillance."

"I see… So if I squeal on you, you'll get the same treatment?"

Even at that casual threat, the guard didn't flinch.

"That's right. Then, before long, a replacement is bound to appear."

"…How do you pull that off? If you tell me that, they might let me off this island tomorrow."

"Why don't you ask Master Huey directly? He might tell you."

As they walked down the passage, the guard kept speaking, still smiling.

"Even with a traitor like me here, he can't break out easily. You saw the heavy guard at the door to the Dungeon."

"…Yeah, that's true."

Even if he did get out of here, the ways to get up to the surface from the Dungeon were probably limited. He'd heard that the warden of this prison was competent. Unless more than half the guards were his henchmen, breaking out would be an extraordinarily knotty problem.

"That said… Apparently, he is planning to leave soon."

"…Leave this island?"

"There is nothing Master Huey can't do."

*Hey, c'mon, hold up a minute…*

This was only his second day here, but Firo had picked up on the prison's extraordinary security all too well. Even if he was immortal, would he be able to swim across the strong currents in that ocean without being targeted by sharks? Practically speaking, escape had to be nearly impossible.

Still, Firo's misgivings weren't due to the issue of whether it was impossible.

If Huey managed to successfully crush out of here—

*—then what happens to me?*

Firo was here on the understanding that he would solve Huey's mystery. If Huey disappeared from the island before he did that—

*They wouldn't shut* me *up in this cellar instead, would they?!*

The nasty idea made the queasiness he was feeling even more noticeable.

While he was mulling over this, before he knew it, the two of them were standing in front of the door, and the guard's hand was on the lock.

After opening several locks, the guard took a step back and motioned for Firo to enter.

"…Hey, I'm not going to end up with a hand on my head the second I get this heavy door open, am I?"

"If that was what we were after, we would have chained you up in the Dungeon first and laced your food with drugs to knock you out."

Glaring at the guard, who'd answered his quip with more sarcasm, Firo reluctantly opened the door himself.

He kept his defenses up, but when he saw the figure of a man sitting in a chair through the cracked door, he relaxed and pushed it open the rest of the way.

However—

"Hey, Firo! What, they called you here, too?"

"Wha...?"

*Isaac?!*

Realizing that Isaac had been the one sitting in the chair in the center of the room, Firo gave a full-body shiver and took a big leap backward.

And then—

—an arm reached out from the shadow of the door, passing right through the spot where he'd been a moment ago.

"...!"

Firo immediately got his breathing under control and sent orders to all the muscles in his body.

Enemies, enemies, everything he could see was the enemy.

However, when he tried to analyze the situation calmly—his urge to kill faded in an instant.

He'd realized the hand that had stretched from the door's shadow... was a left hand.

After a moment's pause, the right hand joined the left, and then both came together in light applause.

"I see. Excellent agility. Your explosive power and judgment are quite impressive as well... You may be the equal of Nile or Denkurou."

The first half was unstinting praise.

During the last half—which was an analysis spoken to himself—a man poked his head out from the shadow of the door.

Unlike the one that had been supplied to Firo, the prison uniform he wore was odd, very nearly pure white.

"It's a pleasure to meet you. Or, from the perspective of your memories, perhaps I should say, 'It's been a long time, Firo Prochainezo.'"

Neither his voice nor his attitude seemed suited to a prison. The man turned a nearly emotionless smile on Firo.

Confirming that the face matched the memories of the various alchemists who slept nested inside him, Firo answered, although his wariness didn't even flicker.

"I'd like to make it 'good-bye' real soon... Huey Laforet."

⇔

"Now then... you look as if you have a few things you'd like to ask."

A mere thirty seconds after their first meeting.

Beckoned by Huey, who'd advanced to the center of the room, Firo warily went farther in. However, there wasn't any particularly unusual equipment inside, and except for its size, it didn't seem all that different from the other cells.

Huey was near the wall on the opposite side of the room, while Firo stood as far from him as he could get, with Isaac between them. He didn't even try to hide his irritation, and his words were saturated with sarcasm.

"Well, let's see. You look like you know all and you act like you think you're God, so I'll ask you where you want an ordinary guy like me to start digging."

"All right. You must be wondering why Isaac is here... I'd like you to start with that one, if you would."

Firo was still radiating murderous intent. In contrast, the white-clad prisoner smiled quietly and spoke without hesitation.

He didn't seem evil. He didn't seem like a swindler, either.

However, somehow, Firo didn't like the man. Why not? There were all sorts of reasons, including their meeting a moment ago, but his feeling wasn't anything so trivial. For some reason, his instincts—his experience living in the underworld as part of his syndicate—wanted nothing to do with the guy.

An uncomfortable aura swirled between Firo and Huey.

The guard was waiting outside, and Isaac, who was being made to sit in the middle of it all by himself, completely failed to read the room. He looked interested only in the fact that his name had come up.

"What's this, what's this? What? What about me?"

"… Well, why are you here?"

Possibly because he'd wanted to break off his conversation with Huey and get his bearings again, Firo spoke to Isaac instead.

"Huh? Me? The guard called me in a little while ago, and I've been talking to this goblin fella."

"… Goblin?"

In the sense that he wasn't human, in a way, that might not have been wrong. Why had Isaac used a word like that, though?

As Firo wondered about this, Isaac began to relate knowledge that was as skewed as usual, looking as proud as he always did.

"Listen, in the Orient, people who secretly live in the hidden rooms of houses, like this one, are called the *shiki-warashi*. If you chase them out, you'll have bad luck, and if you meet one by the side of the road, you're supposed to put your shoes on its head and prostrate yourself to it! It's lucky, so you worship him lots, too, Firo!"

"… Ahhh, dammit. It's a nice change of pace not to have Miria chiming in, but somehow I want to hit you twice as bad."

Possibly because he'd noticed the angry veins standing out on Firo's forehead, Huey took a step away from the wall and spoke kindly to Isaac, who was sitting in the chair.

"Isaac, thank you very much for today. It was truly interesting, hearing all those stories… I'm going to talk about something secret with Firo for a little while, so it's time to say good-bye for now."

For just a moment, Isaac looked sorry, but he quickly regained his smile and responded with words that were far too innocent.

"I see! In that case, make the people in this prison happy, would you?! Everyone looks kinda gloomy for some reason. I bet something bad happened to all of them!"

"Yes, I do hope they find happiness. Oh, that's right: Don't tell anyone about what happened here… It would chase away the good fortune, you see."

"You betcha! Just leave it to me! I may not look like it, but I'm particularly good at keeping secrets!"

*If you were really good at it, you probably wouldn't be here right now.*

Firo thought the words, but making the retort would have been pointless, so he didn't actually say them.

Oblivious to his cares, Isaac nimbly got up from the chair.

With Huey's soft smile at his back, Isaac went away with the guard who'd been outside. He'd probably spend a night in the Dungeon, then be returned to his cell the next morning as if nothing had happened.

As he listened to the sound of the door closing behind him, Firo took another look at the other man's face.

The smile the man wore now was substantially colder than the one he'd shown Isaac.

Wearing a smile that was as mechanical as a doll's, Huey motioned to the chair in the center.

"Please have a seat."

"You have a seat."

"Very well."

"……"

Without hesitating, Huey went over to the chair and sat down. The act intensified Firo's suspicion that this guy would be *hard to deal with.*

He exhaled deeply, trying to curb his irritation, and just as he did so, Huey spoke quietly.

"I was rude to you back there, and I apologize. Sometimes I find myself wanting to indulge in childish mischief."

"…? …Oh, that."

Realizing that by *mischief,* he meant the fact that he'd hidden by the door and stretched out his left hand; Firo pretended to be calm as he responded, although his expression was still stiff.

"Don't worry about it. That Victor guy did something similar to me."

"I see. That does sound like Victor. However, despite your answer, your glare clearly indicates that *you* are worrying about it."

"…Didn't you call me here because you wanted to talk about something? I'm going to walk out."

If he went back now, he'd be the one most inconvenienced by it, but even so, he wanted to leave.

He knew that he couldn't get sucked into this man's rhythm, but Firo hit him with his own question anyway.

"So? Why did you call Isaac here?"

"Yes, well, I knew he was apparently also an immortal, and I wished to speak with him for a little while… He certainly is an interesting fellow, isn't he? I'm intrigued."

"Did you call me for the same reason?"

"That was part of it, naturally, but…" After a moment's pause, Huey crossed his legs and continued. "I had a little something I wanted to ask you. I believe you have questions for me as well, aside from what Victor wanted, correct?"

"…Well, great; that'll make things go faster. And no… I don't have anything to ask. It's just something I want to say."

With his back to the wall, Firo crossed his arms and, glaring at the man who was sitting a few yards away, bluntly made himself clear.

"Don't mess with Ennis or any of the other people around me. That's all."

As Firo calmly stated his demands, he was remembering the Mist Wall incident, which they'd gotten pulled into a year previously.

"Listen," he continued. "I don't care what you're trying to do, and I've got no intention of eating you. Maiza doesn't have anything against you, and even if you make an enemy out of the whole U.S. of A or take a whack at world domination, as long as it doesn't affect our business, then I have no problem. So don't get us involved. I'm already ticked off about having to come all the way to this backwater island."

"I see… You're fond of Ennis, then."

"…That's not the point."

Firo averted his eyes slightly as he answered, and Huey responded quietly.

"Last year… It does sound as though my subordinates committed a discourtesy. I expect Christopher and the others have a special affinity for Ennis."

"Like I care."

"I have no particular need to do anything with Ennis, either…"— the chair creaked, and the cold smile on Huey's face deepened ever so slightly—"provided you cooperate with me."

"Cooperate?"

"Szilard Quates's memories and you yourself are both truly valuable."

"……"

At this, Firo scowled openly.

He'd half expected as much, but that meant this guy already knew he'd consumed Szilard. Either that, or he'd deduced it and was now sure.

"I dunno… Either way, I can't imagine we're worth much."

"No, no. Szilard's memories hold the knowledge that created Ennis and information about the failed liquor of immortality. They're of great value to me."

"……"

"Besides, I'm fascinated with you as well… I haven't experienced eating another immortal myself yet. Szilard ate many people, dozens of them. What changes did doing so trigger, or fail to trigger, in your mind? …Both your past and your future are truly intriguing."

The man was gazing at Firo and smiling, and Firo answered with annoyance. "Shut up, asshole. And stop coming on to me. No matter what happens or how, I'm me."

"…But wasn't there a time when you couldn't say that with confidence?"

In spite of himself, Huey's words left Firo at a loss.

He'd probably suspected already. When he saw how Firo looked, Huey smiled and explained his own reasoning.

"The memories you inherited from Szilard wouldn't consist of knowledge alone. I don't know if you've tried it, but if you attempted to drive a car, your body should move naturally to perform the task, without having to intentionally call upon Szilard's knowledge."

"……"

"Gradually, those past memories and knowledge will blend together. In the end, can you truly declare with certainty that you are yourself? You say that you are the same as you were before you took his knowledge, but have you never doubted yourself, even for a moment?"

Huey wasn't threatening him or attempting to unsettle him. He just kept asking questions with perfect indifference.

The questions were genuine; he wasn't trying to corner Firo. He asked them as frankly as if he were giving a survey, and his calm eyes seemed to be hoping for answers just as candid.

Yet Firo sensed something bottomless and eerie in the depths of those eyes, and he felt sweat breaking out along his spine.

"What…are you trying to do?"

The question had slipped out involuntarily. Huey thought about it for a little while, and then—

"What indeed… My ultimate goal is…to create that 'demon' with my own hands. However, perhaps that's only true at the present stage. No…but…"

By the latter half of the sentence, he was practically talking to himself, as though he was verifying his own thoughts.

After a short pause, he turned his eyes to Firo and murmured with some lingering uncertainty in his voice.

"I may want to know…what comes next. I think."

"What comes next…?"

"I *simply want to know*, that's all."

Hesitant, Firo thought the man had said something odd.

"Know what?"

"To know *something*. The subject doesn't matter."

Huey uncrossed his legs, then crossed them again and began a long, long soliloquy, both for his own benefit and for Firo's.

"Why was I born? What is the meaning of life? Why is it wrong to kill people? You sometimes encounter people who intentionally ask these things, questions that have nothing to do with our instincts. When I was very young, I too once thought such things with pretentions of being a philosopher—but I soon tired of them. And it wasn't because I found no answers. I found too many, in fact. Scores of them, many different kinds. In the end, I could phrase these answers in any number of superficial ways to reach any interpretation—and I just cannot find interest in such things. Even if I know the answers are inside me, that fact alone means little to me at my core.

"However...I like learning the answers other people have found. For example, philosophers, innocent children, the wicked, the good, the contrary, the fools, the sages... It's only natural for different people to find their own meanings in human life and truths of the world. However, for me, it's simply...everything. I simply want to know all of it."

"...All of it?"

"People living now, those who have lived in the past, those who will be born in the future...or all people who might have existed, even if they were never born, in the end—I want to know the minds of these others... And that is merely one example. In addition, there's the question of what lies at the end of the universe. Is the smallest unit of matter a particle or a string...? ...Is it possible to travel back in time? Does the multiverse really exist? Questions such as these have no bearing on the daily lives of humans, but I also want to answer those. What is the truth behind that theft? Who was Jack the Ripper? What is the identity of Ice Pick Thompson, the murderer who electrified New York a few years ago? How long should you cook whitefish to make it fall apart? Does ESP exist? What lies over the rainbow? ...All of it, yes, *all of it*."

The inflections of the prisoner in white gradually grew more pronounced, and he spoke with an excitement that bordered on lunacy.

"Once I know all that, what will I think? Will I find boredom there, or a shock? Or will it be a new mystery, one peculiar only to those who've learned everything? I simply... I simply want to reach it."

"... What's the point of that?"

"There doesn't need to be a point. It's possible that having reached it is the sole definite point. Even the answer to that still lies in the darkness. And so... I exist only to learn everything. I love learning—so much so that if this world won't allow it, I think it should be destroyed. Nothing more."

"If you put that another way, then... you mean you'd be okay with destroying the world if you could learn something from it?"

"If it was for the sake of knowledge, then yes."

"......"

*He's completely nuts.*

Having made that call about the man in front of him, Firo was running mental calculations about how to make his escape, when—

"...Ha-ha..."

—seeing his expression, Huey burst out laughing as though some internal dam had broken.

"Ha-ha-ha-ha-ha-ha! Ah-ha-ha-ha-ha-ha-ha-ha-ha!"

"...?"

*Has he lost it?!*

Deciding that he had, Firo was backing away when Huey put on a childlike smile—and shrugged.

"...I'm kidding."

"...Huh?"

Firo's mouth hung open. Reverting to his calm tone, Huey said, "Did you think I was acting on such pathetic motivations? Good grief. I was a child when I believed the world should be destroyed."

"Huh?"

Firo was growing more and more confused, and Huey continued without concern. "You see, other people seem to see me as a terribly mysterious person. I thought you might think so as well. Just take what I've said with a grain of salt, if you would."

At that point, Firo finally realized that he'd been *teased*, and he was filled with a muddled mess of anger, embarrassment, and ... just a little relief.

"Wh-why, you ..."

"Didn't I say so earlier? Sometimes I feel like playing pranks."

*...... If I jump him, I lose. If I jump him, I lose ...!*

Listening to his own muscles creak, Firo tried desperately to keep his cool.

"I bet you were pretty unpopular with the other alchemists, too."

"I had only one friend."

"That guy was either a total saint, a hypocrite, a moron, a weirdo, or a masochist."

"No. He's a lunatic and a false villain."

As he murmured those words, Huey quietly averted his eyes.

He spoke with a slight trace of loneliness, thinking fondly of someone who wasn't there.

"He is completely insane. The only thing he thought about was what he could do to bring joy to everyone in the world he saw. He seriously thinks there's a way to make everyone on the planet—with their different mind-sets and religions and positions, good people and villains alike—happy."

"Well, sure, he sounds weird ... but I think I'd get along better with him than with you."

Firo very nearly drew the face of one peculiar alchemist from Szilard's memories. However, deciding it wasn't particularly relevant now, he kept it locked away in his heart.

Before long, having completely returned to his original pace, Huey slowly got up from his chair.

"At any rate ... I would like to form a partnership with you. Simply allow me to ask you a few questions from time to time. If you would like to sell the research results in Szilard's memories, I will pay. If you'll settle for an amount I can afford."

"......"

"That way, I'll have no reason to involve Ennis, and I don't believe there's any harm in it for either of us. I'll order Christopher never to approach Ennis again."

It was the first specific proposal Huey had made.

Firo thought about it for a little while, but before he could come to a decision, Huey set a concrete time limit.

"I *plan to stay here for a few days longer*. In the end, I'll summon you here one more time. Give me your answer then, please."

In other words, he meant that he was going to break out of jail in a few days, but at this point, Firo wasn't surprised.

"If you agree, in lieu of an advance payment, I'll provide you with information regarding my methods of making contact and how I make allies of the guards. I expect that's more or less what Victor is concerned with, isn't it?"

The man had seen through everything. Firo still had several things he wanted to say to him, but—

—in the end, Firo could only ask a single question.

"... What the hell are you?"

In response to that simple inquiry, Huey put a hand to his mouth and thought for a few seconds. Then he gave the safest answer he could manage.

"I'm... merely a researcher.

"Although, Victor and *that senator* don't seem pleased with the idea."

⇔

The guard had returned at some point, and after he'd escorted Firo out of the room—

—a young girl's voice sounded from the bed.

"Good work, Father!"

"Yes, thank you, Leeza. How did things go on your end?"

"Um... There's this one person who's really bad news, and he keeps getting in the way! He's a weird guy with a wrench as long as an arm! He's funny in the head! But he's reeeeeally strong, and even the Lamia members can't do anything about him... Oh, but it's okay! I learned all about him, and it's perfect! *I found a perfect hostage*, so we'll be able to do something about him soon!"

"You will, hmm? That's wonderful."

Huey was smiling gently, but abruptly, he realized that his daughter's expression was different from usual.

"…? What's the matter?"

"I've never heard you laugh like you were having so much fun before, Father! When you were talking with that Isaac person and when you were talking with that spy, Firo, you sounded like you were having lots and lots of fun!"

Leeza's voice held a mixture of surprise and jealousy. Huey smiled at her quietly.

"Ha-ha. Leeza, were you jealous that I was getting along so well with people I'd just met?"

"Uh-huh! I was jealous! I was so jealous, I went *grrrr*! They should just go die! So hey, can I kill them?"

"No, you can't. In any case, they're immortals. You couldn't kill them, Leeza."

"Urgh…"

Leeza looked down, frustrated. She didn't seem convinced yet, though, and she kept hounding her father.

"But you know, Father, you really were a little different today."

His daughter's statement sounded uneasy, and Huey gave his response quietly.

"While I talked with Isaac…it reminded me of the past."

As he recalled his old friend, and himself in distant days—

"He…resembles him, doesn't he? His personality, or perhaps the way he's out of his mind…"

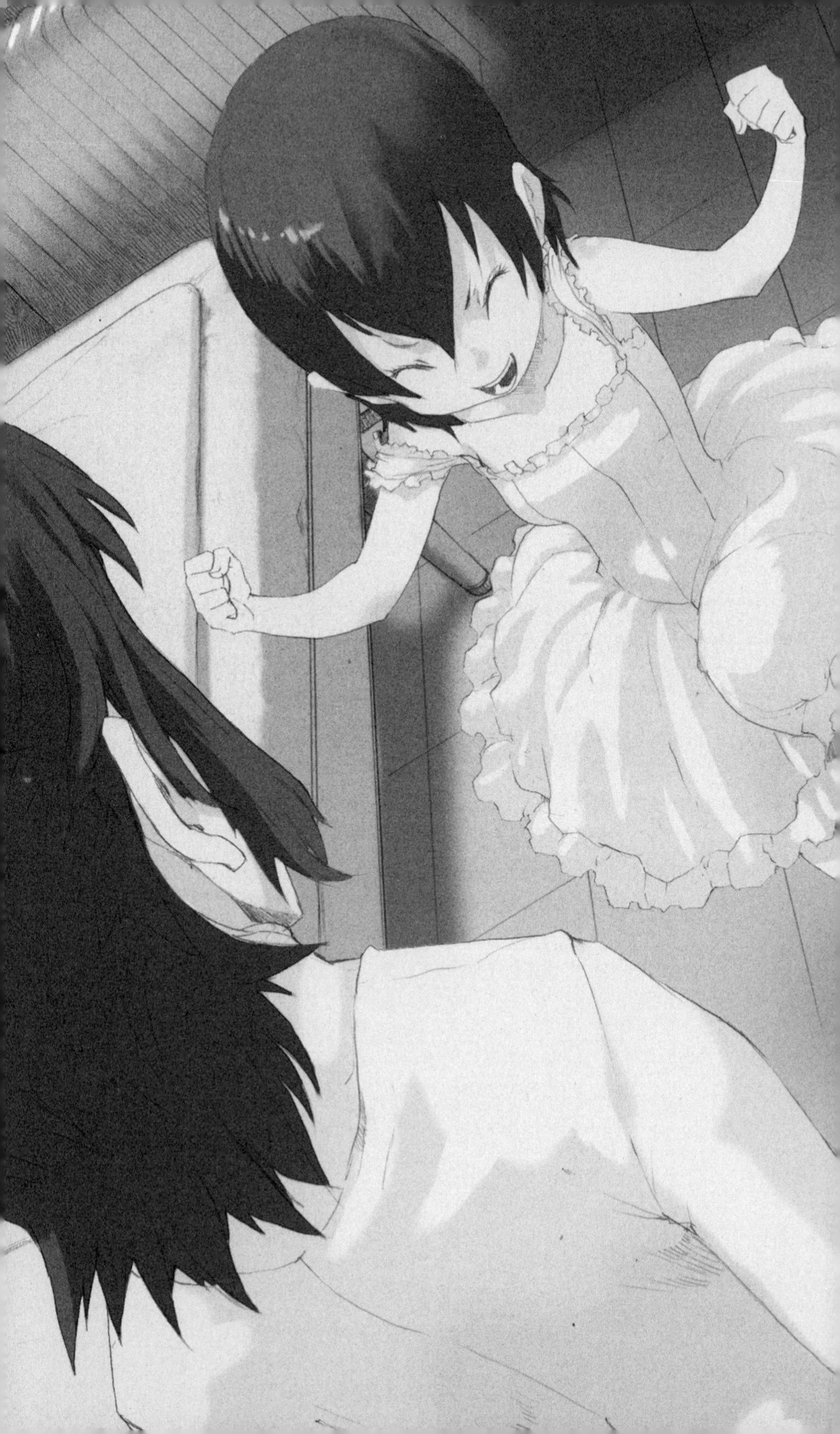

## CHAPTER 4: BACK

# LET'S DISCUSS, LET'S DO THAT

Madison Square Park

"You made Chané cry, didn't you?"

A girl in a black dress and a young man with red hair, surrounded by men in black.

In story terms, this configuration would have signaled a crisis—but the redhead looked completely relaxed.

"Fellas…I'm going to punch your eyes into jelly and make you shed just as many tears as her, so keep that in mind."

"Huh? Uh, nah, she ain't crying."

In response to Spike's criticism, the red-haired young man shook his head sadly.

"Can't you hear it? Can't you hear Chané's voice as she cries, over-whelmed with sadness? That voice, calling for help… The voice that only I can hear, technically!"

"Hey, c'mon, what's with this ignoramus? Are you a dope addict or something?"

"Don't be an idiot. I don't lean on drugs. As long as I've got a heart that believes, I can send my mood soaring as high as I want, and that way, I can hear Chané's voice, too."

"Hey, Mr. Former Felix, did you seriously sell your name to a loon like this?! And actually, is this guy a hitman or something, too?"

The former Felix's only response to the blind man's shout was a heavy sigh.

Meanwhile, the redhead—Claire Stanfield, the current Felix Walken—was looking at the blind man, seeming mystified.

"Oh, I remember."

"…?"

Claire's voice completely betrayed the mood, and Spike frowned, listening to him.

For the past little while, an incomprehensible siren had been wailing in his heart, but…

…the moment he heard what Claire murmured next—

"You're the sniper who was on that train, aren't you?"

—the volume of the alarm increased explosively, toppling the leeway his group's superior numbers had given him.

Easily. Far too easily…

"What, seriously? After I dropped you face-first and everything… I'm impressed you survived, fella."

$\Longleftrightarrow$

Somewhere in New York     The special offices of the Bureau of Investigation

While the men in black were being thrown into confusion in the park, there was another location where the confusion was even worse.

Although the office had escaped going up in flames, it was smoldering and sputtering, sending up black smoke. Inside the room, several figures slowly sat up, coughing.

Although Victor had gotten caught by the blast and toppled over, he'd managed to get by without blacking out.

"Dammit… Are you okay, men?"

When he looked around, although the wind of the blast had done awful things to the desktops, the desks themselves hardly seemed to have moved at all.

"Uh… Physically, I'm fine. Mm-hmm."

"What was that…?"

When he saw his two unscathed subordinates poke their heads out from under the desks, Victor sighed with relief in spite of himself.

"So you're okay. That's great."

"Mm…"

"……"

"? What's the matter?"

His two underlings were gazing at him with mystified expressions, and they responded to his question with absolutely no hesitation.

"Well, it's just, that was the first time you'd acted concerned for us like a normal person, so…"

"Yes… I've been your subordinate for a long time, sir, but I'm so touched… Uh, may I cry?"

"… Y-you jackasses…"

Victor's face went bright red and he ground his teeth. He remembered their current situation almost immediately, however, and walked over to the center of the blast.

"Hunh… To think he'd try to keep us pinned down with a bomb. Did he think he could do something about us with a thing like that? So did the guy already run off?"

There wasn't anything left where the man had been standing just a moment ago. He'd probably fled the scene in the nick of time.

Just as Victor was about to come to that conclusion, as if to dash cold water on him, Bill droned, "Uh… No, I think he's managed to pin us down extremely well."

"What? What do you mean?"

When Victor turned around, Bill was by the window, gazing at the scene outside.

This room was on the first floor, and the situation on the street was in full view.

Following his subordinate's gaze, Victor peered out the window.

The man from earlier, who seemed to have been sent flying by the blast, was on the ground outside the window, covered in blood.

His limbs were twisted oddly, his neck was bent at an abnormal angle, and he wasn't moving. From the amount of blood splattered over the pavement, hoping that he was still alive was probably a waste of time.

Even worse—he was surrounded by several dozen rubberneckers who'd been drawn to the noise of the explosion… And now that Victor had poked his head out the window, they were staring at his face from a distance.

From a good ways away, they heard the hoofbeats of the horses the patrol unit rode— And one of the blood vessels in Victor's brain burst, but since he was immortal, it regenerated immediately and no harm was done.

"Now you've done it, Huey Laforet!"

He looked down at the mute lump of meat, repeatedly grinding his teeth in frustration.

"I knew it… I should've eaten him the moment I collared him…!"

⇔

Millionaires' Row      The Genoard mansion

"WAAAaaaAAAAaaaaah, Graham is… Graham's going to…!"

"No, none of that, stop crying. I'm sure Graham's going to be just fine."

As he'd listened to the news that streamed from the radio, Jacuzzi had grown frantic again.

The people who'd been trying to comfort him had turned on the radio in an attempt to find a fun topic of some sort, and that's when they'd heard the news about Chicago. Even the people who weren't Jacuzzi had been unsettled by it. However, Nice smiled brightly and kept soothing the young tattooed boy all by herself.

"B-but, but, Nice! Three hundred, they said! Three hundred! No matter how you think about it, it's weird for there to be that many bombs! I bet Chicago's going to disappear any minute!"

"It's fine, Jacuzzi. Three hundred is nothing impressive."

"Wh-why?"

Nice's words were filled with confidence, and Jacuzzi looked blank as he asked his question.

At that, the girl with the eye patch and glasses smiled with an expression that seemed vaguely rapturous, and…

"Well, I've got about five hundred just in my room…"

"Aaaaaah, don't say it, don't say any more! It's scary, so don't say iiiit!"

Jacuzzi covered his ears, shaking his head vigorously.

The scene that was playing out in the mansion was routine, but just then, the doorbell rang, and an ambience that wasn't at all routine filled the room.

*Di-ding    di-di-ding*

At the sudden sound of the bell, the delinquents looked at one another.

This was a second residence, and it almost never got packages. On top of that, most of the time, friends of Jacuzzi's group didn't bother to ring.

"Who is it?"

"Whoever it is, guests who show up when Jacuzzi's crying never mean anything good."

"Yeah, when Jacuzzi cries, his voice summons trouble."

"Dammit, Jacuzzi, not again!"

"Would you knock it off already?!"

"Don't you see that your sadness is making more people sad?!"

"Live like your tears are a divine miracle, wouldja?!"

"Control yourself!"

"Hya— Happy thoughts!"

His friends were saying whatever they wanted, and Jacuzzi involuntarily stopped crying to protest.

"Huh?! Why are you blaming me?!"

Drying his eyes and grumbling to himself, the leader of the delinquents crossed to the front door.

"Good grief … Calling them 'trouble' is rude to our guests!"

Then, with a smile in his red, swollen eyes, he flung the door open, and—

"Hey. It's been a while."

His shaved, tattooed head and glasses made the man who stood there far too distinctive. He raised his right hand to Jacuzzi, as if he'd missed him.

"… Tim!"

"Oh, that's great! You're okay! I'm so glad!"

A man and a woman had been standing outside the front door.

One was Tim, the man with the shaved head and glasses.

The woman, Adele, looked timid and carried a long bundle on her back.

They were both acquaintances of Jacuzzi's, and it was thanks to an invitation from them that he'd gotten pulled into the Mist Wall incident a year ago. However, as if he'd forgotten this inconvenient piece of information, Jacuzzi cried out in simple, genuine delight over the fact that his friends were all right.

"And your wounds healed up, Adele! That's wonderful…"

When Jacuzzi suddenly smiled at her, the girl who'd been hiding in Tim's shadow gave a bewildered response.

"U-um… I… Uh…"

"? What's the matter? D-did I say something weird?"

Seeing that Adele looked openly flustered, Jacuzzi glanced at Tim anxiously. Tim sighed, gazing back at Jacuzzi with an expression that held a mixture of disgust and admiration.

"You're a real piece of work. I'm seriously impressed that you can worry about somebody who came this close to killing you."

"Huh? …Oh!"

Maybe he'd finally remembered what had happened a year ago:

As he looked at Adele, Jacuzzi went a little pale, but even so, he kept talking, and he didn't let his smile falter.

"B-but, you know, everything was really confusing back then, so there wasn't any avoiding what happened! Besides…it's not as if we've never killed anybody…"

As he said that last bit, his voice faded until it was barely audible, and he fell silent for a moment. However, he recovered promptly and asked his sudden guests what had brought them there.

"U-um, what did you need today?"

In response, Tim simply stated the answer he'd had waiting, without adding any particular emotion to it.

"You know Graham Specter, right?"

"Huh…?"

Not only did he know him—Jacuzzi had been crying out of worry for his safety up until a moment ago.

Graham Specter.

Without giving him time to feel uneasy about why that name had come up now, Tim calmly began to speak about the organization they belonged to.

"You know about our group, right?"

"Um, wasn't it Chané's father's…?"

Nodding as if to say that would make the conversation go faster, Tim went on, looking a bit troubled.

"That's right. Huey Laforet. There are people acting on the boss's orders in Chicago, and…apparently, your pal Graham is causing them some grief."

"Graham is?!"

At that abrupt remark, Jacuzzi gave an involuntary shriek, and the delinquents who'd been watching from the hallway looked at one another.

"N-no! Trouble? Why?! What are they planning to do to Graham?!"

"No, no, other way around. The fellas in Chicago are having trouble because they can't do a thing about Graham. Frankly, it sounds like they're completely stuck."

"Oh."

"So, uh. The Lamia people got an idea. They want to *take Graham's friends hostage and get him to listen that way.*"

He had a really bad feeling about this.

As sweat broke out on his back for some mysterious reason, Jacuzzi fearfully asked the young man in front of him a question.

"Um… Before I ask this, let me say very, very, very firmly that I think it would be better if you didn't take a hostage, because that's awful… Uh… Who would it be?"

"We hear you guys were pretty tight with Graham."

"AaaaaaaaaaAAAAAAaaah! I knew iiiit!"

Jacuzzi screamed and backed away, and in response, tension ran through the delinquents.

However, Tim held up his hands to show he meant no harm. He murmured, smiling wryly, trying to set them at ease.

"Settle down. Don't worry. At the very least, I'm not planning on pulling you people into this."

"Huh?! D-do you mean that?"

Jacuzzi, who'd obediently relaxed, smiled as if he was relieved from the bottom of his heart—but as if to erase that smile, Tim said something that promptly fanned his nervousness again.

"That said, I'm not running this particular show. I can't say for sure that Lamia doesn't have its eyes on you."

"No!"

"Well, it looks like you've got lots of tough friends… And besides, Leeza was saying something about *having found somebody who'd be easier to take hostage,* so I think you can probably relax."

After making them as uneasy as possible, Tim turned on his heel, as if to say his job was done.

"There's no telling what might happen, though. Be careful not to get dragged into this. The twins are *always right there.* That may not necessarily be the case, but it's better to act as if it's always true."

On that odd note, Tim left the Genoard mansion behind him.

"If there really is a twin there… The guy may not actually be a traitor, but you'll definitely have an information leak on your hands. That's what the twins—Sham and Hilton—are like."

"Um…Jacuzzi…I… Earlier… I'm very…sorry about that…"

As Jacuzzi watched Tim go, looking stunned, Adele, who'd stayed behind, bowed her head again.

"Huh?! Oh, uh, it's okay! It really doesn't bother me anymore."

As he spoke, Jacuzzi waved his hands and shook his head energetically. Adele gave a little smile, then left the Genoard mansion, following Tim.

As she went, as if in apology for that earlier time, she murmured something strange to herself.

"The twins are…peculiar beings. One name controls a thousand faces. The reverse is…also true.

"It isn't about…whether the twins are…strong or weak… Even I… Even that monster Felix… *Even if we killed them, we probably couldn't actually kill them.*"

## CHAPTER 5:
## FRONT & BACK

# LET'S GET
# OUT OF JAIL!

Alcatraz Island    Broadway        Late at night

"What a nasty day."

In the darkness after lights-out, Firo was curled up in his blanket, muttering to himself.

It was several days after his meeting with Huey.

Firo had gone on silently living as a convict.

Being oppressed by the low ceiling when he woke.

Head counts sixteen times a day.

Monotonous prison work.

Strict regulations.

He was sick of all of it, and he felt deep sympathy for the guys who'd been locked up on this rock for life.

After that incident, he'd experienced a night in solitary, and his frank impression had been, *Maybe this is what being "merchandise" on a slave ship felt like.* To be honest, he never wanted to go there again.

Except for his conversations with Isaac during meals, the only occasions he felt a bit of relief were the brief periods of free time they were given, and his encounter with a big, helpful Italian guy in the library who'd told him stories about Naples, where Firo's father was from.

He'd considered telling Misery about the guard who was Huey's underling, but, as a prisoner, he had no way to contact him. Misery had probably decided that it would be dangerous to summon a regular prisoner like Firo too often, but that meant Firo ended up having to live through several pointless days during which he was unable to say anything, which put him in a deeply dismal mood.

Today had come to an end as well, and as he kept an ear out for the footsteps that occasionally echoed down the corridor, he murmured to himself, half-asleep:

"Is one of those three…actually…here on orders from somebody else…?"

Firo had spoken relatively loudly, and he could technically have been heard in the next cell over, but his eyes didn't fly open in panic.

This was probably because he knew there was nobody in the cells on either side of him right now.

Today, Dragon—who would normally have been next to him—had been taken to the Dungeon.

Firo had been there when it happened. The ghastly sight had been branded on his eyes, and he'd been splashed with the victim's blood.

It was afternoon, in the recreation yard.

Firo had run into the gap-toothed man who'd taunted him by calling him "young lady" on that first day, and he'd been thinking about how to break his neck, when…

…he saw the guy was leering, and he seemed to be messing with Dragon.

Dragon's lean face twisted, and he put his mouth up close to the other man's ear.

It wasn't clear whether he expected him to whisper something or if he was hoping he'd blow in his ear, but the gap-toothed man's leer warped further, and just then, with no hesitation whatsoever—

—Dragon bit off that ear.

"Agh! …? Huh…? Uh…?"

There was sudden pain and a shock. The man didn't know what had happened. As he turned around, stunned, Dragon spat the pieces of his chewed-up ear right into his gap-toothed face.

"Aaaaaah!"

The man found himself abruptly blinded by red and flesh-colored meat fragments. Panicking, he tried to wipe his face with his hands—

—but the guy bit another chunk of meat out of his arm…and a corner of the recreation yard was buried in screams and spraying blood.

The surrounding area was in an uproar, but Dragon said, "It's tasty, but…mmf…it grosses me out to think it's that guy." He spat out the flesh, then turned his usual twisted smile on Firo, who'd walked up to him, wiping off the blood he'd been spattered with.

"Hey, Firo. Got some on you, huh? Sorry 'bout that."

"Seriously, what are you doing…?"

"Well, that perv cracked some stupid joke like 'I guess it's true that even grown-up Asians look like little kids.'"

"So he really was one of those kinds of guys, huh?"

Firo didn't seem particularly surprised. He just shook his head, looking disgusted.

"I figured I'd show him hell, but…"

Speaking half sarcastically and half in earnest, bloody lips still twisted in a grin, Dragon thumped Firo on the shoulder.

"Well, y'know, anybody would have worked."

"…?"

He was about to ask what he meant, but the guards immediately came running up and surrounded them. The gap-toothed man was taken to the prison hospital, while Dragon went straight to the Dungeon.

Remembering the afternoon's atrocity, Firo found himself quietly contemplating.

It was only natural that Dragon wasn't here, but Gig—the big black man from the cell on his other side—hadn't come back from the Dungeon yet, either. There were rumors that, after showing that kind of defiance, he was bound to be in there for ten days at least.

There was one more strange thing.

He hadn't seen this directly, but he'd heard that the little white man was currently in the Dungeon as well.

Apparently, he'd been saying, "That big lug is gonna kill me…!" and had attempted a jailbreak.

When they'd fired warning shots, he'd promptly passed out, and they'd carried him right down to the Dungeon, where Gig, the guy he was afraid of, was waiting.

That said, the rooms were separated from one another with thick walls, so there probably wasn't anything they could do to each other—and if that had been possible, it was likely that Ladd and Gig would already have been having a knock-down, drag-out fight to the death.

*Still, to think that the three guys who came in with me and the first fella I became pals with are all in the Dungeon together…*

On the one hand, he thought it was terrible luck, but it was true that something about it felt very strange.

*If one of those three is somebody special…what do they want?*

As Firo thought, footsteps echoed down the cellblock. He'd forgotten how many times people had come down that evening.

In combination with the distant sound of rifle shots, the noise formed a duet that stole through the iron bars, fraying the convicts' nerves.

However—that warped performance stopped dead.

The rifle shots still rang out, but the sound of the footsteps had broken off as if their spring had wound down.

"…You again, huh?"

The footsteps had stopped right in front of the bars Firo lay behind. Arrogantly, their owner ordered the guards in the corridor to open the door.

With an inorganic noise, the door opened. Then his blanket was ripped away.

It was the exact same sequence of events that had woken Firo several nights ago.

When he slowly opened his eyes, he saw…

…the face of the guard from the other day, who had just taken a gleaming silver knife from the folds of the blanket.

The guard sent Firo a private, ironic smile, then spoke in the strict tones of a jailer.

"This time… you might not get out for a while."

⇔

Alcatraz Island     The Dungeon

In deep darkness, where not a single light reached him, Ladd was fiddling with the chains at his feet. His eyes were wide open.

*Clank-clank, clank-clank, clank-clank*

The only thing convicts could do in that blackness, with the exception of sleep, was make that noise.

The monotonous sound echoed in the cramped space between the brick walls, skewing the sense of distance in this dark, blind world.

At the earliest, these cells turned people into madmen in less than a week, but Ladd had spent about half of his prison life up till now in solitary.

Not only had he not gone crazy, it didn't even seem to have weakened him. Most of the other cons had admired him for his tenacious willpower, but—

—some of the jailbirds, the ones who'd lived through many bloody massacres, had picked up on Ladd's true nature ages ago.

*That guy was crazy to begin with, and he never saw light in the first place.*

The warp inside Ladd was in a completely different dimension from the lunacy brought on by darkness, enclosed spaces, and loneliness. He was already twisted to the limit—and it probably wasn't possible for anyone to make him any crazier.

"……"

Today as always, that lunatic had been clanking his chains continuously, but…

*      *      *

...this time, in the darkness, an incredibly cute voice spoke.

*"Say..."*

"......"

*"You're Ladd Russo, aren't you?"*

As he moved the chains—*clank-clank, clank-ank-ank*—Ladd realized the voice was coming from right on the other side of the door.

"...Are you the Tinker Bell Isaac was talking about?"

*"Tinker Bell? So that dim-looking guy was going around saying that...? He's just like a little kid. That's funny."*

"Well, it doesn't matter. So...what do you want with me?"

A little girl's voice, echoing in a prison.

Considered normally, you'd probably assume you'd gone nuts. However, ever since he'd entered this prison, Ladd had been sure of one thing: If the man he wanted to kill really existed—then anything, no matter how weird, could happen here.

And right now, he was hearing an impossible voice, right in front of him. Not only that, but his ears caught the sound of the padlock being released—and the door slowly began to swing open.

*Clank, clank-ank-ank, clank-ank-ank-ank*

Ladd kept right on playing with the chains. In front of him, a lantern held in a small hand appeared, its pale flame glowing...

"You've got a good friend named Graham Specter, right, mister?"

The black-haired, golden-eyed girl who'd appeared from behind the door gave an innocent smile and said something cruel.

"I'm about to go kill him...so I want you to be my hostage!

"And then, and then ... After that, I want you to die!"

⇔

"Well, well... You're late."

They were below the Dungeon.

Firo, who'd been brought in by the guard, was facing the prisoner in white again.

Huey Laforet was sitting in the chair, looking just as he had the other day. When he saw Firo, he folded the newspaper he'd been holding.

"The warden here is competent, as well as strict, so I wasn't able to look at magazines or newspapers at all. However, since Mr. Misery was placed directly in charge of me, there are more amusements in my room. It's wonderful."

He'd tossed the newspaper down beside him. Intriguing words danced across it—*Chicago*, and something about explosions and kidnappings—but Firo showed no particular interest. He just gazed straight at Huey.

Huey watched him, seeming deeply intrigued by his attitude, and broached the main subject in a matter-of-fact way.

"Well? What do you say? Did you think about it?"

"...On one condition."

"Condition?"

"I've offered my life, past, and future...to my great leader, Molsa Martillo, and his syndicate. If you make this an official transaction with my organization, then I'll cooperate as much as you want. I can't sell what I know to somebody else based on a decision I made on my own."

On hearing Firo's stiff answer, Huey drew a breath, then responded:

"Then coming to this island to save Ennis wasn't a personal decision?"

"She's family."

Firo made that declaration boldly, and Huey continued to face him, his expression unchanged. "I see... The idea of dealing with your organization is intriguing, but considering Maiza's personality...it may be difficult to earn their cooperation."

"That's about the size of it."

"Then you don't need my information, either?"

"...I've got a pretty good idea already."

Firo shook his head, smiling wryly, and confronted Huey with the facts he'd deduced from the strangers' memories that slept deep in his own mind.

"Last year...your guy Christopher told me something. He said, 'We were made using techniques stolen from Szilard.'"

"...My, my. That was indiscreet of him."

"And so, when I saw the guard outside the door just now, I had an idea. Maybe your contact method is—"

Just as he was about to say something he was very nearly certain of ...

...Firo heard the door open behind him.

When he turned on reflex—

—outside the door, the guard who'd brought Firo in was lying facedown, and a man appeared, stepping over his body.

When he saw him, Huey murmured, although there was still no change in his expression.

"Well, well. I don't believe I summoned you here..."

Then, with a very faint smile, as if something made sense to him now, he asked the intruder a question.

"In other words...you're the hitman Nebula sent? Felix Walken, assuming my information is correct."

In the midst of an atmosphere that had grown a bit colder—the little white man spoke with a bitter smile.

"I sold that name to somebody else a long time ago."

"Now...I'm nameless."

⟺

New York     Madison Square Park

Let's turn back the clock a few days.

"Ah! ...Ah... Dammit, hold on... Wait just a minute! Y-y-you've gotta be kidding me, c'mon!"

On learning the other man's identity and the reason behind the alarms that were going off inside him, Spike's hands tightened on the staffs he held, and he immediately issued an order to the surrounding men in black.

"R-retreat!"

"Huh...?"

The order to withdraw had been far too abrupt.

There were only two opponents here. They were retreating from a situation in which they should have had an overwhelming advantage. Confused, the men in black looked at Spike.

Possibly because he'd heard their breathing, Spike turned on his heel by himself and continued to yell for a retreat.

"Idiots! Never mind why, just fall back! I'm telling you to run for it!"

Moving at a speed that made it hard to believe he was blind, Spike took off running, and the men in black followed him, their minds filled with question marks. On seeing this, Claire cracked his neck, then broke into a run.

"C'mon, you really think I'd let you go...?"

The next instant, just as he had started to run, he flipped and rose into the air.

Before Claire was aware of it, a man in black—the former Felix Walken—had appeared beside him. He'd bent forward, and as Claire had accelerated, he'd dexterously caught his leg and then vigorously straightened back up.

Watching the scene from behind them, Chané gasped involuntarily, but things didn't play out the way they had with her a few minutes earlier.

Claire, who'd been on the verge of revolving in midair, took his right hand, set a finger against the former Felix's lips—and stopped the other man's movements, simultaneously righting himself nimbly and landing in front of his opponent.

Just as Claire touched down, the man swiftly tore Claire's finger away. Without so much as twitching an eyebrow, he spoke to the redhead in front of him.

"There's something I'd like to ask you."

"...You're good."

In response, Claire stared at the other man's face.

He wasn't glaring. He looked genuinely impressed.

The man in black narrowed his eyes, then simply asked his question.

"You called yourself Felix Walken. Who did you inherit that name from?"

"Me? Well, I can't give you the details, but…*I bought it from a real smooth doll* who was about thirty."

Chané was standing a short distance away, and at Claire's words, her eyes went round.

She'd heard that he'd gotten the alias "Felix Walken" from another hitman, but from the name, she'd just assumed the other one had been male.

The man in black narrowed his eyes even further and spoke to himself.

"I see… It's *changed hands* quite a bit in such a short time."

Then the man turned his back on Claire and began walking toward Spike and the others, who were just starting their cars.

"I'll come again someday."

"Hey, wai—"

Claire reached out, trying to stop him, but Chané caught his arm first and held him back.

"Hmm? What's the matter, Chané? D-does something hurt?!"

"……, …, ……, ……!"

"You're worried about Jacuzzi's crew? …… Yeah, that's true… Okay."

At the sight of Chané's serious expression, Claire raised his hands in surrender.

Then, hugging her shoulders tightly and pulling her close, he called after the black-clad man's retreating back.

"Hey, give your boss a message from me."

"What is it?"

"Tell him to take a look at the other guy before he picks a fight."

"…I'll tell him."

The former Felix Walken raised a hand, and the current Felix asked him something that had been bothering him a bit.

"By the way…what sort of guy did you sell it to? Your name. Felix."

At that point, the man stopped in his tracks. He looked up at the sky, as if thinking nostalgically of his former self, and responded:

"I...didn't sell it to one person."

"They were an Asian man, a black man, and a white man."

⇔

A few days later    Alcatraz Island    ·  The special cell

From behind the little white man appeared...

...an Asian with tattoos on both arms.

And a big black man who was covered in scars.

"Hey, Firo. We meet again, huh?"

"Dragon..."

In response to Firo's murmur, Dragon grinned and winked at him.

The wounds the black man had gotten from Ladd didn't seem to have healed up yet. His face was badly swollen, and he gazed at Huey wordlessly.

"...I see."

When he saw the three men, Huey's eyes narrowed as if something now made sense to him.

"In other words...it's all three of you?"

"Huh?"

Looking as if he had no idea what was going on, Firo turned from the three men to Huey and back.

Ignoring Firo, the three newcomers slowly dispersed into the room.

The small man, who was standing with his back to the door, shrugged.

"Don't ask me. You don't need to know about that."

The man gave a small, fearless smile. He seemed completely different from the way he'd presented himself in jail, the coward who was constantly jittery.

In response, Huey thought about the situation for a short while, and then...

"No… Someone led you here, so taking that person into account, there must be four of you."

"You really are sharp. That figures."

The small man snapped his fingers, and another shape emerged from the shadows of the door. It was a different guard, not the one who'd brought Firo here.

The rifle he held in his hands made the room, which should have been spacious, feel as if it couldn't possibly be smaller.

"In terms of being sent in, then, the guard was the main thing, and not the prisoners?"

Huey smiled faintly as he spoke, and in response, four different expressions appeared on the intruders' faces. Dragon, who was smiling thinly, answered for all of them, clicking his teeth together as he did so.

"Well, that could be it."

"C'mon, no, wait, wait just a minute." Firo, who was now the odd man out, spoke to Huey. He was wearing a complicated expression. "Hey… what are these guys?"

"Felix Walken. You've heard the name at least, haven't you?"

"Huh? Uh… Well, yeah."

Firo nodded with a very odd look on his face. Huey spoke to him quietly.

His expression seemed relaxed, but he might have looked that way even in a crisis.

As Firo was mulling that over, another familiar name jumped out at him. This one belonged to a company.

"They're exclusive hitmen employed by Nebula. That said, I hadn't learned more than the name myself, and so…I had no idea they were a group of four."

"That intel's not accurate." Dragon smiled at Firo and Huey, baring his teeth, and puffed out his chest proudly. "Before, it was just a symbol for hired killers. We were the ones who created the name 'Handymen' in New York."

"You're talking too much."

The man in the guard uniform reprimanded his companion in an intimidating voice.

Then, without relaxing that intimidation, he pointed the rifle he held at Firo and stared at him. His expression was nearly devoid of emotion in a way that was completely different from Huey's.

"And? What're you?"

"…I really don't know how to explain. Any chance you'd give me a little time?"

"Sorry, but no. We'll decide whether or not to dispose of you later. For now, you let us do our job."

Ignoring Firo, the three men were slowly closing the distance between themselves and Huey. It wasn't clear what kind of skills the little guy actually had, but at the very least, Dragon and Gig were definitely experienced fighters.

Huey's face was still calm, but after thinking for a short while, he directed a rather timid question at Firo.

"I'm not good at fighting. I don't suppose you'd help me?"

"Sorry, but no."

When he mimicked the guard's remark, Huey smiled with an expression that seemed to say, *I thought not.* Slowly, he set a hand on the chair.

Tension flashed across all the hired killers' faces, and the air grew thin as they waited to see who would make the first move—

—but a sound intruded on that tension.

*Tak…*

*Tak…*

*Tak…*

It was the sound of footsteps.

A shoe-wearing enigma was approaching from the depths of the gloomy hallway.

After the guard had entered, the door had been closed partway, so there was no way for them to see what was happening outside. They could see the window, but it reflected the light from inside the room, and they couldn't see into the dark hallway.

*Tak...          Tak...          Tak...*

It was a regular rhythm, like the hand of a clock, or a pendulum.

The mechanical noise raised the tension in the room to nearly unbearable levels. Everyone was focused on the source of that sound, and all eyes were trained on the half-open door.

In that instant—

—the footfalls stopped, and after a pause that lasted for the space of a breath, the sound of an explosive impact echoed in the room.

"_____!"

The noise was so enormous that their ears and their bodies all shrank from it—but the sound wasn't the only thing that had ricocheted.

Along with the noise of the impact, the half-open door buckled, and the broken doorknob shot off, bouncing across the floor with a pleasant metallic sound.

After that flashy moment, what appeared through the now-open door was—

"Good evening, good evening. Also, it's nice to meet you, and on top of that, good-bye. Captive Peter Pan. Eternal boy."

In this prison...

...more naturally than anybody...

...seeming more entertained than anybody...

...and with a smile more warped than anybody else's, a blood-thirsty killer appeared.

There was an iron chain wrapped around his misshapen claw—and at the end of it, tangled up in the chain, was a little girl's body.

"Leeza..."

When he saw the girl, Huey murmured. Hearing it, the killer—Ladd Russo—knew for certain which one was Huey Laforet.

Then, as if he'd just met a woman he was passionately in love with,

with a smile that was filled with insanity and was also incredibly pure, he spoke clearly. His voice echoed in the underground room on the prison island.

"The ticking crocodile who ate the Captain's hook is here—and he's coming to eat you, too."

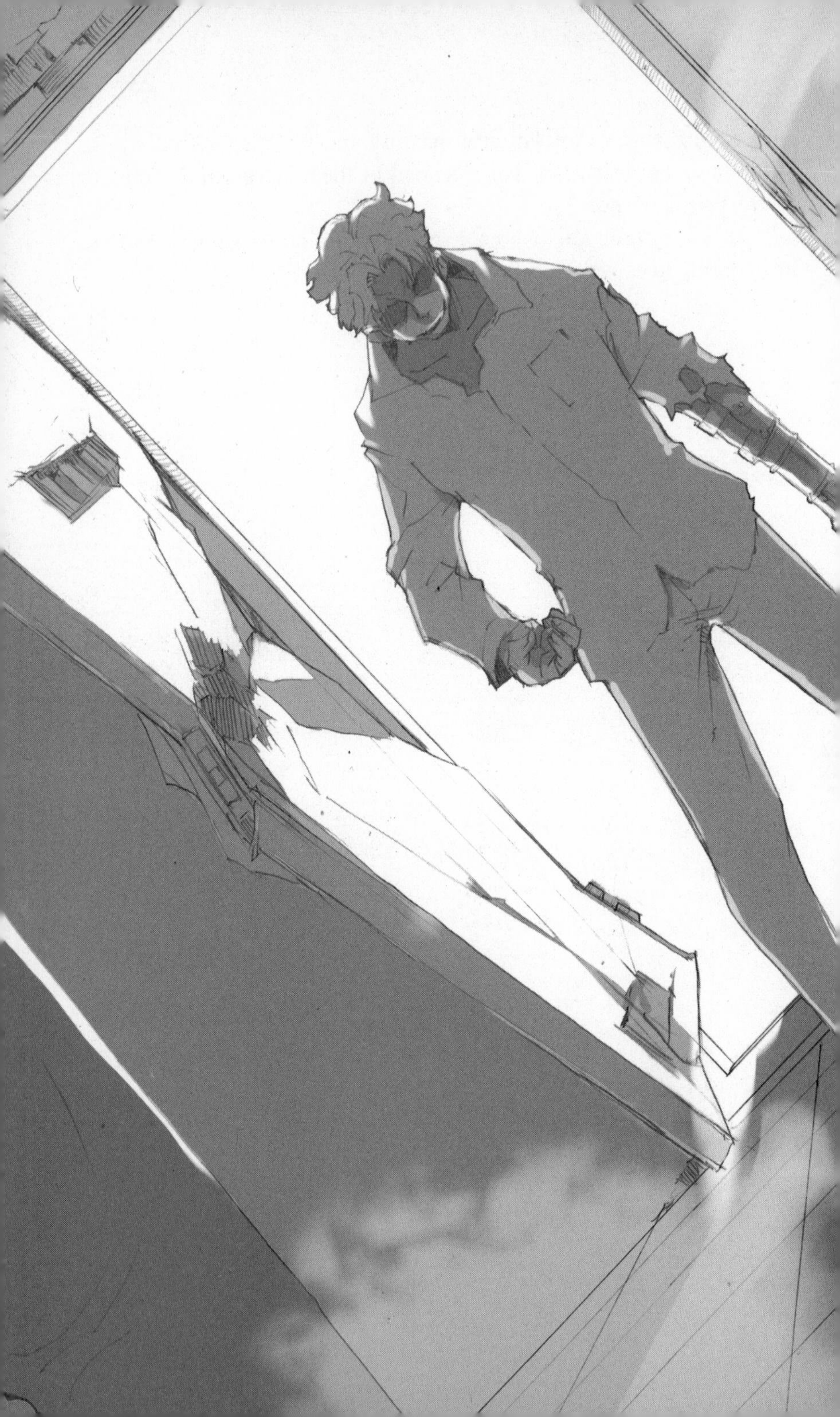

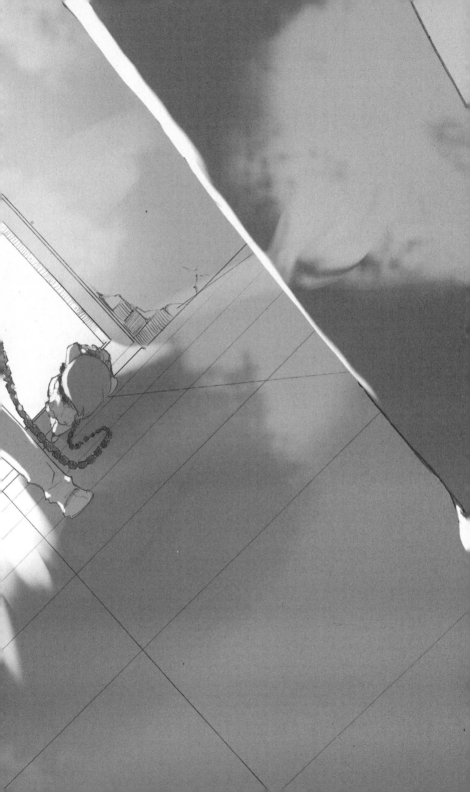

⇔

A few minutes earlier    The Dungeon

"Okay, I'm not sure what you'd do to me if I went closer, so I'll take you hostage from here!"

Standing near the door, where she assumed Ladd's chained hands couldn't reach her, the artless girl took several disks from some unknown place.

The shining silver disks had holes in their centers, like doughnuts, and the girl was spinning one of them on the tip of her finger.

The closer you got to the outer edge of the rings, the smoother their gleam became, and someone with keen instincts would probably have picked up on the fact that they were sharp, ring-shaped blades.

With only the light that crept in from the hallway to rely on, there was no telling whether Ladd realized this or not. He kept right on jangling the chains at his feet, just as he'd been doing before the door opened.

"How does it feel to be chained up so you can't move?"

In time with the clanking noises, Ladd quietly muttered to the girl in front of him.

"Say…the light's behind you, so I can't tell real well from here, but…"

"What, hmm?"

"Right now, I bet you look like you're sure you'll never die."

"…? You're not making any sense, but that's right. In a situation like this, there's no way you could kill me. I'm the one who's doing the killing right now."

The girl gave a cackling laugh, but Ladd kept on making those clanking noises.

"I dunno what you're fighting with Graham for, but listen—that guy doesn't kill, but in a straight-up fight, he's tougher'n me. You'd better watch yourself."

*Clank-clank, clank-clank, clankety-clank*

"I know. That's why I'm taking you hostage—"

"Me, though… I can kill."

*Clank-clank, clank-ank-ank*
"Anybody's fine. The point is, I can kill somebody."
*Clank-ank-ank*
"Broads or rugrats—anybody who ticks me off."
*Clank...*
Abruptly, the sound of the chain stopped.
Ladd had only been reeling the chain in, toward himself. However, to Leeza, the end of the chain seemed to have left the ground.
"Huh...?"
"I can kill, see."
At the same time, Ladd stood up smoothly. Eyes shining in the gloom, he let the chain he'd wrapped around his right hand dangle to the floor, clanking.
At that point, for the first time, Leeza noticed the slight but crucial abnormality in the room.
*That chain... It's not attached to his legs—*
The chain came down, forcibly shutting off her consciousness—
—and afterward, only the killer's ferocious mutter remained.

"I can kill."

⟺

A few minutes later     The special cell

To Firo, the man—Ladd Russo—had appeared far too abruptly and far too unfairly, and he wore an aura that was far too violent.
Ladd spread his arms wide and grinned, then flung the girl's body against the wall with his right hand.
With a light thud, the girl tumbled to the floor, and she didn't move a muscle. It wasn't clear whether she was alive or dead. However, without so much as glancing at her body, Ladd spoke words without a shred of tension in them.
"My switch got flipped." He spoke easily, holding his arms out to either side. "That's all."

From the elbow down, his prosthetic left arm dangled awkwardly, but Ladd didn't seem to care. He spread his arms even wider.

"Did you know? People have switches. Real simple switches that decide whether they can kill people or not. When those get flipped… anybody can kill. Anybody can end a life. That's all it takes to determine whether or not somebody can kill: whether or not that switch gets flipped. Can you believe that?"

Muttering something that didn't make much sense, Ladd put a hand to his own temple and gestured as though he were pushing something in.

"Click," he said. Just one word.

However, he pressed his finger against his temple over and over and over.

"Click, click, click, click, click, click, clickclickclickclickclickclick-clickclickclickclickclickclickclickclickclick clickclickclickclickclick-clickclickclickclickclickclickclickclickclickclickclickclickclickclick-clickclickclickclickclickclick, until finally it sounds like applause. The switches just keep flipping on. The many, the dozens, hundreds, thousands, tens of thousands, hundreds of thousands of switches inside me! In other words, I've just gotta kill. See?"

*He's nuts.*

That was Firo's genuine impression, and around him, the Felix Walkens apparently felt the same way. They didn't seem to know what to make of the guy.

Only Huey kept gazing at Ladd, as if he intrigued him. His attitude rubbed Ladd the wrong way; shrugging, he took a step into the room. Looking straight at Huey, he announced something simple, unfair, and completely insane:

"So, well, there you have it: Die for those hundreds of thousands of switches I just flipped. Don't worry; you just have to die once."

Returning Ladd's shrug, Huey gazed at his face steadily. He was interested, but from the look in his eyes, he seemed to be trying to grasp who the other man was. "Abruptly barging into someone else's room… You're a pretty unreasonable fellow, aren't you?"

"Guys who say 'I'm about to head over to your room now' before-hand don't get called murderers."

He spoke with simple indifference.

"They're just crazy."

However, his tone gradually grew more cheerful, and Ladd let his ego bleed into the room's atmosphere.

"My body and brain are finally warmed up."

Cracking his neck, he pressed his right fist against his limply dangling prosthetic, and the sound of his knuckles popping echoed lightly in the room.

"Okay… Okay, okay, okay! How do you want to get killed? I'm going to kill you to death until you die. I'll give you a choice between dying or kicking the bucket, at least, so it'd be great if you'd make your decision before I'm done taking you apart!"

At this point, Huey was all Ladd could see, and he started across the room with bold steps.

"Hey, you… What are you trying to…? Uh?"

By the time the guard with the rifle asked the question, setting his finger on the trigger—

—his target was *already right in front of him.*

Up until then, Ladd had been completely focused on Huey and had been walking straight toward him. However, his steps had abruptly turned light, and he'd closed in on the guard with the rifle in an instant.

"You're in my way."

There was a nasty noise, and all the strength went out of the guard's body.

"Not that you were actually blocking my path or anything. Your observation of me was in my way. Your killing intent was in my way. Your voice was in my way. Your existence was in my way. Being in my way meant you were in my way, which puts you in my way, you goddamned obstacle."

Ladd's words penetrated the guard's eardrums—and the pain hit him right after that.

*Something* had happened to his arm.

The only sensation left in that arm was pain, but before he could look at it, the muzzle of a gun appeared right in front of his face.

The black, glossy tube was the end of the rifle he'd been holding a moment ago.

"Yeah, I'll take the rifle. Thanks, pal."

At that point, the guard finally realized the situation he was in.

The man who'd abruptly appeared in front of him had caught the barrel of the rifle—and had wrenched it out of his hands by force.

The guard looked at his wrist and fingers, which were twisted at awkward angles, but he didn't even have time to scream.

"Okay, I appreciate it, so die."

Without hesitating or taking time to terrorize the guard, Ladd squeezed the trigger, and—

—a gunshot echoed in the prison.

The roar rebounded off the walls, and even Firo cringed despite being used to hearing such sounds.

*This guy...!*

At the same time, blood sprayed into the air—but the amount was far less than he'd been expecting.

Even though he'd been lugged with a rifle at point-blank range, the only things the human lug had lost had been consciousness and his right ear.

Ladd had shifted his aim, blowing the guard's ear off, and the man's upper body swiveled as he crashed to the cold floor.

The guard hadn't fainted from pain or fear. He'd passed out from more direct causes.

As it skimmed past the guard's ear, the rifle bullet had sent a shock through his temple directly into his brain. In combination with the roar right next to his eardrum, this had shaken the contents of his head violently.

The guard had blacked out without even understanding what had happened to him. Around him, clear wariness came into the eyes of the remaining prisoners, and they surrounded Ladd on three sides.

Even so, the three of them didn't jump in right away. Seeing this,

Firo, who was standing a little apart from the action, quietly analyzed the current situation.

*They can't jump him out of hand, that's for sure.*

The strange aura that radiated from Ladd was warped, but it was truly pure.

If letters had appeared in that atmosphere, 80 percent of the air would probably have been made up of the string of letters *K-I-L-L* instead of nitrogen.

Even then, strangely, Ladd wasn't giving anybody any openings. Firo was directly behind him, but the air was clammy with the feeling that even if he leaped at his back, the next instant, he'd be staring down the muzzle of that gun.

The tension in the room skyrocketed immediately. In the midst of it, Ladd chuckled to himself, kicking the unconscious guard in the face.

"Ha! That 'die' was a joke. Just kidding. I wouldn't bother killing a two-bit punk like you right now. You think I'd *blow all this energy* on something stupid like that?"

Ladd turned a vicious smile on the ceiling, and Dragon—who was standing right in front of him, on the other side of the guard—bared his teeth in a complicated expression.

"Hey… What the hell are you do—?"

"Okay! Shut up!"

Summarily cutting off Dragon's remark, which had seemed likely to morph into a taunt, Ladd let the rifle hang limply, pointing at the floor.

"I get it. I don't get you people, but I get it. Don't talk, can it, shut your mouth and kiss the ground."

"Wha—?"

"Shutting up is important. You know those idiots who keep handing out souvenirs for the afterlife and end up giving the other guy a chance to counterattack? I've seen it tons of times, in books and musicals, and in actual life-or-death fights. For some reason, even though it's a fight to the death, the more used to stuff like that guys are, the chattier they get. *The thing is, I'm that type myself!* So, well, you know, I'm not looking for that stuff from you people. Frankly, I'm tired of it, so don't talk. Swallow your souvenirs for the afterlife. Choke on 'em and die."

That incredibly unfair sentiment left Dragon unable to put away his sharpened teeth.

Firo stared in wide-eyed amazement, and Huey was still studying Ladd with deep interest.

Then, from behind Ladd on the right, a low, heavy voice rumbled, and a huge shadow took a menacing step forward.

"Dragon...let me take this guy."

It was the big black man, Gig. As he spoke, he'd lumbered closer to Ladd.

"I couldn't get serious last time, see. It's rude if I don't hit you with everything I've got, right?"

No sooner had Gig finished muttering the words than he launched himself at Ladd.

*He's fast!*

When Firo saw the movement, a light shock ran through him from head to toe.

With a speed that was impossible to imagine from his big frame, the giant rushed at Ladd like the wind.

*This is on a whole different level from when he went berserk in the mess hall.*

Moving in a way that clearly showed he practiced some sort of martial art, the big man charged straight at Ladd's knees like a low-flying cannonball.

The rifle still hung limply. He hadn't moved it yet.

Gig grinned, sure of his victory, and in that instant—

—the rifle fell to the ground with a clunk.

"?!"

Right before Gig's eyes, Ladd retreated, displaying some magnificent footwork—

—and the next moment, there was a fist in front of him.

By the time Gig realized that Ladd had unleashed an uppercut on a super-low trajectory, that fist was already sinking into his face, deeper and deeper—

"Forget 'everything you've got—'"

Ladd, who'd casually tossed away the weapon that gave him an absolute advantage, looked down at the silent Gig, whose nose he'd just caved in.

"You're being rude the second you take a swing at somebody. Obviously."

"Why, you..." "You piece of ..."

The little white man and Dragon muttered at the same time, but Ladd yawned as if he was bored.

"So, what? What are you fellas?"

"You... What are you? We—"

"Yeah, don't talk."

Interrupting the small man, Ladd shrugged as if he wasn't interested, then coolly spat out words that held a trace of melancholy.

"I don't care who you are or how amazingly strong you are, so don't talk. I don't care if you're way tougher than me or if you're some kind of god or devil who could blow my head off with a one-word curse—don't talk."

Ladd was clearly leaving them all sorts of openings, and the small man and Dragon jumped him from both sides at once.

The small man reached for the rifle that lay at Ladd's feet, while Dragon went for his throat, attempting to sink his fangs into it like a mad dog.

"Your pasts, your positions, your trump cards, your grudges against me, your bragging and spell chanting and fairy-tale legends—"

As Ladd spoke indifferently, his movements were completely economical and abnormally violent.

He'd been speaking slowly, and maybe they'd been fooled by the rhythm of his words: The other two waited a moment too long to deal with Ladd's actions.

Ladd stuck his right fist out toward Dragon's face, and grinning with eyes that seemed to say *You fell for it*, Dragon vigorously bit down on his hand.

His mouth was open so wide that he seemed to have unhinged his jaw, and no sooner was Ladd's fist sucked into it than he chomped down with the force of a bear trap.

First came the impact of something striking the bones of his fist. Then pressure and pain, as if it was being squeezed in a vise.

But Ladd didn't even flinch.

On the contrary, as if he'd been waiting for this, he gave a fiendish smile—

—and without letting it bother him, he twisted his upper and lower body to the max and cut loose with all the power he'd stored up.

"I'll listen to all that stuff next time I kill you."

When the small one, who'd picked up the rifle, heard that sarcastic voice and looked up—he saw a shadow bearing down on him.

It was Dragon's face, his eyes wide with astonishment.

Dragon's teeth were still clamped down on Ladd's right fist. Using the man as a boxing glove...

...Ladd struck the small man's head with a downswing that had all his might behind it.

"...? That all you got?"

The four former Felix Walkens had been taken out in a literal instant, and an odd silence fell over the room.

Huey, who had watched the whole thing, murmured to himself as a small doubt surfaced in his mind:

"A group that uses the Felix name, taken down this easily by a single human being...? Well, in this case, perhaps I should say that their opponent was beyond human..."

As Huey gazed at Ladd, murmuring, the object of that look clenched and unclenched his hand, which was dripping with blood. The killer's smile returned to his face.

"What are you muttering about? Practicing begging for your life?"

Ladd taunted him, and Huey answered, smiling slightly.

"I've developed a little interest in you."

"What a coincidence. I've been feeling the urge to kill you this whole time."

In contrast to Huey, who was chuckling quietly, Ladd wore a truly chummy smile.

Firo had been completely left behind in this situation. He stood with his back to the wall in a position where he could look to either side and see one of the two, watching to see how the situation played out.

In the midst of an atmosphere that was on the verge of congealing, Huey started the conversation again.

"You...called yourself the ticking crocodile."

"Yeah, come to think of it, I guess I did."

"In the story of Peter Pan, Peter is a symbol of completely cruel children who ignore concepts of good and evil. In contrast, although he is evil, Captain Hook is a symbol of logical adulthood. What, then, is the role of the ticking crocodile? From what angle do you intend to turn that urge to kill on me?"

Huey wasn't really expecting an answer, but as if to say *You're asking about that?*, Ladd shook his head and stated his position without a moment's hesitation.

"Unadulterated strength, amoral bloodlust, and unstoppable hunger. Disaster, in other words."

"......"

"I'm a murderer, and I like killing. If heaven and hell exist, then I'm probably going to hell. I've never given much thought to good and evil myself, though. Say you've got a murderer who has no urge to kill, no malice, not even a motive. The one who decides whether he's good or evil is the victim. The side that inflicts the damage doesn't have the slightest intention of talking about that. They just follow their appetites, eat and spit it back out... What I mean is, I'm only thinking about me. That's all it is. And I hear you don't die, and I thought killing you sounded like a whole lot of fun. —Yeah, that's all. That's all it was."

At that oddly calm response, Huey narrowed his eyes as if impressed and gave Ladd an honest compliment.

"I thought you were just a barbaric murderer, but you're quite the poet."

"Would you listen to that?! Calling the likes of me a poet... Don't you think that's pretty rude to poets?"

Clenching his fist, Ladd smiled that vicious smile again, exuding a sticky, murderous intent.

"Here, lemme go ahead and settle the score for those poets you just insulted."

"Still—in that case, shouldn't you direct some of that urge to kill somewhere else?"

"Hunh?"

"You like killing people who believe they won't die, correct? That's why you're targeting me, an immortal. If that's the case..."

After pausing for the space of a breath, Huey gave a cold smile and went on.

"Firo Prochainezo over there is immortal, just like me."

*That slimy little—!!*

The one those words stunned was Firo himself.

Up until that point, he'd been a complete outsider, but he'd just been dragged right into the middle of their conversation. Huey was probably scheming to divert part of that murderous intent and forcibly turn him into an ally.

Having deduced this, Firo ground his teeth and glared at Huey. Then he sighed in resignation and turned to face Ladd.

"...Is that for real, Firo Prochainezo?" Ladd muttered.

In response, Firo slowly walked over and stood behind and to the right of Huey.

Then, deliberately, he set a fingertip against a canine and bit down hard, ripping into it.

The taste of blood spread through his mouth, and he felt a throbbing pain as that blood dripped to the floor—but it was over in an instant, and as if time were running backward, the taste of blood and the blood itself were drawn into the wound again.

Ladd was seeing the peculiarities of an immortal body for the first time, and his eyes widened slightly, but it wasn't possible to read whatever lay in the depths of that emotion.

"Sorry. That's how it is."

It felt as if he was selling out a man he'd gotten close to, and that hurt, but it did seem like it would be best to cut ties with this type as soon as possible. As Firo looked at the little girl who'd been thrown into the corner, he felt some misgivings.

Meanwhile, Ladd's face remained expressionless for a bit, and then—

"…Ha-ha."

—he gave an abrupt bark of laughter, then spoke up loudly and happily.

"Ha-ha-ha-ha-ha-ha-ha-ha-ha! I see, I see, I see, so that's what it is, huh?! Wow… Thanks, Firo! You just told me something real good!"

*Huh? Did I say something just now?*

Firo stood there, not understanding what he meant, and Ladd snapped his fingers, speaking as if he was really and truly enjoying himself.

"Remember what I told you? The only guys I kill are the ones who think they're never gonna die, no matter what! And I said this, too, right? I told you that you weren't like those soft fellas!"

"Yeah…? So what?"

"Hey, Firo. You're immortal, too, but somewhere in there, you're still scared of dying. Your eyes ain't soft. Right now! Right this instant! You're keeping a wary eye on that Huey fella over there! Like you might get killed any minute! …That tells me one thing."

After a moment's pause, Ladd put the certainty he'd reached into words.

"There is *a way to kill* you immortals. Ain't that right?"

"…!"

"Well, whatever. For now, if you both want to jump me at once, go right ahead. While you're doing that, I'll grill you… about what a guy would have to do to kill an immortal…"

As he spoke, Ladd soundlessly began running through pugilists' footwork, shadowboxing lightly right on the spot.

"If you want some time to talk it over with each other, I'll give you that."

"Well now…you heard him. What should we do?"

Huey directed that question at Firo, over his shoulder. He didn't seem very troubled.

In response, Firo exhaled deeply—then spoke firmly.

"Hey. Huey Laforet."

"What is it all of a sudden?"

"You asked me whether I thought Szilard and the other alchemists in my memories had hijacked my mind."

Firo had abruptly said something odd, and Huey watched him curiously but didn't stop him. He just listened to him with interest.

"Even if that's true…I don't care. Just as long as I don't suddenly start thinking like that damn old gink and doing something ugly to Ennis or my friends."

"……"

"I don't care about myself. As long as the world around me stays peaceful, I don't care who I am… Even if I'm just a dream somebody near me is seeing, that's fine."

*…Come to think of it, I used to fight about that opinion with Claire a lot.*

Remembering his childhood, Firo smiled, laughing at himself.

"Why would you bring that up now, under these circumstances?"

Huey was dubious—naturally—and Firo smiled a little as he responded:

"Well, we don't know how this is going to turn out, so…"

"Either way, I wanted to make sure it got said before we parted ways."

⇔

New York    A police station

Three men were sitting in a New York Metropolitan Police reception room. Each wore a different expression.

The initial on-site inspections and inquiries regarding the explosion were over, and the agents had finally been released.

However, until the incident calmed down and people who were further up in the hierarchy than Victor finished their dealings with one another, practically speaking, they wouldn't be able to leave New York.

Victor was gazing up at the reception room ceiling as if he loathed it.

"In the end…I guess Huey got us. If things are like this, I bet he either ate the kid I sent to Alcatraz or flipped him and made him his underling."

"I'm not so sure about that."

Edward responded to his boss's pessimistic guess with a low mutter.

"What, Edward? Come to think of it, you started to say something right before the suicide bomber showed up."

In response to Victor's question, Edward was quiet for a little while, but…

Before long, as if he couldn't take it anymore, he responded with his opinion on what had been said earlier, about not being able to expect anything from the guy.

"With all due respect, Assistant Director, that Firo kid didn't move up in the world through sheer luck or by default."

"…You really do think highly of him, huh. So it's okay to hope a little?"

"No. You shouldn't hope for anything."

Edward had spoken decisively, and Victor scowled.

"What are you getting at?"

"I'm saying it would be better not to ignore him."

Remembering the way that Firo punk had risen through the ranks of the city's underworld, he spoke firmly, as if reminding himself as well.

"You really can't expect anything from him—but you should *keep your guard up.*"

"After all, at the end of the day, he's a gangster... Just a villain."

⟺

Alcatraz Federal Penitentiary      The special cell

"While I'm at it, there's one more thing I want to say."
"What is it?"
They were facing Ladd, and Huey, who was standing in front, didn't seem to be paying much attention to Firo's murmur.
"Listen. Earlier, when you said the Felix who'd come after you was really a group of four guys..."
"Yes?"
As Huey responded, he was watching Ladd, who'd turned ferocious murderous intent on him.
The sound of a very small thud struck his eardrums.
"...?"
The next moment, a sharp chill began to seep through his back.
"...?!"
In an instant, the cold changed to heat, then morphed into pain that shook his brain violently.
An impact as if something had pierced his spine made his whole body shudder, and immediately afterward, Huey realized that the sensation had promptly vanished.
Simultaneously, he noticed that he couldn't move his arms or legs...
As he pitched forward, he saw Ladd staring at him, eyes round. At that point, he was certain that the other man had nothing to do with this situation.
The moment his body hit the floor, he heard Firo's cold voice.

"...*There were five of 'em*, actually."

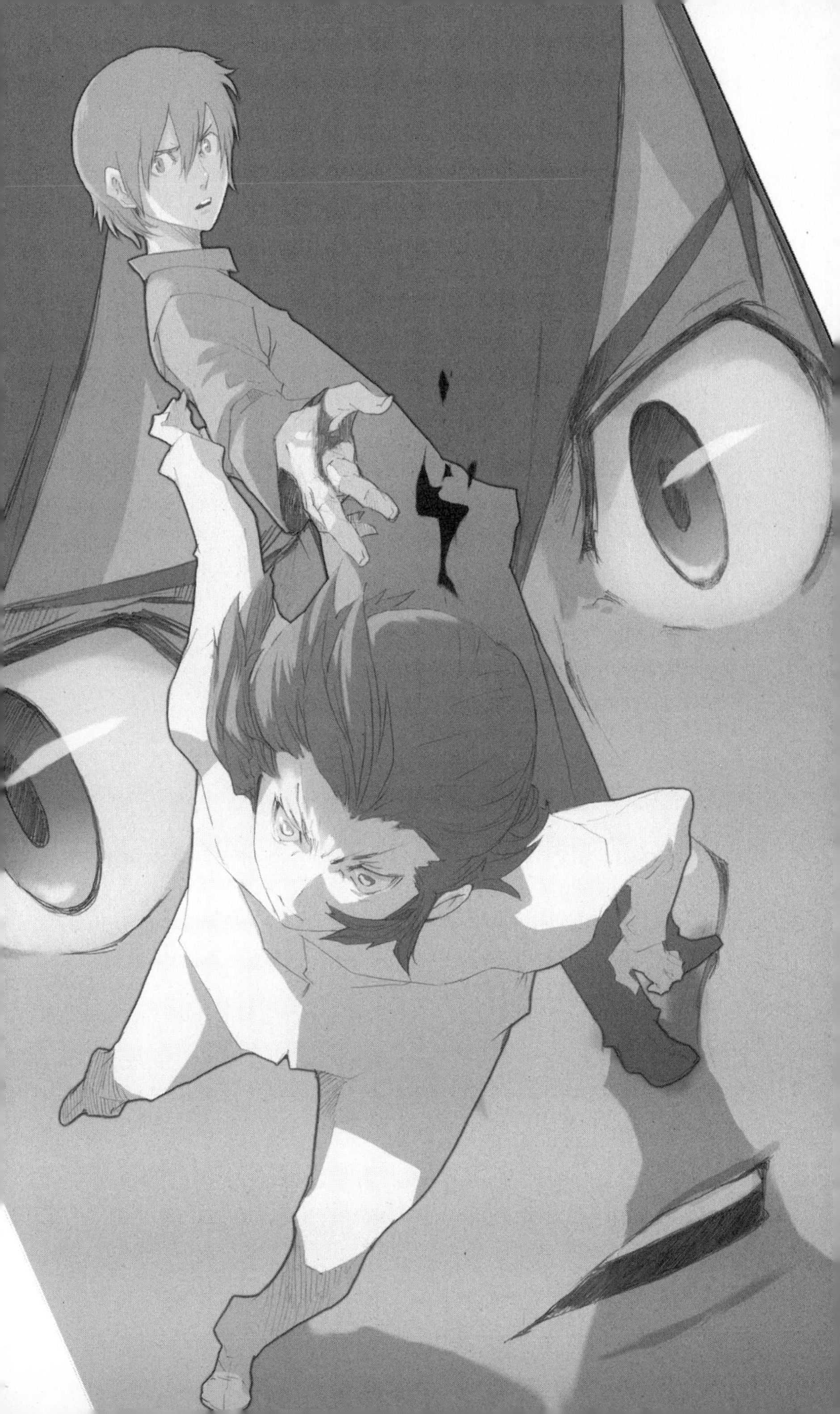

\*   \*   \*

Slowly, in order to steal Huey's consciousness completely, Firo reached for the man's head with his right hand.

Huey had fallen with his face turned sideways, and as he watched the shadow cover his field of vision, he thought:

*I completely failed to predict this.*

*I thought I had a certain number of things well under control, but…Once in a while, this sort of uncertain element turns up.*

Little by little, it was getting harder to breathe, and as his consciousness rapidly faded…

…thinking of his old friend's face, Huey murmured, smiling ironically.

*Elmer. It's just as you said.*

"This…is what makes the world interesting."

⟺

In a space where silence reigned…

The small figure that had been lying in the corner of the room flinched and shivered.

"…Uu…nn……!"

As before, almost as soon as she regained consciousness, Leeza was wide-awake and upright.

How long had she been out?

She wondered for a moment, and then, in the next instant—

"A whole hour and twenty-seven minutes…!" she muttered, *judging the passage of time with perfect accuracy*, although there was no clock nearby.

"Father…!"

Realizing that this gloomy place was her father's cell, Leeza immediately examined her surroundings.

The first thing she saw was the door. It was open, and she noticed a familiar guard lying facedown outside it.

However, that didn't matter to her at all. Her searching eyes had spotted a figure in white lying on the ground, and her heart lurched violently.

"Father!"

Leeza jumped to her feet and ran over to her father, who lay on his stomach.

A knife had been plunged deep into his neck, and it looked as though his spinal cord had been completely destroyed.

"Nooo… Noooooooooo!"

Nearly crying, the girl set her hands on the knife and pulled with all her might.

With a nasty, crunching sound, the blade came free, scattering blood.

The blood that spouted from her father's body gave the girl a significant shock—but when she saw it promptly begin to writhe and return to the wound on his neck, her heart calmed down a little.

*Oh, good! He's alive!*

Even though she knew that Huey was immortal, seeing him with a knife planted in him had unsettled her quite badly.

"Nng…"

"Father, Father! Wake up… Please wake up…?!"

"Oh… Is that you, Leeza? …What about the others?"

As he asked the question, her father sat up slowly, and Leeza gasped and took another look around.

However, there was only the lone guard, collapsed in the hall. She didn't see any other figures.

"It's okay, Father! There's nobody here, nobody's here!"

"Is that right…? I just assumed he'd eat me. I'd steeled myself for it."

Huey got up slowly, checking himself over, but…

Abruptly, he noticed that something felt wrong, and he turned to Leeza, who was beside him.

"That's strange. My left eye won't open… Leeza, would you look at it for me?"

He was fairly certain of the results already, but Huey had his daughter check anyway.

He simply wanted to know how the girl, who thought of him as a perfect person, would react when she saw it.

"Fa...ther...?"

Puzzled, Leeza ran her fingers over her father's closed left eyelid—

And from below it, a hollow, dark, red cavern appeared.

The eyeball that should have been there was gone—and red-black darkness stared back at her.

As he listened to his daughter's screams, the man forgot that his left eye had been gouged out. Impassively, he engraved the girl's reaction into his memory.

Reflecting on his own behavior...

...Huey realized, once again, that he was a terrible human being, and—

—smiling with delight, he decided to resume his experiment.

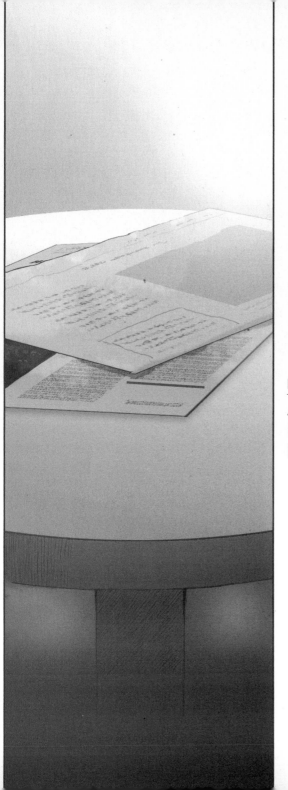

**LINKING CHAPTER**

# AT THE INFORMATION BROKERAGE

New York    The Daily Days office

All right... I believe I'll break off my tale here for now.

Just consider it an advance payment.

Didn't I say as much earlier?

I was present in several situations.

There were others in which I was absent.

Most of what I've told you was focused on the prison. 'Cept there's a few key things I haven't told ya yet.

Those items are deeply connected to what happened in Chicago, this incident's other stage. Unless I relate the events there, the other items won't make sense.

I'll tell you what happened after this point—once you've told me what you know.

You understand, don't you?

This incident won't be complete unless you add the events that happened in the other location, Chicago.

Who is Graham Specter?

How did that murdering bastard Ladd Russo get those chains off his getaway sticks?

Why the heck did that kid Firo gouge out Huey's eye?

What happened to Firo and Ladd after that?

As to Master Huey's method of contacting the outside world...I imagine you already have some idea about that.

Well, above and beyond those various questions, we'll get nowhere unless I tell you the truth behind the Chicago incident.

Sorry. To be honest...I do want to tell you about it, and I wanna know what happened in the places where I wasn't. I do indeed.

I want to pick up the intel only you information broker fellas know, guess at the dirt even youse guys don't have, and fill in those missing puzzle pieces.

In that sense, I suppose I am similar to Master Huey after all.

...Whoops. Are you closing for the day already?

In that case, I'll take my leave.

The me who returns tomorrow may be a different person, or I may not come at all, then.

That may seem weird to you, but the thing is, if I run into Mr. St. Germain, that'll take care of everything.

Yes, that's right. At all times, I am seeing something.

Regardless of my wishes, I'm compelled to continuously see more than people ever do.

That is the destiny given to myself and Hilton... To the twins.

And so, at the very least...I would like to convert that destiny to cash. You see?

Well, let's keep up this nice, friendly relationship we've got going, Mr. Intel Broker.

For better or worse, you see—I believe all the information will complete my world.

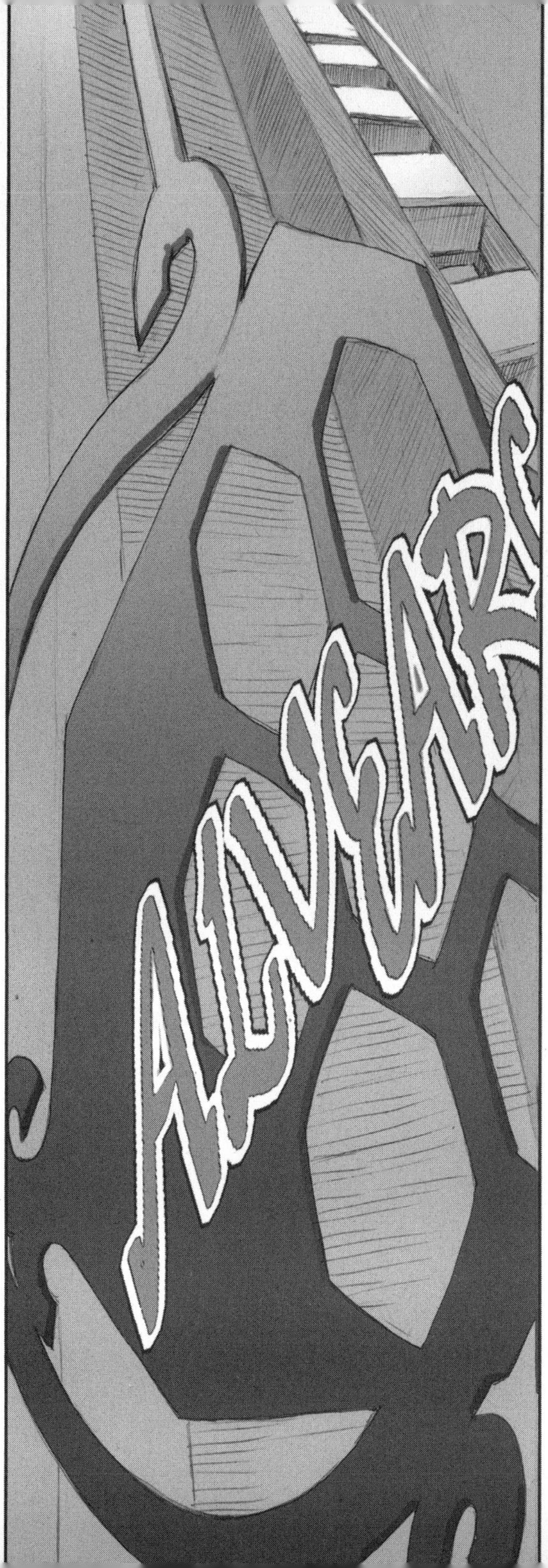

## DIGRESSION

# OUT OF JAIL!

San Francisco Bay    Alcatraz Island

"You're being released today, aren't you? Congratulations."

In response to Misery's words, Isaac laughed, looking self-conscious.

"Really, I can't thank you enough. I mean, you took care of everything for me!"

"...You're the third person I've been directly in charge of admitting. So far, I've only done the entry procedures for the other two; they haven't been released yet."

"Wow, amazing! You mean I'm the only one?! No, hang on: I was in prison, so there's no way I'm amazing... Maybe it's not me! Maybe you're the amazing one, Warden!"

"No, I'm not the ward— Well, yes, it's true that Warden Johnston is an amazing person."

Misery, who'd been thrown off his stride, murmured this, then turned the conversation back to Isaac's release.

"It's incredibly unusual for someone to leave this island after such a short time, unless it's as a corpse... Well, this is true for paying for your crimes in prison as well, but how you live in society after your release determines whether you've actually atoned. From now on, turn over a new leaf and live for the good of society and for America. For the sake of your loved ones as well."

"Yessir! I'll do my best!"

Isaac delivered that remark with the energy of a little kid. Misery exhaled, impressed, then drew an envelope from his jacket.

"Hmm... I never thought the day would come when I'd be saying things like this. At any rate, these are your wages for one month of prison labor, so take them without reservation. There's a little extra as a parting gift."

Isaac, who'd accepted the envelope, smiled happily and thanked him over and over.

"Say, thanks! Wow, I'm thrilled! Really, thanks so much, Warden!"

"No, as I said, I'm not the warden..."

"Then you're some kinda big shot?"

"... Well, erm, I wouldn't say that characterization bothers me."

Smiling wryly, Misery saw him off, and Isaac left the office.

Then, escorted by a guard just as he had been when he'd arrived, Isaac put the little island behind him.

The cliffs were tinted orange by the sunset light, and they encircled the island's scenery in a truly beautiful way.

"How pretty..."

As he looked at Alcatraz Island, which he'd seen countless times as a small child, Isaac remembered his past—

—and more than make him anticipate his freedom, it just made him want to see Miria.

⇐⇒

"Well, drat. This isn't enough money to get me back to New York."

After going through several formalities at a Bureau of Investigation branch office, Isaac finally had his freedom.

In most cases, after leaving Alcatraz, people did their remaining time in other prisons. Since Isaac hadn't gone through a formal trial, though, they'd simply released him.

Originally, Victor had been scheduled to come and meet with him, but apparently, there'd been some sort of trouble in New York, so instead, Isaac was released after speaking with a man who said he was Victor's superior.

The news about the Chicago incident was playing on radios all over town, but Isaac didn't hear it.

His wallet and the clothes he'd been wearing when he was arrested had been returned to him, and he immediately combined the wages he'd been given with the contents of his wallet and headed for the station.

…Carrying only his desire to see Miria again soon.

However, no matter how he figured, he didn't have the cash to take a transcontinental train back to New York.

The pay for prison labor was meager, and on top of that, Isaac had worked for only a month. Even with the extra Misery had thrown in, plus everything in his wallet, his travel funds would run out partway there.

Up until now, Isaac would have decided, "I know! I'll steal it from some bad people!"—however, as far as he was concerned, Misery was an amazing person, and Misery had told him to "turn over a new leaf…for the sake of your loved ones." Remembering that exhortation, he stopped himself in the nick of time.

For just a moment, he remembered he was currently very close to his family home…but then he thought of Miria's face and immediately discarded the idea of going back there.

"After all, if they find me…they just might kill me."

Muttering something deeply significant to himself, Isaac decided to make a phone call from a nearby facility.

The switchboard operator connected him to Alveare.

There, Seina passed the phone on to Ronny, who told him where he could find the person he was looking for, so then he dialed the other place.

The operator connected him once again, and this time, the voice that answered belonged to a familiar tattooed youth.

Jacuzzi sobbed and told him how glad he was, and after that—

—he heard a voice he'd missed very much.

The voice he'd most wanted to hear.

Even choked with tears, that voice gave vent to all the happiness it could hold, and it brought a smile to Isaac's face.

Isaac had worried quite a lot over what he should say to her and where he should start, but—

—he abruptly remembered something, and just as he always did, he shouted without even taking the time to think about it:

"Miria, I'm sorry! That wallet—it was in my pocket."

He wasn't trying to deceive her or hide his embarrassment. He'd simply thought, *I've got to apologize.* In answer to his frank words, on the other end of the line, without a moment's hesitation, Miria's voice responded: *"It's okay! I'm not mad or anything!"*

Her words relieved Isaac, and he went on to say the rest of his reunion speech, as if it wasn't easy to get out.

"The thing is…I don't have enough money to get back there… see… Erm, this is pretty hard to say, but, Miria…do you think you could get the train fare out of my piggy bank and bring it to me…?"

"——. ——, ——!"

Through the receiver, Miria's voice was so enthusiastic that she seemed ready to head right over.

As Isaac listened to her, he thought it would be rough on Miria to make her come all the way here, so he decided to take the train as far as he could on his own.

Isaac checked his notes on timetable and fare information, and his eyes fell on the name of a station he'd visited once before.

The name of the city in which he and Miria had dressed up as major leaguers and had rendered gangsters speechless.

"Then…let's make it Chicago! I can get that far!"

Hearing vigorous agreement through the receiver, Isaac let his thoughts run to his journey east. He felt invigorated.

"Yeah, I'll hop on a Chicago-bound train right now. Let's see, where should we meet…?"

As he put the note with the meeting place and time in his pocket, Isaac was filled with hope for the next day.

His thoughts went east, and the sun went west.

Isaac, who'd been set free, spoke firmly into the receiver.

Very, very simply.

He wasn't thinking of a single thing besides meeting Miria.

For that very reason, his words were decisive—and they relieved the listener on the other end of the line.

"Well then...see you in Chicago!"

To BACCANO!
1934: Streets (Chicago)

## AFTERWORD

To those of you I haven't met before, it's nice to meet you. To those of you (probably the vast majority) for whom it's been a while, it's been a while. Also, apologies for the wait!

This is the first *Baccano!* in nearly two years. Although there was a mid-length novel project for a CD drama in the middle, it really is the first *Baccano!* in a long time, and I'm a bit nervous about it myself.

Well, in this volume, the prison arc ends, and the scene shifts to the outside world.

I think the composition will end up being a bit different from the 1931 Local and Express volumes, so although it's going to be a long sequence, I hope you'll stick with me until the end.

That aside, this really was the first *Baccano!* in a very long time.

Even I've forgotten some of the details about past stories, and it's freaking me out—although I do remember things that completely don't matter, like the whiskered pig's lines.

So this is the first *Baccano!* in two years, and…

…I've got an announcement for the readers.

Let's see. Those of you who read the book band and *Dengeki Kanzume* probably already know about this, but—they're turning *Baccano!* into a manga in the magazine *Dengeki Comic Gao!*

Heh-heh-heh… Ha-ha-ha-ha-ha!

It's been over half a year since they first told me about the manga project. Every time I saw opinions online like *It's just not possible to turn Narita's stories into manga* and *I bet it won't happen unless his sales numbers go up*, I thought, *Heh-heh-heh… You people have misread the era!* I had the urge to release the information on my own website, but for reasons of confidentiality, I couldn't do it. Actually, now that I think about it, that would have been way too immature, so I suppose I should probably be grateful for that obligation to keep quiet.

So the serial starts in the issue of *Gao!* that goes on sale in late December, but I have yet to meet Ginyuu Shijin, who's drawing the manga. In exchange, the other day, I did meet Mr. Ogino, the manga's editor.

This is the first time I've had a project turned into a manga, after all. If I said I wasn't worried about what they were going to do to my story, I'd be lying. For the sake of the fans of the original as well, I marched into Media Works, fully intending to let them have it—"If you don't stay faithful to the spirit of the original work, we're going to have problems... *Phooo.*"—while puffing on a cigar or something.

It was our first meeting, and these were the first words out of Mr. Ogino's mouth.

Ogino: "With *Baccano!*, do you mind if we 'break' the original work, change its vibe?"

Me: *See?! I knew it! There it is! No, we can't have that, gweh-heh-heh...* "Ha-ha-ha, break it? Uh, in what way exactly?"

Ogino: "The *Weekly Shonen Champion* way."

Me: "......"

Ogino: "A bit like turning Norio Nanjo's *The Bout Before an August Audience at Suruga Castle* into *Shigurui: Death Frenzy.*"

Me: "......"

Ogino: "We've already given Ginyuu Shijin, who's drawing the manga, other books and told him to try for that sort of tone. We sent him all of *JoJo's Bizarre Adventure*, all of *Shigurui*, and all of *Hellsing.*"

Me: "...Bueno!"

I shook Ogino's hand firmly, and then we talked for ages about how fascinating *Champion* is, until Mr. Wada, the novels' editor, got disgusted with us and said, "Excuse me, I can't follow this at all..."

... The problem is that I feel kind of bad for getting all excited by myself when I haven't met the manga artist yet. I also think that having to read all the volumes in those three series at once might result in some pretty serious brainwashing! I'm incredibly worried about a manga artist I haven't even met; what's up with this situation?! Ginyuu Shijin, please do your best not to get taken out by Ogino's raged attack!!

So I'm looking forward to the new serial, which will be running in *Gao!*, and I hope you'll look forward to it as well!

Well, the next book is about the "outside world," so I'm planning to keep the mood free and easy. I'd like to write in a supercool way that takes the dark, heavy prison atmosphere in this volume and flips it 180 degrees. As I write this afterword, I'm still working on it, so I can't say anything about how it's going to turn out yet, but...

...in any case, the *Baccano!* series is still ongoing, and I hope you'll continue to support it!

*The usual thank-yous begin here.

To my editor, Wada-san (Papio), for whom I'm constantly making trouble, and to Chief Editor Suzuki and the rest of the editorial department. To the copy editors, for whom I'm always causing problems by being late, every single time. To the designers, who make my books look good. To the people of the publicity department, the printing department, the marketing department, and Media Works as a whole.

To my family, friends, and acquaintances, who always take care of me in all sorts of ways, and particularly to everyone in S City.

To Katsumi Enami, who colored the world of *Baccano!* with superb quality, even though I forced an insane schedule onto him.

And to all the readers...

Thank you very much!

August 2006
I bought a new car and am raring to go, but it's crunch time at work, so I can't go anywhere.

Ryohgo Narita